He looked at her for a long moment, and she found herself staring boldly back. As she gazed into his deep blue eyes, Brigitte suddenly astonished herself with the understanding that she really cared for Rowland. He was rude and abrupt and sometimes cruel in his remarks. But he was also strong and decisive and fair-minded, and she liked more about him than she had admitted to herself.

Besides, she thought, he looks at me with tenderness and, yes, even with love. He pretends he is merely taking what is his, but there's more to this assault than that, much more . . .

Rowland was thinking how lovely she was, and how much he wanted her. He would never admit as much to Brigitte, but she was special, charming, and he took delight in her strong spirit. No, it would not do to tell her so, but Rowland was beginning to care for her deeply. He kissed her lovely face, and then moved slowly down her neck . . .

Johanna Lindsey

# So Speaks the Heart

**CORGI BOOKS**

# SO SPEAKS THE HEART
## A CORGI BOOK 0 552 12305 6

First publication in Great Britain

PRINTING HISTORY
Corgi edition published 1983

Corgi Books are published by
Transworld Publishers Ltd.,
Century House, 61–63 Uxbridge Road,
Ealing, London W5 5SA

Printed and bound in Great Britain by
Cox & Wyman Ltd., Reading, Berks.

*For my grandma*

*WHO HAS PROVEN ROMANCE IS WONDERFUL AT ANY AGE.*

# Chapter One

France, A.D. 972.

Brigitte de Louroux sighed, keeping her blue eyes on the fat goose lying on the work table before her. Frowning with concentration, she plucked the feathers as she had been recently taught. It was a new chore to the seventeen-year-old girl, but only one of many that she was slowly getting accustomed to. She wearily wiped a tendril of flaxen hair away from her face.

Blood from the slaughtered goose was splattered on her apron and also on the hem of her brown woolen tunic beneath. Brigitte's wardrobe of fine gowns was nearly all ruined from the filthy chores that were now forced on her. This drudgery was her own choice though, she reminded herself, her own stubborn choice.

Across the table stood Eudora, whose task Brigitte was doing. Eudora's brown eyes were sympathetic until Brigitte looked up and smiled almost apologetically.

"It's not right!" Eudora hissed, her eyes suddenly round with anger. "I, who have served in your father's house all my life, and happy for it, must stand idle while you work."

1

Brigitte lowered her gaze, her blue eyes misting. "Better this than my giving in to Druoda's plans for me," she murmured.

"That lady is cruel."

"I am inclined to agree," Brigitte said softly. "I fear my brother's aunt does not like me."

"She is a bitch!" Eudora replied heatedly.

Eudora's mother, Althea, crossed the kitchen waving a large spoon. "You are too kind, Eudora. Druoda forces us to call her lady, but she is a slothful cow. She gets fatter and fatter while I have lost weight since she came here. She has said she will cut off my fingers if I taste while I cook, but what cook can cook without tasting, I ask you? I must taste what I am cooking, yet she says I must not. What can I do?"

Eudora grinned. "You can add chicken droppings to her food and hope she doesn't find out, that's what you can do."

Brigitte laughed. "You would not dare, Althea. She would beat you, or even banish you. She might even kill you."

"Ah, no doubt you are right, milady." Althea chuckled, her large body jiggling. "But it was nice to think about it, to savor as I would a sweet cake."

Eudora quickly grew serious again. "It has been terrible for us since Druoda began to rule here. She is a cruel mistress and that cowardly husband of hers does nothing to stop her. Lady Brigitte does not deserve to be treated like the lowest serf on the manor." Eudora became even angrier. "She is the daughter of the house, and her half brother should have made provisions for her after their father died. Now that he—"

Eudora stopped and lowered her head in shame,

but Brigitte smiled. "It's all right, Eudora. Quintin is dead, and I realize that."

"I only meant to say that he should have made arrangements with his liege lord. It's cruel that you should fall under the will of a woman like Druoda. She and her husband came here to beg the mercy of Lord Quintin as soon as the Baron died. He should have turned them away then. Now it's too late. They seem to think this fief is theirs instead of yours. Your stepbrother was a great man, but in this case—"

Brigitte silenced her with a sharp look, her bright blue eyes fierce.

"You do Quintin wrong, Eudora. My half brother could not know that Druoda would keep me from Count Arnulf. But the Count is our liege and my rightful guardian now, no matter what Druoda says, and he will settle my estate. I have only to reach him."

"And how will you reach him when Druoda will not let you leave the manor?" Eudora asked heatedly.

"I will find a way." Brigitte's voice lacked conviction.

"If only you had family somewhere." Althea shook her head, sighing.

"There is no one. You should know, Althea, for you were here when my father became lord of Louroux. His family were few, and the last perished in the King's campaign to regain Lotharingia. And on my mother's side there was no one, for she was ward to Count Arnulf when she married the Baron."

"Milady, Druoda already makes you toil as if you were a mere serf. Soon she will beat you as one, too," Eudora said gravely. "If you know a way to reach

Count Arnulf, then you must do it quickly. Could you send a messenger?"

Brigitte sighed. "Who, Eudora? The serfs would gladly do as I ask, but they need permission to leave the manor."

"Leandor would help you. Or one of the vassals," Eudora persisted.

"Druoda keeps Leandor tied to the manor as well," Brigitte said. "She will not even let him go to the Abbey of Bourges to buy wine. And she has convinced my brother's vassals that her husband, Walafrid, will be seneschal here once she marries me off, and that she will find a husband for me who will not dispose of them, so they will not disobey her for my sake.

"Count Arnuff of Berry is more than a day's ride from here. How can I get to him?"

"But—"

"Be quiet, Eudora!" Althea snapped with a warning look to her daughter. "You are upsetting our lady. Would you have her travel the country *alone?* Be prey to thieves and criminals?"

Brigitte shivered despite the heat of the cooking fires and the sweat beading her brow. She stared dismally at the half-plucked goose, thinking that her prospects for the future could not be worse.

Eudora gazed compassionately at the Baron's daughter. "Why not go out and feed Wolff, milady? I will finish the goose for you."

"No. If Hildegard came in and saw that I was not working, she would run to Druoda. When Mavis protested my doing this work she was beaten and banished. And I could do nothing to help my old friend. The soldiers are following Druoda's orders, not mine.

And then to hear that Mavis had died on the road, killed by thieves! Losing Mavis was like losing my mother again." Brigitte's composure was rapidly crumbling.

She quickly wiped at her tears. Mavis had been her maid from the day she was born. The old Celtic woman had been a second mother, and had been a comfort and help to her young charge ever since her mother died.

"Go, milady." Althea gently pushed Brigitte away from the table. "Feed your dog. He always cheers you."

"Aye, go, lady." Eudora came around the table to take Brigitte's place. "I will finish the goose. And if Hildegard comes in here, she will get her ears boxed."

Brigitte smiled at a picture of Druoda's fat servant spy getting her ears boxed. She picked up a tray of scraps for Wolff. She let Althea fasten her own woolen mantle over her shoulders, and then left the cooking room carefully, checking first to see that the great hall was empty. Fortunately only two servants were there, scattering new rushes on the floor, and they did not look up.

She knew all of the house serfs by name, for they were like family; all except Hildegard, who had come with Druoda and Walafrid. It had been a happy household before Quintin's unexpected death and his aunt's unwelcome change from guest to mistress.

Outside the air was brisk, and the smells of the animal pens to the west drifted on the wind. Brigitte headed that way, passing the horse and goat stables and the sleeping quarters of the house servants across from the stables. Beside the stables was the cow barn, with the sheepfold beyond and the pigsty behind it.

Wolff was locked with the other hunting dogs in a large pen on the side of the barn. Druoda had ordered that. Wolff, Brigitte's pet dog, who had never known anything but freedom, was now as much a prisoner as Brigitte was.

Her father had found Wolff seven years before in the forest that covered most of the land between Louroux and the Loire River. Brigitte had only reached her tenth year when the Baron brought the puppy home. It was obvious how huge the animal would become, and he had certainly not been intended as a pet for Brigitte. But she had fallen in love with Wolff at first sight, and, though she was forbidden to go near the dog, could not keep away. It was soon discovered that Wolff was equally devoted to Brigitte, and that there was no cause for worry. Now that Brigitte was all of five feet two inches tall, her chin did not come far above Wolff's huge white head. And when he stood on his hind legs, he towered a foot above her.

Wolff had known she was coming and sat waiting impatiently by the gate of his pen. It was uncanny, but Wolff always seemed to know whatever Brigitte was doing. Often in the past he had known when she left the manor, and, if tied, he had broken loose and joined her on the road. It had always been impossible for Brigitte to go anywhere without Wolff. But she didn't go anywhere anymore, and neither did he.

Brigitte smiled at him as she opened the gate, let him out, and then closed it. "Feel like a king, do you, not having to wait with your friends there for the marshal to feed you?" She bent to hug him, her long flaxen braids falling over his large head. Though most women in Berry clung to the long linen mantle,

Brigitte had always disliked mantles. Her braids were not immodest, she had decided, and she liked the freedom of not having her head draped all the time, though she always wore a white linen mantle to church.

Her undergowns were usually brown spun wool or, in warm weather, a light cotton wool dyed blue or yellow. Her overtunic was usually blue, a light linen blue in summer and a darker wool blue in winter.

"You can thank Althea for pushing me out of the house, or I would not be here to see you now."

Wolff barked once in the direction of the house before he attacked his food. Brigitte laughed and sat down beside him, leaning back against the dog pen. She stared over the high wall surrounding the manor.

It was hard to see over the wall unless she looked straight up at the treetops. The entire manor, stables, servants' huts, and gardens were walled in by two-foot-thick stone walls, long ago blackened by age and scarred by warfare. In Brigitte's lifetime there had been no siege against her home, but her grandfather had fought several battles to keep his fief, and in his youth her father had seen many assaults on his inheritance. The past twenty years had seen so many battles with the Saracens that almost nobody in France had the men to mount attacks on his neighbors. Brigitte could just barely make out the top of the orchard to the south. The last time the fruit trees had blossomed, her life was entirely different. A year ago she had still had Quintin and Mavis. The fief that she had lived on all her life had gone to Quintin, but she had had her marriage portion. Now it was all hers, but she could not rule it. She must have a husband, or ownership of the fief would revert to Count Arnulf.

Brigitte considered her inheritance. It was a wealthy demesne, acres of fertile land in central France, game abounding in the forests, a well-kept village. And for twenty-seven years it had belonged to Thomas de Louroux, her father.

The manor house was a fine one. Lord Thomas had built it himself, on the same site as the old manor, the old house having burned down in a raid by a recalcitrant vassal of Count Arnulf. Half the village next to the manor had also burned, and many serfs had died. The wattle and daub huts of the village were easy to replace, but not the serfs. Over the years, however, the village had grown, and now there were many serfs bound to the land and Louroux. A keep had been built for the protection of all, spread on a bare hill a half mile to the north.

Brigitte looked that way now and saw the tall tower lit by the afternoon sun. Quintin had been born there. An unlikely place for a birthing, but Thomas de Louroux's first wife had been inspecting the stores there when her pains had come upon her.

Lord Thomas had married Leonie of Gascony soon after he became vassal to Count Arnulf. Lady Leonie was the daughter of a landless knight, but her poverty had not deterred a man in love. She gave him much happiness and a fine son soon after their marriage. But their happiness did not last. When Quintin was four years old, his mother traveled to Gascony for the marriage of her only sister, Druoda, to a clerk, Walafrid of Gascony. She and her whole entourage had been massacred by Magyar raiders as they trav-

eled through Aquitaine on the journey back to Louroux.

Thomas was beside himself with grief, and Count
Arnulf, distressed to see his favored vassal so mo-
rose, pressed him to marry his beautiful ward, Rosamond of Berry. After a proper mourning period,
Thomas did so, and the lovely Rosamond won his
heart. Her generous dowry also blessed Louroux. Was
any other man so lucky as to love two women and find
happiness with each?

After a few years Rosamond gave birth to a daughter, whom she and Thomas named Brigitte, and indeed her august beauty was apparent even when
Brigitte was only a baby. Quintin was eight then
and already page to Count Arnulf and learning his
warrior skills at the Count's castle. Brigitte was a
happy child, loved by her parents and adored by her
half brother, Quintin. Though she saw him only on
his visits home, she could not have loved him more
if he had been her true brother and had been there
always.

Life was wonderful until Brigitte's mother died
when Brigitte was twelve. In the same year she was
further devastated when Quintin, knighted two years
before, left with Count Arnulf on a pilgrimage to the
Holy Land. Her father consoled her as best he could,
though his own grief was tremendous. He spoiled
her terribly during those next few years. Brigitte
became haughty and quick-tempered, but for her
pride she was punished when her father died three
years later.

Fortunately Quintin returned home in 970, shortly
after the Baron died, and took over the lordship of
Louroux. A few months later Druoda and her hus-

band arrived, beseeching Quintin to take them in. He did not refuse his aunt and her husband. Druoda was meek and unassuming. In fact, Brigitte hardly noticed her presence in the house except at meals. Her brother was home to stay, and that was all Brigitte cared about. They consoled each other over the death of their father.

Then, several months earlier, the Abbot of the Burgundian monastery of Cluny was kidnapped by Saracen pirates as he crossed the Alps on the Great St. Bernard pass. The Count of Burgundy was enraged and asked his neighbors for help in ridding the country of Saracen robber bands, who had terrorized all the western passes of the Alps and southern France for more than a century. Count Arnulf had never been harassed by the Saracens, but he needed Burgundy as an ally, so he sent many of his vassals and their knights to do battle with the Saracens. Quintin had gone, too.

Quintin was delighted. A knight's life was war, and he had been idle for more than a year. He took most of his own vassals and their men, and half of the soldiers who manned the keep. He left behind only Sir Charles and Sir Einhard, who were old and prone to frequent illness, and Sir Stephen, one of the household knights.

And so Quintin rode away one bright morning, and that was the last Brigitte ever saw of her half brother. She could not say exactly when it was that Quintin's squire, Hugh, brought the news of Quintin's death. She knew only that it had been several months since she came out of shock and was told that weeks had passed that she was unaware of. She could remember Hugh's words clearly enough. "Lord

Quitin fell when the French nobles attacked one of the pirate bases at the mouth of the Rhone." Her pain never left her.

Brigitte was too stunned by all the deaths in her family to see the changes taking place in her home, or to wonder why Quintin's vassals did not return, or why Hugh had gone back to the south coast. Mavis tried to tell her that she had to notice the changes, particularly the change in Druoda. But it was not until Brigitte found Wolff penned up with the other dogs that she began to understand.

Brigitte confronted Druoda. It was then she realized for the first time that Druoda was not the woman Brigitte had assumed she knew.

"Do not bother me with trifles, girl! I have important matters on my mind," Druoda said imperiously.

Brigitte's temper rose. "By what right—?"

"By every right!" Druoda cut her off. "As your brother's only kin, as *your* only kin, I have every right to assume authority here. You are still a maiden and must have a guardian. Naturally, Walafrid and I shall be appointed."

"No!" Brigitte retorted. "Count Arnulf will be my guardian. He will see to my interests."

Druoda was six inches taller than Brigitte, and she moved closer to tower over her. "My girl, you will hardly have a say in the matter. Maidens do not choose their guardians. Now, if you were without kin, then Count Arnulf, as your brother's seignior, would be your guardian. But you are not alone, Brigitte," Druoda smiled and added smugly. "You have me and Walafrid. Count Arnulf will make us your guardians."

"I will speak to him," Brigitte replied confidently.

"How? You cannot leave Louroux without an escort, and I can see that I will have to deny you one. And Count Arnulf will not come here, for he does not know yet that Quintin is dead."

Brigitte gasped. "Why was he not told?"

"I thought it best to wait," Druoda said carelessly. "Until you are betrothed. No need to bother such a busy man with finding you a suitable husband, when I am perfectly able to do so without his help."

"You choose? Never!" Brigitte's voice rose indignantly. "I will choose my own husband. My father promised me my choice, and Quintin agreed. Count Arnulf knows this."

"Do not be absurd. A girl your age is too young to make such an important decision. The idea!"

"I will not marry at all then!" Brigitte said impulsively. "I will enter a nunnery!"

Druoda smiled and began pacing, thinking as she spoke. "Will you indeed? A lady who has not labored at anything more difficult than a spinning wheel? Well then, if you wish to be a novice, you can begin your training immediately." Druoda smiled again. "You did not know a novice labors day and night like a common servant?"

Brigitte raised her chin defiantly, but she did not reply.

"You can begin your training here and now. Yes, it might do much to improve your attitude."

Brigitte stubbornly agreed. She would show Druoda that she would make a fine novice. Nor did she back down a few days later when she returned to her chamber to find her possessions gone and Druoda waiting to tell her that novices were not allowed fine lodgings and that she would henceforth live in one of the servants' huts across the courtyard.

Still, Brigitte never considered leaving. Not even when she asked Sir Stephen to take a message to Count Arnulf and he refused did she think of going to the Count alone. But when Mavis was turned out with only the clothes on her back, Brigitte had to be locked up to be stopped from going with her. After three days, Brigitte was released.

The time lost did not stop Brigitte. She went directly to the stable, unmindful of the consequences of leaving the manor alone. The dangers were pointed out explicitly by Leandor, the Louroux bailiff, when he found her readying her mount.

"Leave and risk rape and murder," Leandor had said, angry at Brigitte's foolishness. "Lady, I cannot let you go alone."

"I *will* go, Leandor," Brigitte had said determinedly. "If I cannot find Mavis near, then I will ride to Count Arnulf's castle and enlist his aid. It is way past time he knew of the foul deeds of my brother's aunt. I should have gone sooner."

"And if you are attacked?"

"No one would dare. The penalty for harming a lady is too great. I must find Mavis."

Leandor lowered his head. "I did not wish to tell you this, but your maid was found last evening. She is dead."

Brigitte backed away. "No," she whispered, shaking her head. "No, Leandor."

"A woman is not safe alone, not even a gentlewoman such as Mavis. And you, milady, with your beauty, would risk more than murder."

The death of her friend had nearly broken Brigitte

all over again. And Leandor's dire predictions had ended her determination to leave the manor alone. She would wait. Count Arnulf would come eventually.

In the meantime, Druoda had to think she was still intent on a nunnery. Perhaps that would forestall Druoda's matchmaking endeavors, at least for a while.

# Chapter Two

Arles, an old city in the heart of Provence, had been built on the Rhone River many centuries before. Once a major Roman community, it was called little Rome, and Roman antiquities were still present, including a palace built by Constantine and an amphitheater and an arena still intact.

Arles was a new city to Rowland of Montville. But a strange new place would be no difficulty for the young knight. Since leaving his home in Normandy six years before, Rowland had encountered many challenges and had learned how lacking his education really was.

Rowland had been taught letters, which many nobles were not, and he was a skilled warrior. But many an untutored French noble called Rowland a churlish rustic, for he was not refined. Rowland was like his father, who was and would always be a coarse country lord.

Rowland was well aware that he lacked polish. In the years since leaving Luthor of Montville, he had cursed his father more than once for failing him in this area. Ladies were affronted by him. Knights of lesser standing laughed, which had caused more than a few brawls over the years.

Rowland tried. He had his squire teach him proper court behavior, but his newly acquired manners were stiff, and he felt foolish. How did one rid himself of eighteen years of coarse breeding? It was not easily done.

In Arles, Rowland was surprised to meet up with another knight tutored by Luthor. Roger of Mezidon had a black soul if anyone did, and Rowland had hoped never to see the man again. Rowland had not recovered from this surprise when he was accosted by Gui of Falaise, who had come to Arles in order to find Rowland.

"Your father's orders were explicit as usual," Gui said after he and Rowland embraced and exchanged news. They had not seen each other for six years, but had once been the closest of friends. "If I could not find you, I was not to return to his manor!"

"In that case, you have not failed your lord," Rowland replied dryly.

He was not pleased that Gui had sworn allegiance to his father, but he realized that Gui did not know Luthor as well as Rowland did.

"Well, finding you was only half of my mission," Gui admitted. "The other half is to bring you back with me."

Rowland was shocked and hard pressed not to show it. "Why?" he demanded sharply. "Has my father grown soft in old age? Does he forget he banished me from my home?"

"Are you still bitter, Rowland?" Gui's green eyes showed deep concern.

"You know I only wanted to fight for the King of France, who was our Duke's seignior. But Luthor refused. He made me a strong warrior, but he would never let me test my skills. My God, in my whole life I had not left Montville once, and there I was, eighteen years old and newly knighted, and my father wanted to tie me to home as if I were a swaddled babe. It was too much for me to bear."

"But your fight with Luthor was no worse than any other," Gui replied. "He beat you, as he always beat you, hand to hand."

Rowland's dark blue eyes grew darker. "Yes, you saw that, but you did not hear the words spoken afterward. I was as much to blame, I admit it, for he provoked me with his smug assurance that he would never lose a match to me, not even when he approached his grave. If he had not bragged about that before his wife and daughters, then I would not have said I would leave without his permission and probably never return. But I said so in anger, and he said, 'Do so and be damned! I will never call you back.'"

"I never knew it had come to that. But that was six years ago, Rowland, and words spoken in anger should not be remembered forever."

"Yet he said it, and my father does not back down. Even when the man is wrong and knows full well he is wrong, he will not back down."

His friend frowned. "I am sorry, Rowland. I didn't know the extent of your quarrel. You left, and I knew you had fought with Luthor, but he would not talk of it after you went away. I understand now why he was never sure whether you would come home or not. But I know the old warrior has missed you. I'm sure he would have sent for you sooner if he had known of a way to do so without losing face. You know Luthor. He's all pride."

"You have yet to tell me the reason my banishment has been lifted."

"Your father wants you near to claim his fief if he dies," Gui said abruptly.

The color drained slowly from Rowland's face. "Luthor is dying?"

"No! I did not mean to imply that. But there is trouble brewing. Your stepsister Brenda has married."

"So the hag found a mate at last." Rowland chuckled. "The fellow must be a dullard and hideous to look at."

"No, Rowland, she married Thurston of Mezidon."

"Roger's brother!" Rowland cried.

"The same."

"Why? Thurston was a handsome fellow, and the ladies liked him very much. Why would he want Brenda? Not only is she a shrew like her mother, but she's homely as well."

"I believe her dower drew him," Gui offered hesitantly.

"But her marriage portion was not large."

"I have heard she led him to believe otherwise, so enamored of him was she. It is also said he nearly beat her to death on their wedding night, after he found her dower was less than half what he had expected."

"It was no more than she deserved, I suppose," Rowland said offhandedly.

It was no secret that there was no love between Rowland and his two older stepsisters. He had suffered cruelly at their hands from earliest childhood, with no one to protect him. He truly had no feelings for them now, not even pity.

"And my sister Ilse," Rowland continued. "Do she and her husband still live with Luthor?"

"Oh, yes. Geoffrey would never leave his cups long enough to build a manor on his small fief," Gui said contemptuously. "But there is one important change. Geoffrey has suddenly developed a close friendship with Thurston."

"And?"

"It bodes ill for Luthor. He has one son-in-law who is furious over Brenda's marriage portion and who wants more of Montville. His other son-in-law lives under his roof and is friendly with Thurston. Luthor feels he must guard his back now, as his two sons-in-law are probably allied against him."

"What has Luthor to fear? He has men enough."

"Do not underestimate Thurston. He has enough ambition and greed for two men. He plunders in Brittany and Maine, and he has amassed quite a large army, large enough that Luthor strengthened Montville because of him. Open warfare is certain if Luthor is not simply murdered first."

"You think Thurston would resort to that?"

"Yes, Rowland, I do. There has been one accident already that cannot be explained. And if Luthor should die without you there to claim Montville, Thurston and Geoffrey would claim it for themselves, and you would need an army as large as the Duke's to win it back again."

"And if I do not want it?"

"You cannot say so, Rowland! To give up the horses you love, the land that Luthor means you to have."

Rowland ran a hand through his thick, wavy hair. There was no reason to pretend. "You are right, I want it. It's the *only* thing I want of Luthor's."

"So you will return home?" Gui asked hopefully. "Even though you said you would not?"

"I am like my father in many ways, Gui, but when I make a foolish statement, I will not stand by it to my grave. A few years, perhaps, but not always." Rowland chuckled. "Though he too has relented, or so it seems."

"You have changed, old friend. I can remember many fights with Roger of Mezidon because you would not retract a remark. Have you met up with that blackguard in your wanderings?"

"He is here, with the Count of Limousin."

Gui was surprised. "We have heard of Roger's prowess. He has amassed land all across the country. I wonder how he has time to serve so many lords."

"He is as greedy as his older brother, Thurston."

"And have you spoken with Roger?" Gui asked eagerly.

Rowland shrugged. "Yes, I saw him. He did not antagonize me as much as he used to, but he is no longer assured of besting me."

"You have grown more since last I saw you. You're taller and more muscular as well. I would wager you are even taller than Luthor now, and I have yet to see a man look down on him."

Rowland grinned. "I have surpassed Roger, at any rate, much to his chagrin."

"But have you changed otherwise?" Gui ventured, his green eyes twinkling mischieviously. "Have the Franks made you soft?"

Gui ducked, anticipating the mock blow. "No? I suppose we shall have two Luthors at home now?"

Rowland grunted. "At least *I* only strike when provoked, which is more than I can say for my father."

It was true. Luthor of Montville was a hard, gruff man, a man to whom other lords sent their sons for training, for their boys returned strong, capable warriors.

Rowland was Luthor's only son, his bastard. Luthor shrugged that off, but Rowland despised his state. Rowland's mother had been from a nearby village. A woman of no standing and without family, she had died in childbirth, so Rowland was told, and the birthing woman took the infant Rowland into her care. Luthor was not even aware that he had a son until a year and a half later, when the old woman who had kept Rowland was near death and sent for Luthor.

Luthor had no other son, so he brought Rowland home to his wife, sneering at Hedda once more because she had given him only daughters. Hedda hated the baby Rowland and had nothing to do with him until he was old enough to feel her malice. From the time he was three, she and her daughters beat Rowland for any reason.

Luthor did not attempt to stop the cruel treatment of Rowland. Raised harshly himself, he felt he owed his strength to his hard youth.

From Luthor, Rowland learned to suppress tenderness and control all feelings except anger. He was trained to run, leap, swim, and ride, to dart the javelin or battle-ax with unerring aim, and to wield sword and fists with brutality and skill. Luthor taught the boy well, giving blows for mistakes, and praise very grudgingly.

Rowland's childhood was marked by beatings from inside the home and out, for the nobles' sons given to Luthor for training were a spiteful lot, especially

Roger of Mezidon, who was two years older than Rowland and had come to Montville when Rowland was five. Daily beatings continued until Rowland gained enough strength to protect himself. And as Luthor did not stop Hedda and his two daughters from beating Rowland when he was young and defenseless, so he did not stop Rowland from striking back when he grew large enough to do so.

His life was easier after the first time he hit back. After that, he did not retaliate anymore against the women of the house. He preferred to ignore them. He had no need to fear their abuse anymore and had only to fend off the older boys and Luthor.

"Can we take our leave in the morning?" Gui asked as they arrived at Rowland's tent on the outskirts of Arles. The city had been taken over by celebrations now that the battle was won, and there was no reason to stay. "The sooner we leave the better. It has taken me nearly a half year to find you."

"And what led you to me here?" Rowland asked.

"The battle here, of course." Gui grinned widely. "If I have learned nothing else I have at least learned that wherever there is a battle, that is where you are to be found. You must have as many fiefs as Roger, after all your battles."

Rowland chuckled, and his eyes sparkled like sapphires. "I fight for gold, not land. Land needs caring, and I like the freedom to roam where I will."

"Then you must have a fortune in gold."

Rowland shook his head. "Alas, most was spent on women and drink, but I do have some wealth."

"And plunder from the Saracens?"

"That too. Those pirates had silks and glass works, gold plates and lamps, to say nothing of jewels."

"And the battle?"

"There were many battles," Rowland replied. "The Saracens had bases all along the coast. But the biggest was at Nice. They did not make a good showing, however, for they fought without armor. They fell like peasants against skilled knights. Some escaped in their ships, but we plundered their bases and then set fire to them."

"I suppose I came just in time then."

"Yes. My service to the Burgundian duke is over. We can leave in the morning. But tonight, tonight I will show you a fine time, *mon ami*. I know of a decent alehouse by the north gate, where they serve an excellent spiced pottage and the ale is sweet." Rowland suddenly laughed. "You cannot imagine how much I have missed my father's ale. The French can drown in their cursed wine, I will take ale with the peasants any day."

Rowland strapped on his scabbard, sheathed his long broadsword, and gathered a long woolen mantle around his broad shoulders. His mail and armor were left behind. He had grown into a fine figure of a man, Gui thought appreciatively. Rock hard, firm and strong, Rowland was truly a man of war. Luthor would be proud to have this son by his side in battle, whether he admitted it or not.

Gui sighed. Rowland had grown up without the love of a single soul. It was no wonder he was surly at times, bad-tempered and bitter, he had every right to be. Yet Rowland did have good qualities as well. He could show as much loyalty to one man as he could hate to another. And he was not without humor. In truth, he was a good man.

"I must warn you, Gui," Rowland said now as they

entered the city. "Roger of Mezidon has also discovered the merits of the alehouse where we are going, for a certain maid has caught his interest there."

"And yours, too, no doubt," Gui remarked in amusement. "You and he always were attracted to the same women. Did you compete over this one?"

Rowland grimaced, the memory recent. "Yes, we fought. But the sly varlet took me unawares, after I had raised one too many cups."

"So you lost?"

"Did I not just say so?" Rowland snapped. "But that will be the last time I fight him over anything so insignificant. Women are all alike and too easy to come by. He and I have enough reasons to go at one another without making women one of them."

"You have not asked about Amelia," Gui ventured warily.

"That is right, I have not," Rowland retorted.

"You are not curious?"

"No," said Rowland. "I broke my claim on Amelia when I left. If she is still free when I return, then perhaps I will claim her again. If not..." He shrugged. "I will find another. It matters little to me."

"She is free, Rowland. And she has waited faithfully for you for these six years."

"I did not bid her do so."

"Nonetheless, she has. The girl hopes for marriage with you, and even Luthor is not opposed. Already he treats her like a daughter."

Rowland stopped and scowled. "She knows I have no inclination to marry. What did marriage do for my father but give him two nagging daughters and a shrew for a wife?"

"You cannot compare all women to your stepmother," Gui pointed out. "Surely your travels in France have shown you that all women are not the same."

"On the contrary. I know a woman can have sweet words when she wants something, and that otherwise she is a bitch. No, I want no wife nagging at me. I would sooner rot in hell than marry."

"You are being foolish, Rowland," Gui risked. "I know you have said this before, but I thought you would have changed your mind. You should marry. You will want a son one day. You must leave Montville to someone."

"I will no doubt have a bastard or two. I need not marry for that."

"But—"

Rowland's dark blue eyes narrowed. "I feel strongly about this, Gui, so do not prick me about it."

"Very well," Gui sighed. "But what of Amelia?"

"She knew how I felt when she came to my bed. She is a fool if she thought I would reconsider." They started walking again, and Rowland's tone lightened. "Besides, she is the last woman I would recommend for a wife. Comely she is and finely shaped, but fickle. Roger had her before me, and no doubt many others before him. You have probably tasted her yourself. Come now, and admit it."

Gui's face reddened, and he quickly changed the subject. "How much farther to this alehouse?"

Rowland laughed heartily at Gui's discomfort and slapped him on the back. "Relax, *mon ami*. No woman is worth fighting a friend over. You can have any woman I have, with my blessings. As I said before, they are all the same and too easy to come by, including Amelia. And as to your question, the alehouse is just up ahead."

Rowland pointed to a building at the end of the street. Two knights were leaving, and they waved to Rowland.

"They fought by my side in the last battle," Rowland explained. "Burgundians from Lyons. It seems the whole country has contributed to the ousting of the Saracens. Even Saxons sent their knights."

"Would that I had come sooner," Gui said wistfully.

Rowland chuckled. "Have you yet to taste your first battle? Surely Luthor has not been idle all these years?"

"Nay, but only skirmishes with brigands."

"Then you must be looking forward to the confrontation with Thurston."

Gui grinned as they reached the alehouse. "In truth, I have not given it much thought. The only thing on my mind since I left home was what I would do if you refused to come back, for then I could not return either."

"Then you must be much relieved, eh?"

"To be sure." Gui laughed. "I would rather face the devil than Luthor's displeasure."

They went inside and found the alehouse crowded with knights drinking alongside their squires and men-at-arms. The alehouse was large, at least two hundred feet square, and made of stone. It was full. Men stood near the great fireplace in which meat was roasting, or stood in groups talking. There were twenty hardwood tables with stone benches, and most were filled. Despite the presence of two doors, one at each end of the large room, the place was smoky and very warm. Nearly all the knights wore leather and mail, and their squires wore leather. No one seemed comfortable.

At home, away from battle, Rowland and his neighbors, Gui and Roger and Thurston and Geoffrey, all favored the three-sided cape over undershirting and leathers. Fastened on one shoulder, it allowed free access to the sword these men always wore, but was not nearly as cumbersome as mail or a leather overtunic. Rowland did sometimes prefer the tunic, however, as he had never quite gotten used to the cape. It seemed womanish, and the fact that Roger of Mezidon postured so in his made the garment even more suspect in Rowland's eyes.

Roger of Mezidon was there, with two of his vassals and their squires. Gui had traveled without his squire, and Rowland's squire had fallen under a Saracen's scimitar and had not been replaced.

Rowland knew one of Roger's vassals, Sir Magnus, who was a ward of Roger's father. Sir Magnus, like Rowland, was twenty-four, and he had taken his training with Gui and Roger and Rowland.

Roger, at twenty-six, was the oldest of them, and from their first days together, he had been the leader. He had been a bitter youth, knowing that, as a second son, he would have to make his own way in the world. He envied Rowland because Rowland was assured of having Montville one day, bastard or not. That a bastard should inherit while Roger, a noble's son, would not, rankled deeply. Rowland and Roger competed against one another in all things, and Roger, being the older, usually won. He gloated every time. They fought and bickered throughout their youth, more than if they had been brothers, and the fighting did not stop with age.

Roger spied Rowland first and decided to ignore him. But Sir Magnus saw Gui and jumped up to greet them.

"By God, Gui of Falaise, the runt!" Magnus called exuberantly. "It has been years since I saw you. Did you not take old Luthor of Montville as your liege?"

"Yes," Gui answered stiffly.

He bristled at the nickname given him in his youth and never forgotten. *The runt.* He was short of stature, and he could not change that. It had made him the brunt of jokes as a youth and an easy target for men like Roger and Magnus, who threw their weight around. Rowland had taken pity on him and tried to protect him, fighting often in his stead. It had made a bond between Gui and Rowland, and Gui felt that he owed Rowland his loyalty because of it.

"And what brings Luthor's vassal to Arles?" Roger asked.

"There is trouble—"

Before Gui could get any more out, Rowland elbowed him in the ribs and broke in. "My father has missed me," Rowland said lightly, causing Magnus to choke on his ale. Everyone present knew the statement was ludicrous. Roger scowled at the answer, and Rowland anticipated a battle sooner than the one awaiting him in Normandy.

Rowland sat down on a stone bench across the table from Roger. A serving girl, the same one he and Roger had fought over, brought ale to the newcomers and then hovered nearby, aware of the tension her presence was causing and reveling in it. She had been fought over before, but never by two so brutal yet desirable men as these were.

Gui stood behind Rowland, wondering at Roger's black scowl. He was a handsome man with the distinctive blue-eyed, flaxen-haired looks of the Normans, but Roger's face was etched now with hard, angry lines. He seldom laughed except in derision, and his smile was always closer to a sneer. Rowland and Roger were much alike in stature, both brawny, well-fit young men of considerable height. But Rowland's countenance was not as hard as Roger's. Handsome by any standards, Rowland also retained a sense of humor and a hint of kindness.

"So your father misses you, does he?" Roger remarked laconically. "But why send a knight to call you home, when any lackey could have found you?"

"You show an untoward interest in my affairs, Roger," Rowland said flatly.

Roger offered a sarcastic grin. "My brother has married your sister," he said, reaching for the serving girl and pulling her onto his lap with a sideways glance at Rowland. "A mismatch, I do believe."

"I hope you do not think that makes us kin," Rowland growled.

"I would not claim kinship with a bastard!" Roger spat.

The silence was heavy. Then Roger's derisive laughter filled the room. "What? You have no reply, Rowland?" Roger goaded. Hugging the girl he held on his lap, he added, "The bastard has lost his nerve since I defeated him."

An explosion ought to have accompanied the sudden blaze that appeared in Rowland's eyes, but he spoke calmly. "A bastard I am, that's well known.

But a coward, Roger? I had begun to suspect that of you. The last time you attacked me, you made sure I was besotted with drink before you fought me."
Roland started to rise, throwing off the girl, but Rowland's sharp gaze impaled him. "I was wrong, Roger. You are not a coward. You tempt death with your words, and you do so with purpose."

"Rowland, no!" Gui gasped, and he tried to stop his friend from rising.

But the volcano inside Rowland could not be stopped. He shoved Gui aside, stood, and drew his sword, moving so quickly that he pushed the stone slab bench from its supports. It crashed to the floor, scattering the others.

The attention of the whole room was on the combatants, but Rowland and Roger were oblivious to everything but each other. In an act of bravado, Roger swiped the table clean of ale. But the ale splattered over a drunken knight, and the man attacked Roger before Rowland could.

Rowland waited impatiently, his anger simmering, but he did not wait long. The combat between Roger and the knight sparked others to fight, and in moments the room was a battlefield. Drunken warriors attacked, while sober ones defended. Two soldiers attacked Rowland without cause, and he lost sight of Roger in the confusion. Gui came to his aid and the two friends made short work of their foes.

Rowland was about to turn to search out Roger when, behind him, he heard the sharp clang of steel. He turned to see Roger standing, surprised, his sword knocked out of his hand. Beside him was a knight Rowland did not recognize. The stranger faced Rowland and was about to speak when suddenly Roger retrieved his sword and ran the man through.

Rowland was too outraged to move against his old enemy. Before he could recover, a sodden squire came upon Roger from behind and bent the flat edge of his sword over his head. Roger crumbled at Rowland's feet, next to the knight he had wounded.

"Leave him, Rowland." Gui stayed his hand.

Rowland glared at him. "Did you not see? He meant to run me through the back, and this good man prevented him."

"I saw Roger approach you, Rowland, that is all. Surely he would have given warning before he struck."

"I know Roger better than you, Gui, and I say his intent was to kill me without warning," Rowland growled.

"Then challenge him when he recovers," Gui beseeched him earnestly. "But do not resort to murder. Let it go for now."

Rowland had never killed a helpless man, and he agreed. He bent over the knight who had come to his aid, who had probably saved his life.

"This man is still alive, Gui," he cried. "We will take him to the surgeon at my camp."

Gui hesitated. "What of Roger?"

"Leave him," Rowland said in disgust. "One of these men here may run him through and save me the trouble."

# Chapter Three

Rowland waited anxiously outside the physician's tent. Gui paced the ground near him, vexed.

"It has been three days, Rowland," he said impatiently. "If the man dies, he dies. You can do nothing to help him."

Rowland stared at Gui irritably. They had been through this once already, earlier that same day.

"We must be on our way, Rowland. Roger crept off in the night, so you cannot challenge him now. As it is, we will not reach home before the first snow."

"A few more days will not matter."

"But you do not even know this man."

"Your impatience does you no credit, Gui. I am indebted to the man."

"You cannot be sure of that."

"I can."

Finally the tent flap opened, and the Duke's physician approached the two men wearily.

"He was conscious for a few moments, but it's too soon to know if he will live. The flow of blood has ceased, but I can do very little for the injuries inside him."

"Did he speak?"

The physician nodded. "He woke and thought he

was in a fishing village. I believe he spent many weeks on the coast recovering from injuries."

Rowland frowned. "Injuries?"

The physician shook his head. "That young man must be cursed. To be left to the mercy of peasants. He barely survived. He claims he did not awaken for a week, and that he could not move or speak for many more weeks. He took a bad blow on the head."

"Who is he?" asked Rowland anxiously.

"Sir Rowland, the man is gravely wounded. I did not press him, I only listened to what he volunteered. He was in a frantic state. When I insisted he could not get up, he tried to explain about the injury. He said something about a sister, his worry over her, but he collapsed before he could tell me what it was about. He was quite upset."

"May I see him?"

"He is unconscious again."

"I will wait in the tent until he awakens. I must speak with him."

"Very well."

Gui continued his urgings after the doctor left. "There, the leecher does not seem overly worried. Let us leave for home. You can do no more here."

Rowland had lost patience with his old friend. He was honor bound to stay. "Be damned, you are like a woman with your nagging! You are so eager to be off, then go—go!"

"Rowland, I only see the urgency of haste. It may already be too late. Thurston of Mezidon may have attacked while I was away, before the cold set in."

"Leave now. I will catch up to you on the road."

"But I cannot let you travel alone."

Rowland looked at his friend sharply. "Since when

do I need an escort? Or is it you do not trust me to follow? I can see you do not." Rowland chuckled. "Take my possessions with you, then. Leave only my horse and armor. That should assure you that I will follow. Unhindered, I should join you between the Rhone and the Loire rivers. If not there, then just after you leave the Loire. Do not wait if I fail to catch up."

Reluctantly, Gui left, and Rowland sat by the cot in the tent for the rest of the afternoon. That evening his vigilance was rewarded when the injured man opened his eyes. He tried to sit up, but Rowland stopped him.

"You must not move. Your wound will bleed again."

The man's light brown eyes focused on Rowland. "I know you?" He spoke clearly in French, then answered his own question. "From last eve at the alehouse."

"That was three nights past, my friend."

"Three?" the man groaned. "I must find my men and return to Berry immediately."

"You will not be going anywhere, not for some time." The man groaned. "Do you need the physician?"

"Only if he can perform a miracle and heal me this minute," the man whispered.

Rowland grinned. "What can I do to help you? You saved my life and have suffered for it."

"I suffer from my own carelessness. Only twice in my life have I raised my sword for earnest combat, and each time I have ended near death. I do not listen to warnings. I always think that men will fight fairly. I have learned the lesson at great expense."

"I understand you recently recovered from a head wound. The Saracens?"

"Yes. I and three others were after a fleeing band. They turned to fight when we caught up, and my horse crumbled, throwing me. The next thing I knew, I was in a fishing village, with a headache I would wish on no man, and told I had been unconscious for a week. I came to Arles as soon as I was well. I have had no luck in finding my vassals. I had thought to find one or two at that alehouse, but I saw none of them."

"But fortunate for me you were there."

"I could do no less than fight when I saw that knight creeping up behind you," the wounded man declared.

"Well, you have saved the life of Rowland of Montville. What can I do in return?"

"Pray for my quick recovery."

Rowland laughed, for the man kept his humor despite his condition.

"I will indeed pray for you. And your name? I must have it if I am to entreat the saints."

"Quintin de Louroux."

"A Frank?"

"Yes, of Berry."

"Your family is there?"

"My parents are both dead. I have only my sister left and—" He paused. "And there is one thing you could do for me."

"You have only to name it."

"My vassals, the three I brought with me. If you could find them for me, I will be grateful. I would send one home to tell my sister that I am alive but that I shall not be home for some weeks yet."

"Your sister believes you dead?"

Quintin nodded weakly. "I think she must. I had thought it would be only a matter of a few days to round up my men and leave for Berry. Now the physician tells me that I must keep to this bed for three weeks. I cannot bear to think of my sister grieving over me."

Such concern for a woman was beyond Rowland. "She must be very dear to you."

"We are very close."

"Then rest easy, my friend. I will find your knights and send them to you. But you ask too little of me. I would consider it an honor if you would let me bring the news to your sister. Putting your mind at ease would be small payment on the debt I owe you."

"I cannot ask that of you," Quintin protested.

"You offend me if you do not ask it. I must travel north at any rate, for my father has called me home to Montville. I delayed only to see how you were faring. And have you not heard of the destriers of Montville? My mount would put your knight's horse to shame, and the good news would reach your sister all the sooner."

Quintin's eyes brightened. "You will find my home easily. You need only ask once you near Berry, and you will be directed to Louroux."

"I will find it," Rowland assured him. "You must rest and regain your strength."

"I can rest now," Quintin sighed. "You have my thanks, Sir Rowland."

Rowland stood up to leave. "It's little enough for you, and nothing at all compared to saving my life."

Quintin protested, "Your debt is paid. Do not tell my sister I have been wounded once again, for I would cause her no more anguish. Tell her only that I cannot leave the Duke's service as yet, but will return to her soon."

It was only after Rowland had left Arles that he realized he did not know the name of Quintin de Louroux's sister. But no matter—he would find her.

# Chapter Four

*D*ruoda of Gascony lounged on a long green couch in her new chambers, eating dried grapes and drinking their nectar in sweet wine. It was late afternoon, and, although the winter had been mild thus far, Druoda was used to the warmer climate of southern France, and she insisted on a brazier of hot coals to warm her room.

At Druoda's feet knelt Hildegard, preparing her mistress's nails for painting, another of many practices Druoda had learned from the carefree women of the south. It was not so very long ago that both women had been strangers to luxury. Only recently they had catered to travelers, working day and night laundering other people's travel-stained garments and cooking. This deplorable labor had been necessary, for Druoda's father had left her nothing. Her husband, Walafrid, possessed a large house, but had no money to maintain it. So they had turned the house into a hostelry, hiring Hildegard to help.

Thanks to the death of Druoda's nephew, Quintin, their days of hard work were over. It had been a calculated risk, assuming guardianship of Brigitte de Louroux and keeping the news of the Baron's death from his liege lord. Druoda gloated over having rid herself of the only person who might tell Count Arnulf of the Baron's death. Hugh had returned to the south coast on Druoda's orders to verify Quintin's death. Druoda did not really need the verification, but she needed time, and waiting for Hugh and Quintin's vassals to return with Quintin's possessions was giving her the time she needed to marry Brigitte without Count Arnulf's interference.

If there was a betrothal before the Count knew of Quintin's death, then there would be no need to appoint the girl a guardian, for she would have a husband. It only remained to keep the lady from crying to the Count, and that could be arranged by simply keeping them apart. Once the wedding took place, the Count would not step in and try to run things. No, he would leave the estate to Brigitte's lawful husband, who would be controlled by Druoda.

The husband, ah, that had been the most difficult part! Finding a man who wanted Lady Brigitte enough to agree to Druoda's demands had been Druoda's greatest challenge. She had a long list of possibilities, a list obtained from the servants, for Brigitte had been asked for many times over the years. Druoda believed she had finally found the right man in Wilhelm, lord of Arsnay. He had come to ask for the lady two times in recent years, but Thomas and Quintin had refused his request, for they would never have considered giving their precious Brigitte to a man older than her father, and a man with Wilhelm's unsavory reputation.

Lord Wilhelm was perfect for Druoda's plans. A man who seldom left Arsnay, who would not come often to Louroux to inspect his wife's estate, a man who wanted a beautiful young virgin so much he was willing to give Walafrid free reign at Louroux was just the thing. The old fool thought only a virgin bride could give him the son he so desperately wanted. It was not Brigitte herself he wanted, though he was delighted with her beauty. It was her innocence he demanded. And what other young woman would have such an old husband? Lord Wilhelm was also Count Arnulf's vassal, so the Count would not question Druoda's choice.

Druoda lay back and sighed with satisfaction. Wilhelm was the answer to Druoda's plans, and she was extremely pleased with herself, for only last night she had concluded the arrangements with him. Wilhelm was so smitten that he would no doubt pamper Brigitte. And after a year or so, Brigitte would have a most unfortunate accident, for it would not do for her to outlive Wilhelm and be in a position to threaten all Druoda had worked for. Druoda had gotten rid of Mavis with perfect ease, and she would get rid of Brigitte. Brigitte would die, Wilhelm would be Lord of Louroux and Walafrid still seneschal, and Druoda would always rule Louroux.

"When will you tell her, Druoda?"

Hildegard's question brought a smile to Druoda's round, pasty face. "This evening, after Brigitte is weary from working the whole day long."

"Why are you so sure she will agree? Even I would not care to marry Wilhelm d'Arsnay."

"Nonsense," Druoda scoffed. "He may be a little ill-favored in appearance and have peculiar notions about virgins and sons, but he is a man of wealth. And do not forget the lady has no choice." Hildegard looked at her mistress doubtfully, and Druoda laughed. "Let her protest. She can do nothing about this marriage."

"And if she runs away?"

"I have employed two ruffians who will guard her until the ceremony. I brought them back with me last night."

"You have thought of everything," her servant said admiringly.

Druoda nodded grimly. "I have had to."

Druoda had been cursed with the square shape of her father, and a moon face also like his, whereas her sister, Leonie, had been blessed with their mother's looks. Druoda always envied Leonie her beauty, and when she made such a fine marriage with the Baron of Louroux, Druoda's envy turned immediately to hate for her sister and her sister's husband. Now that Leonie and her husband were dead, that hate found a focus in Brigitte.

Now Druoda would have what Leonie had once had. She did not have such a fine husband, however, for Walafrid was a poor example of a man. But that suited Druoda. She had a strong will and could not have borne any man's domination. At the age of forty-three, she would finally have what had been denied her all her life. With Brigitte safely married and out of her way, Louroux would be hers to rule, and she would be a grand lady, a lady of wealth and influence.

Late that evening Brigitte was summoned to Druoda's spacious chamber, the room that had once belonged to her parents. The large wood-frame bed was now draped in gaudy red silk, and ornate lounges had been added to the room. The long wardrobes were filled with the many rich tunics and mantles that Druoda had ordered made. Wooden tables had been replaced with bronze, and candelabra of pure gold adorned many of them.

Brigitte hated the room as it was, filled with Druoda's extravagances. Druoda reclined on her couch with a queenly air, her coarse, heavy body clothed in no fewer than three linen tunics of varying colors and lengths. Small emeralds had been sewn onto the cuffs of the wide sleeves of the outer gown. These gems were rarer than diamonds and cost a fortune. Druoda's girdle was also studded with emeralds, as was the gold ornament she wore in her elaborately curled dark brown hair. No doubt Hildegard had used a vexing iron.

Brigitte had worked the entire day at weeding the manor garden. The chore had always before been given to three or four serfs as part of the labors owed their lord, yet she had done it all alone. And she had also bottled the winter's herbs. She was exhausted and cramped with hunger pangs, for she had been told not to stop working until she was finished, and she had only just finished. Yet there was Druoda with a feast laid out on the table before her. There was more food than even Druoda could possibly eat, succulent pig, several creamed vegetables, breads, fruits, and sweet cakes.

"I would like to retire, Druoda." Brigitte spoke after a few minutes had passed in silence. "So if you will tell me why I am here—"

"Yes, I imagine you are tired and hungry," Druoda said casually, as she stuffed another sweet cake into her mouth. "Tell me, girl, do you feel you are being overworked? But no, you must not think so, for you never complain."

"Druoda, if you would tell me why you have summoned me," Brigitte said tiredly.

"I think your stubbornness has gone far enough, do you not agree?" Druoda did not wait for an answer. "Of course you do. Forget this foolishness about a nunnery. I have wonderful news, Brigitte." Druoda smiled.

"What news?"

Druoda's lips turned down at the corners. "Your attitude toward me has not been all I might have desired. Nevertheless, out of the goodness of my heart I have arranged a splendid marriage for you."

Brigitte was speechless. She had told Druoda several times that she would not marry yet.

"Well, girl? Have you nothing to say?"

"I had no idea you could be so generous, Druoda," said Brigitte, managing a tone that could not quite be taken for sarcasm.

"I knew you would be grateful, and justifiably so, for your betrothed is a man of importance, and you will be happy to know that he also is vassal to your liege, Count Arnulf, so that good man will surely not refuse him. Yes, my dear child, you are truly fortunate."

Brigitte still held her temper in check, though her light blue eyes sparkled dangerously.

"And what of my mourning period? How dare you try to marry me off when I am still in mourning for my brother?"

"Your betrothed is eager for this union and will not be put off. On the morrow we will go to his manor to celebrate your betrothal. I trust you can be suitably attired and ready to leave by midday?"

Brigitte hesitated. To leave the manor, perhaps even to travel toward Arnulf's castle!

"I can be ready," Brigitte said calmly, adding, "but you have not told me his name."

Druoda smiled with great delight. "Your betrothed is Lord Wilhelm d'Arsnay."

Brigitte gasped. Druoda watched gleefully as the color drained from her face.

"You are overcome by your good fortune," Druoda said smoothly.

"Lord Wilhelm!"

"A fine man."

"He is a fat, lecherous, loathsome, disgusting pig!" Brigitte cried, caution gone. "I would rather die than marry him!"

Druoda laughed. "Such a temper! First you choose a nunnery, and now it's death over dishonor!"

"I mean what I say, Druoda!"

"Then I suppose you will have to kill yourself," Druoda sighed. "Poor Wilhelm will be so disappointed."

"I do not have to marry him just because you have arranged it. I will leave here if you insist on it. I do not care what befalls me on the road, for it cannot be worse than marrying the most repulsive man in all of Berry."

"I am afraid that is out of the question. You do not think I would let you come to harm on the road, do you? I have given my word on this marriage, and it will take place."

Brigitte drew herself up, trying desperately to control herself. "You cannot force me to wed that loathsome man, Druoda. You forget one important factor. Whether he is your choice or not, Count Arnulf is still my lord, and he must approve the match. He would never give me to Wilhelm d'Arsnay, vassal or not."

"You think not?"

"I know he will not!"

"You underestimate me, girl." Druoda growled, all pretense gone now. She leaned forward, toward her prey. "The Count will give his consent, because he will think this match is what *you* desire. It is not uncommon for a young woman to choose an old man for her husband, for she is sure to outlive him and will someday have the freedom of widowhood. And you, my girl, with your willfullness, would desire that freedom. Count Arnulf will believe that you desire this match."

"I will tell him otherwise, even if I must do so on my wedding day!"

Druoda slapped her hard then, viciously and with pleasure. "There will be no more outbursts, Brigitte. You will be wed when Count Arnulf is unable to attend your wedding. If you defy me, I will be forced to take harsh measures. A good beating might instill proper respect. Now get out of here. Get out!"

# Chapter Five

*B*rigitte was awakened after only a few hours sleep. Before she was even fully awake she was informed by a smug Hildegard that she would be moved back into her old chamber later that day. How typical of Druoda to allow her to return now, only to prepare to meet her betrothed.

Brigitte spent most of an hour in a large tub, soothing some of the stiffness from her body. But nothing could be done for the roughness of her hands, the broken and chipped nails, evidence of months of toil.

After her bath, she went to her clothes wardrobe. Only two respectable garments were left to her. A smaller chest was inside the larger one, but the costly jewelry it had once contained had disappeared. A spiked comb and a steel looking glass were all that remained of what had once been a fabulous array of jewels. Looking beneath a pile of cotton garments, Brigitte withdrew two tunics of fine blue linen, embroidered with silver threads. The longer tunic was sleeveless, to be worn beneath the shorter outer tunic, which had long, wide sleeves. The outer gown was, she was astonished to see, inlaid with rare sapphires all over the bodice. The gown had been a gift from

her father just before he died. The long mantle that
was made for these gowns was fringed with silver
cord and matched her undergarment, and was clasped
with a large sapphire. Why had the jewels not been
removed?

Brigitte could only imagine that this ensemble
had been overlooked when she moved to the servants'
huts. Why else was she still in possession of such
costly gems? Like emeralds, sapphires were rarer
than diamonds or pearls. The sapphires might even
buy her freedom.

At a little after dawn, a horse was brought around
to the front of the manor house for Brigitte. She was
dressed in her blue gowns, the fringed mantle clasped
at her throat, looking much like her former self. She
looked beautiful and even defiant, her golden hair
braided into two long plaits falling over her shoulders to her waist.

Druoda was mounted and waiting. Also present
were two burly men whom Brigitte had never seen
before. She was offered no introductions or expla-
nations before Druoda led the way through the gate
in the stone wall surrounding the manor. The two
men rode on either side of Brigitte.

It was not until hours later, when they came within
a mile of Lord Wilhelm's domain and Druoda slowed
enough that Brigitte could ask about the two men,
that her suspicions were confirmed.

"They are here to guard you," Druoda informed
her curtly. They will see to it that you do not disappear before your marriage ceremony."

Brigitte was frantic. How could she escape if she
was continually guarded?

The rest of the day was no less dismal. They spent

the afternoon with Lord Wilhelm and his obese daughter. Wilhelm was a grossly fat man, much older than Brigitte's father, with thin tufts of grey hair circling his head. He was ugly, with a red and bulbous nose and beady black eyes that never left Brigitte until the banquet was served.

They dined in the great hall, a barren room except for the trellis tables and the armor which adorned the bleak stone walls. Brigitte could not touch any of the food, and her stomach churned as she watched the others stuff themselves. Druoda was in fine company, among fellow gluttons.

Rare jellyfish and spiced sea urchins were served first and quickly devoured. The main course, broiled ostrich with sweet sauce, turtle dove, mutton, and boiled ham, went just as quickly. Cakes and stuffed dates fried in honey were served last, and were accompanied by wine spiced with myrrh. A banquet customarily took hours, but this one did not last more than one hour.

After the banquet Brigitte feared that she would become sick when she was forced to watch the entertainment Wilhelm had planned, the baiting of a tame dog against a wolf. Brigitte loved animals and was frequently upset by such displays.

She ran from the hall to the courtyard and took deep breaths, grateful to be away from the others. But her relief was short-lived, for Wilhelm's daughter followed her and said abruptly, "I am mistress of this house and shall always be. You will be the fourth child bride my father has brought home, and if you think you can take over here, you will end as the others did—dead."

Too shaken to reply, Brigitte stumbled away from

her. They soon left Wilhelm's house, and Brigitte stammered her good-byes through a blur of tears.

Tears still blurred her vision as they rode off toward home. Brigitte's guards were close by. How could she ride to Count Arnulf if they would not let her out of their sight? she wondered.

But what really did she have to lose if she made a desperate attempt to reach Arnulf? Suddenly she wiped at her eyes angrily and dug her heels into her horse. For several moments, she and her mare flew from the others. But her guards had been expecting this, and they caught up with her quickly, before she passed the last cobbled hut in Wilhelm's village.

They brought her back to where Druoda waited, and Brigitte was met by a blow that took her unawares and knocked her off her horse. She fell into the mud, the breath knocked from her. It brought her rage to the point of explosion, but she did not vent her anger on Druoda. She kept it under control, and as far as Druoda could see, Brigitte was beaten. She wiped at the mud on her face and allowed herself to be handed roughly back up onto her mare.

Brigitte simmered silently. She waited patiently for her companions to relax their guard, careful always to ride slumped in her saddle and give every impression of submissiveness. But Brigitte was feeling far from submissive.

So engrossed in thought was she that she was not aware it had grown dark until the chill of night stung her cheeks. She quickly raised the hood of her mantle and pulled it closer over her head. While doing so, she studied her companions furtively and saw that only Druoda was riding close to her. The guards had gone a short way ahead of the women in order to protect them from night raiders.

This was her chance. With night upon them, she could hide in the dark. She would never be as close to Count Arnulf as she was now. Gathering her reins in a tight fist and moving closer to Druoda, she used them to whip Druoda's mare, sending the horse charging into the guards, while Brigitte spun about and galloped off in the opposite direction.

This time she was able to put a good distance between herself and the guards before they gave pursuit. A half mile down the road she slowed and turned off into the woods, the shadows there black as pitch and perfect for concealment. She quickly slid off her mare and began walking her horse slowly through the dark maze. A few moments later she heard the guards race past her on the old track road.

She knew the forest, for she had traveled it often with her parents when they visited Count Arnulf. On the other side of the woods there was a wider road, the old road between Orleans and Bourges, and that route would take her to Arnulf. She had only to get through the forest. However, that was no small feat.

As her fear of Druoda's guards lessened, the frightening sounds of the forest began to assault her, and Brigitte remembered Leandor's dire warnings about thieves and murderers, groups of brigands who lived in forests. She quickened her pace till she was nearly running, and suddenly she burst through the woods into a clearing. Panic seized her. She looked around frantically, expecting to see a fire with men surrounding it. She gasped with relief, for it was not a clearing she stood in but the road—she had made it to the road!

She drew back into the shadows and hastily shed her gown and tunic, all but an old woolen tunic next to her skin. She then wrapped her other gowns around her waist. Thin as they were, they were not too bulky. She put her mantle back on but did not clasp it, so that if she came upon anyone she could remove it quickly and be left in peasant's garb.

She mounted again and rode south, exhilarated, feeling free. There would be no wedding to Wilhelm. And there would be no more Druoda, for Arnulf would not take kindly to her once Brigitte told him what she had been doing at Louroux. Brigitte felt almost giddy as her sturdy mare quickly put mile after mile behind them. Nothing could stop her now.

But suddenly something did. Her horse stopped and reared up, and for the second time that day Brigitte found herself on the ground, trying to breathe. She scrambled to her feet as fast as she could, fearing her horse would bolt. But the mare stood still, and as Brigitte moved closer, she saw why.

"And what have we here?"

The knight sat ramrod straight on his destrier, a horse larger than any Brigitte had ever seen. The knight was himself quite large, probably six feet tall, even taller. He wore full armor and was a most impressive sight. He removed his helmet and revealed a thick shock of blond hair which fell just below his neck, a style too short for a Frenchman. Brigitte could not see his features clearly.

"Well, wench?"

His deep voice broke through her surprise. "Is that

all you can say, Sir Knight, after you have unseated a lady?"

"A lady, is it?"

Too late, Brigitte remembered her worn peasant's tunic. She decided to say nothing further. Remounting her horse as quickly as she could, she tried to pull the leather reins from his grip. But she could not, for he wouldn't let them out of his iron grasp.

"How dare you?" Brigitte demanded. "Is it not enough you cause my horse to throw me? Now you detain me as well?" He laughed, and she said haughtily, "What is so amusing?"

"You would have me think you a lady, with your haughty airs, but you are not," the knight said derisively. Then he continued, "A lady, alone, without an escort?"

Brigitte's mind whirled, but before she could select a reply, he said, "Come along."

"Wait!" Brigitte cried as he turned her horse around and began to pull it along after his. "Stop!" He appeared not to have heard and she glared at his back in fury. "Where are you taking me?"

"I will take you where I am bound, and others can then return you to your master. I am sure he will be glad to have his horse back, if not his serf."

"You think me a serf?"

"Your mount is too fine for a village wench," he continued. "And even a lord pleased with your favors would not bestow on a serf such a costly garment as the mantle you are wearing."

"The mantle is mine, as is the horse!"

"Your cunning is wasted on me, damosel," he said smoothly. "I care not what you say."

"Let me go."

"No. You have stolen, and I cannot abet a thief."
he said harshly, then added, "Were you a man, I
would as soon run you through as waste my time
returning you. Do not test me further with lies."

Well, all was not lost, Brigitte thought. Wherever
he took her, they would surely know her, and then
this ignoble knight would find out what mistake he
had made. Somehow, she would at least get a message to Count Arnulf.

An hour passed and then another before he left
the road and took them in the direction of Louroux.
Brigitte began to be truly frightened.

To be taken right back to Druoda—she could not
stand it anymore. She would never get another chance
to escape if she failed this time.

Brigitte slid quietly off the horse and dashed frantically into a nearby copse of trees. She tripped and
fell, scraping her palms and the side of her face on
the rough ground. Her cheek burned, and tears sprang
to her eyes. She got up and ran, but he was behind
her and reached her before she could enter the forest
again.

Standing next to her, the knight was an awesome
sight, every bit as large as she had first thought.
How she hated this man!

Brigitte spat, "Who are you? I want to know your
name, for some day I will make you pay for what
you have done to me!"

"And what have I done to you?"

"You bring me to Louroux!"

"Ah! So that is it. It is from Louroux that you are
fleeing." He laughed.

Brigitte stiffened. "And are you pleased that I will
suffer because of you?"

"I do not care," He shrugged. "My business here is with the lady of Louroux."

"What is your business with Druoda?" she asked, assuming that Druoda was the lady to whom he referred.

"Nothing to concern you, wench," he answered disdainfully.

"You have yet to tell me your name," she reminded him. "Or do you fear to give it to me?"

"Fear you, woman?" He was incredulous. "If I am ever addled enough to let a wench do me harm, then it's no more than I deserve. Rowland of Montville, at your service," he mocked.

When he pushed her back toward her horse, panic seized her. She turned and braced her small hands against his chest. "Please, Sir Rowland of Montville, do not take me to Louroux. Druoda will have me locked up."

"Locked up? You deserve a beating for thievery. The lady is merciful if she only locks you up."

"I tell you I stole nothing!"

"Lies!" he thundered. "Enough! My patience is gone!"

He took her reins, and they continued the short distance to Louroux. It was Hildegard who met them in the torchlit courtyard, and her eyes lit up at the sight of Brigitte and the tall knight.

"Will you not learn, girl? My lady has been more than fair with you, but this time I fear you will pay for your foolishness. You had best wait for her in your chamber."

"Which chamber, Hildegard?" Brigitte asked caustically. "My old one, or my recent hovel? Do not answer. I will go to the hovel, for I will no doubt end there before the night is through."

Rowland shook his head as he watched Brigitte walk proudly across the court to a short row of servants' huts and enter one. "By the saints," he sighed in disbelief. "I have never met such an insolent serf."

"What?" Hildegard looked from the hut to him in confusion.

Rowland laughed derisively. "She tried to tell me she was a lady. But I was not so easily fooled. The wench should be punished not only for thievery, but for audacity as well. If she belonged to me, I swear she would not be so haughty."

Hildegard held her tongue. It was clear that the knight thought Lady Brigitte no more than a runaway serf!

"Will you come into the hall, Sir Knight? The Lady Druoda will be pleased that you have returned her...property."

# Chapter Six

*H*ildegard quickly explained to Druoda while the knight sat by himself at a table in the great hall. He was pleased with the wine and food set out for him.

Hildegard giggled, her eye cautiously on their guest. "I gave him wine with a little powder to loosen his tongue."

"You drugged him?"

"We need to know what he has heard of Louroux, do we not? He is still upright, but he will not be for long. Come."

"I will see to the Norman. I have something more important for you to do," Druoda said, glancing venomously in the direction of Brigitte's quarters. "The girl almost succeeded in escaping today, even with those fools I hired to prevent it. If not for the knight, she would have succeeded, and all we have achieved would be lost even now. Ten lashes will make her think before she tries again."

"You want her beaten?"

"Severely. Be sure to bind her mouth. I do not want the whole manor to know about it, but I want her to suffer as much pain as possible so that she will be in no condition to escape again. Do not draw

blood. Wilhelm would not want his bride marred."
Druoda smiled at her old friend. "I am sure he will
take pleasure in marring her himself, if what I have
heard about him is true."

Druoda approached the knight. His eyes were
closed, and his head was tilting downward, as if he
were fighting to stay awake.

"I owe you my thanks," Druoda pronounced imperiously as she came forward.

His eyes opened, but it took several moments for
them to focus. He was a formidable looking young
man, with a rough handsomeness that was striking.
A strong, aggressive chin, beardless, but with a day's
stubble darkening it, sharp, aquiline nose, eyes of a
sapphire hue. Yes, he was indeed handsome.

"You are the lady of Louroux?"

"I am."

Rowland shook his head to clear his vision, but
the image before him did not change. The large, bulky
woman seemed nearly twice his age, and she was
not the picture of Quintin de Louroux's sister that
he had carried in his mind. Why had he expected a
comely lady, or at least a young one?

"I bring you glad tidings, mistress," Rowland
blurted. "Your brother lives."

"You are mistaken, Sir Knight," Druoda replied
curtly. "I have no brother."

Rowland stood up, his vision blurred again, and
he fell back on the bench, cursing the woman silently
for keeping him waiting and for serving such strong
wine. "I know you think your brother is dead, but I
am here to tell you this is not so. Quintin de Louroux
is very much alive."

"Quintin...lives!" Druoda sank down onto the

bench beside the Norman knight. "How—how is it possible?"

"Your brother's squire left him for dead, but the fool was so anxious to be away from the fighting that he did not make sure of his master's death. Your brother was found by some fishermen and taken to their village. It took a long time, but he recovered."

Druoda quickly gathered her wits. There was no need to panic. This man obviously thought she was Quintin's sister.

"Where is...my dear brother now?"

"In Arles, where I have just come from. I was going north, and so he bid me stop and bring you the news since he has been delayed. He was most eager that you not grieve for him any longer than necessary."

"He has been delayed? When can I anticipate his return?"

"A month, perhaps less."

Druoda rose. "You have been most kind in coming here to bring me these joyful tidings. I am indeed grateful."

"Lady, I am in your brother's debt, so this was only a small favor."

"His debt?"

"Your brother saved my life."

Druoda did not care to waste time prodding him for his story. "You will of course be my guest this night. I will send you a young wench for company."

Rowland tried to stand once again, and this time he succeeded. "Thank you, lady."

Druoda smiled, bade him good night politely, and left him to wait for Hildegard, who would show him to his quarters.

She met Hildegard in the courtyard. "Has the girl been taken care of?"

"Did you not hear the howls of her dog because of it? I am glad that beast is penned."

"Be damned, Hildegard! Then someone knows what you were doing!" Druoda snapped.

"Only the dog with his keen hearing," Hildegard assured her. "No one else was there to hear how greatly she suffered." Then Hildegard asked, "What news did the Norman bring?"

"The worst. Hurry and show him to a room, then join me. We have much to do."

Hildegard did as she was told. She found Druoda in her room, nervously pacing the floor.

"What has happened?"

"Quintin is alive."

"Oh, no!" Hildegard cried. "He will kill us!"

"Silence, woman!" Druoda rasped. "I have killed before this. If I must I shall do so again to keep what I have gained. I will not have everything taken from me. My nephew will come here in a few weeks, or so the Norman says."

"If he comes here, Brigitte will tell him everything," Hildegard cried.

"She will not be here to tell him," Druoda said firmly. "I will have her taken to Lord Wilhelm's to await the wedding there. Then I will go to Count Arnulf with the news of Quintin's death. We will have Brigitte married before he returns. And if I can arrange everything as I please, he will never return at all," she said grimly.

# Chapter Seven

Brigitte lay motionless on her pallet, letting her tears fall freely. But crying only made her muscles jerk and the slightest movement was agony.

She still could not believe what they had done to her. She had only just finished washing her muddy clothes when Hildegard and the two guards burst into her room. She was stripped of her worn gown and gagged, and did not even have time to feel humiliated at being exposed to the two men before she was thrown face down on her mat and held fast by the guards. And then came the pain, as Hildegard let loose with her leather strap. It was as if fire licked across her back each time that strap came down, and she could do nothing but cry out against the gag in her mouth. She lost consciousness before she felt the last blow, and when she awoke she found herself alone, still naked.

She began to cry again, but only for a moment. She could not give up! She would just have to get her clothes with the sapphires sewn on them, and some food. Even now she was weak with hunger, not having eaten all day. She would have to force herself up off the pallet and try again to get away. This time she could take Wolff with her.

\* \* \*

Rowland tossed fitfully in his sleep, troubled by a dream that had recurred for as long as he could remember. Dreams could be delightful or disquieting, some were even terrifying, but Rowland did not understand this one at all. It did not come to him often, at least not as frequently as it had in his youth, but it came when his mind was troubled.

The dream always began with a feeling of contentment. And then there would be faces, the face of a young man out of the dark, and then of a young woman, faces that Rowland had never seen except in the dream. The faces would be together, looking down on him from far above. But Rowland was never frightened of them. There was such warmth and happiness in those faces, happiness such as he had never known in his life. But then something would shatter the feeling of happiness, though he never knew what. The faces would disappear, and flashing scenes would take their place, along with a sense of desolation. Rowland would awaken with a terrible feeling of loss and not know why.

It was the same now. His tossing landed him on the floor, and he awoke abruptly, the dream still vivid.

Rowland pulled himself back up on the bed and shook his head. However long he had slept, it had not been long enough to clear the effects of the wine from his body.

He hated wine anyway. Why in the name of the blessed saints had he not asked for ale? Still drugged, he stumbled off the pallet and into the hallway. Rowland moved slowly through the dark corridor. A meager red glow filtered up the stairs from the hall below, creating shadows along the walls. It was several moments before he got his bearings, and he looked in both directions, up and down, to see if anyone was there. He desperately needed some ale to clear his head.

Brigitte held her breath and pressed her back to the wall. She was only a few feet from him. Would he recognize her in the dark? She wanted to run, but her legs would not move. Her back still hurt, and if she ran now, she would have to go without Wolff, without her clothes, and without a horse. All she had managed so far was to gather food, which she had wrapped in a small bag. She stood stock-still, hardly daring to breathe.

Rowland saw her, and, though he failed to recognize her in the dark, he did see the long flaxen hair. He moved toward her. Ale fled from his mind. If he could not clear his head with ale, he could at least pass the night with the lovely young woman Druoda had obviously sent to him. It was, after all, only polite to entertain one's guest with a companion, and while this girl seemed a bit reluctant to join him, he would soon warm her.

Without speaking, Rowland pulled her into his room and closed the door. He did not let go of her for fear that he would lose her in the dark. But he loosened his hold when he heard her crying.

"I will not hurt you," he said gently. "I do not give pain without reason, so you must not fear me."

Rowland, still drugged, did not realize that he was slurring his words and that his French was interspersed with the old Norse tongue his father had taught him long ago.

"Is it my size that frightens you?" he asked, gazing

down at her small form. "I am not much different from any other man." As he stood gazing down at her, he suddenly recognized her.

"Be damned, woman, you try my patience sorely! Have you not given enough trouble for one day? I will cajole you no more, but take what your mistress has sent me and be done with you!"

Brigitte had been terrified from the moment he began to speak, for Druoda's chamber was across from them, and she was sure she would hear. But she could not understand what he was saying. He was obviously drunk, slurring his words, but he was also using foreign words. His tone was harsh, and that was enough to make her see that she was again thwarted. There would be no escape for her tonight.

Her silence led Rowland to think she had acquiesced, and he began fumbling with his clothes. But the wine had slowed not only his wits. Desire was not there. So he toyed with the woman, shoving her down onto the pallet and opening her cloak, not in the least surprised to find her naked beneath. His fingers touched the smoothness of her legs and thighs, and the warmth between her legs. He continued his exploration roughly, moving toward her breasts. They were ample breasts, full and ripe for squeezing. There would be bruises there come morning, marks from the strength Rowland was using without realizing it.

But he was not hurting Brigitte. Nothing could hurt her. She had fainted the moment her back touched the pallet with such brutal force. She had been naked beneath the cloak because she could not bear to have anything touch her back. She had hardly been able to stand the cloak. To touch her throbbing back to the rough pallet had been beyond endurance.

But Rowland did not know she was unconscious. Nor did he realize that his movements were slowing, or that he was nearly asleep. As soon as he positioned himself for thrusting, Rowland passed out.

# Chapter Eight

*E*arly the next day, Hildegard pounded on the Norman's door, wanting the knight away as soon as possible. A second later a terrified scream came from within, and Hildegard quickly threw open the door.

"God in Heaven!" she gasped, seeing Brigitte on the pallet beneath the Norman, their bodies naked and entwined. "Druoda will kill someone for this!"

She hurried from the room, leaving Brigitte and Rowland looking at each other, startled and embarrassed.

Brigitte pushed him away, moaning as she shoved her back into the mattress. The pain was not as bad as it had been, but her back was still sore. She had still not escaped Druoda, and it was this man who had stopped her twice.

All that had happened to her yesterday was terrible enough, and now it seemed she had also been raped. Was there ever a woman as cursed as she was? Raped, but thank God she had fainted and could not recall the act. For that single mercy, Brigitte was grateful.

Rowland got up without a word and dressed quickly. He could not help glancing down at the naked body that had been pressed so warmly against his. He grunted. Her body had been pleasing to lie next to and to look upon, which was more than he could say for the rest of her. She was filthy and bedraggled. He could not even guess her age, though her body was firm and she had a sweetly shaped face. He recalled that her voice was young and musical, but he remembered little else about her. Embarrassed, he turned away from her appraising look.

Brigitte cleared her throat. "Do you know what you have done to me?"

"I know," Rowland answered in a croaking voice. "What difference?" he added a bit more confidently as he strapped on his sword. "I cannot say it has been a pleasure. Frankly, I do not remember taking you."

She was not sure she had heard correctly. "Not remember?"

"I was drunk," he said flatly, there being nothing he could do but admit the truth.

She began to cry softly, and Rowland glanced around as though for help. He looked toward the door longingly, but just then she began laughing, and Rowland turned back to her. "Are you mad, wench?" He sounded bewildered.

"Perhaps I owe you thanks. After all, what is disgrace compared to what you have saved me from? Lord Wilhelm will not want me now that I have been raped by a drunken knight."

Rowland had no time to reply, for Druoda burst into the room just then, Hildegard on her heels. Druoda was in a towering rage, which she turned on Brigitte.

"So! It is true! You have ruined my plans for you by giving yourself to this man!" Druoda screeched. "You will live to regret this, Brigitte!"

"I did not *give* myself to him, Druoda," Brigitte said firmly. "He dragged me in here and raped me."

"What?" Druoda exploded, her face turning a deep shade of red.

Brigitte got to her feet slowly, holding her mantle before her in modesty. She turned to Rowland. "Tell her how I came to be here."

Rowland looked hard at Brigitte and then at Druoda. He began to see that he had made a mistake, had assumed too much at the very least. Not one to let others take the blame due him, he admitted, "It is as the wench claims. I found her near my room, and I assumed that she was meant for me. Hosts usually do send me a..."

"But what were you doing here?" Druoda cried, and Brigitte, thinking quickly, offered a partial truth.

"I came for food, since I ate little yesterday."

"Food?" Druoda was having a difficult time believing all of this.

Brigitte pointed to the floor. "There it is, in that bag where I dropped it." She prayed Druoda would not look inside, for the amount of food there was much more than Brigitte would need for one meal.

But Druoda was not concerned with incidentals. "Why did you not scream, Brigitte? You wanted him to take you so you could ruin my plans for you!"

"No, that's not so!" Brigitte cried, equally frightened and indignant.

"Why did you not cry for help then?"

Brigitte lowered her head and whispered slowly, "Because I fainted."

Rowland burst into laughter. "There is no harm done, mistress, if the wench cannot remember. Why, it is as though it never happened."

"No harm!" Druoda screamed. "She was a virgin—
and promised to another."

"A virgin!" Rowland gasped. This had not, apparently, occurred to him.

What in blazes had he gotten himself into?

His shocked reaction gave Druoda pause. "How
could you not know that?"

"I was too...too drunk to take notice, that is how!"
Rowland said brusquely, furious with himself all over
again.

"That does not alter what you have done," Druoda
moaned bitterly.

Druoda began pacing the floor, ignoring the others. She ought to have killed the girl long ago, but
it was too late now, for her disappearance would be
questioned by the disappointed bridegroom. And what
to do about him? He would not marry Brigitte now,
for he wanted only a virgin.

But she had to get rid of Brigitte, and quickly,
before Quintin returned.

"Druoda." Hildegard stood next to her and whispered, "Give her to the knight and your problem is
solved."

"How?"

"He obviously thought she was a serf, and he still
must think so. Send her away with him."

"She will deny it once they are alone again,"
Druoda whispered in return.

"She has probably done that already, but he did
not believe her. He thinks her a thief and a liar, so
you need only confirm his beliefs. Call her a liar.
Make all the excuses you must so that he will take
her away and not bring her back."

"Hildegard, you are a wonder!" Druoda hissed gleefully.

"First, get him out of this room quickly before he sees that there is no virgin blood on the pallet."

"What!"

"It seems Brigitte has dallied before this."

Druoda stood stiffly, raging inside. Brigitte had fooled them all. Druoda supposed it was fortunate that this had happened, for Wilhelm d'Arsnay would have annulled the marriage as soon as he discovered the truth about his bride. Hildegard's suggestion was perfect. Brigitte would become a serf, and the Norman would take her away.

"Get to my chamber, Brigitte, and wait for me there," Druoda snapped.

Brigitte's head came up sharply. "What of him?"

"Do as you are told!"

Without hesitating further, Brigitte picked up her bag of food from the floor and walked stiffly out of the room.

Druoda followed her to the door, waiting there until the knight's curiosity overcame his silence. She hadn't long to wait.

"What will you do to her?"

Druoda ignored his question and in her most imperious manner, looked about the room in disgust. "It stinks of lust here," she said distastefully, and abruptly left the room.

Rowland took off after her, stopping her as soon as she reached the hall below. "I asked what you will do. She has other faults, I know, but she is innocent of all blame here. Do not hurt her."

"I know who is to blame," Druoda said slowly, her eyes condemning him.

"An honest mistake, lady. You did promise me a woman for the night, unless I remember that incorrectly."

Druoda sighed impatiently. "You should have waited for the girl I intended, not taken this one, whose only value was her innocence."

"A serf's value is not measured by virtue."

"This one's was. She is a teller of tales—a liar, to speak plainly."

"What will you do with her?"

"I will do nothing with her at all. She is yours now, bound with my blessing."

Rowland shook his head slowly. "No, lady, I do not want her."

"You wanted her well enough last night," she reminded him sharply. "I had a lord far from here who was willing to take her simply because she was innocent. Now that is no longer possible, but I will not have her here. If you do not take her, I will have her stoned for the whore you have made of her. I am within my rights as her mistress to do so."

"Surely you cannot do such a thing."

"You do not understand, Sir Rowland." Druoda thought quickly. "That girl was my brother's weakness. He was enamored of her and treated her as he would a lady. That is why she is so troublesome. She thinks herself above her station. She was born a serf, but my brother's attentions made her vain."

"If your brother loves her, then she should be here when he returns."

"And have him learn that the man he sent here in good faith has raped her? He was saving her for himself," Druoda said slyly. "Quintin is a fool when it comes to that girl. I did not want to admit this, for it shames me, but my brother contemplates marriage to her. I must get her away from here. I can't have that girl here when he returns and risk his marrying a serf. You take her—and make sure she never returns here—or I shall kill her."

Rowland knew himself entirely helpless, trapped with a servant he did not need, who would be a hindrance to him on his journey home. Yet he had no choice. He could not let her die.

"I go to ready my horse, lady," he gritted angrily. "Have the girl sent to the stable and I will take her."

"Do not sound so put out, Sir Knight. I am sure you will have better luck than I in breaking her of her haughty airs, and once she is tamed she will serve your needs well."

Seeing that Rowland was not in the least mollified, Druoda added, "I am truly sorry then that your visit has ended this way. And let me advise you about something. You will avoid much trouble with the girl if you do not tell her that her lord lives."

"Why?"

"She thinks Quintin is dead. If she knew that he is alive, she would do anything to find him. If you consider him your friend, I do not think you would want that any more than I do."

Rowland groaned. It would be a fine thing for Quintin to learn that Rowland bedded the girl he had planned to marry, serf or not.

"You have my word. She will never return."

As soon as Rowland had left the hall, Druoda summoned Hildegard. Their amusement knew no bounds.

"Go and help Brigitte gather some possessions. She is to meet her new lord in the stable. He will wait for her, but not overly long, so make sure she hurries." Druoda's face gleamed.

"But what if she will not go with him?" Hildegard asked.

"Tell her that I relinquish my guardianship. She will be so pleased that she will not question her good luck until it is too late. Explain that the Norman is remorseful over what he has done, and insists he be allowed to see her safely to Count Arnulf, who is reported to be visiting the Duke of Maine."

"But Arnulf is not away."

"Of course not, but if she thinks he is, she will not question the direction the Norman takes until they pass Maine. And once she is that far north, even if she manages to escape the Norman, she can hardly return alone to Berry." Druoda smiled. At last, everything had fallen into place!

# Chapter Nine

*B*rigitte approached the stable timidly. That she was leaving Louroux in the light of day rather than sneaking away at night seemed too strange. Her miracle was not perfect, of course. She could go, but she had to go with the man who had taken her, a man she despised, and who knew her intimately when she knew him not at all. She felt a humiliation she had never felt before, but oddly, a deep gratitude as well.

As she entered the stable, she saw him standing next to his big gray steed. The stallion looked none too friendly in the light of day, but neither did his master. Rowland's dark blue eyes blazed angrily as she came forward.

"I have kept you waiting?" she asked timidly.

Rowland checked his temper. "Just get on the horse," he said, sighing with frustration.

Brigitte drew away from him. "On your horse? But I will ride my own."

"By God, you will get on this horse or I will leave you behind!"

Leave her behind? She could not chance that.

"Pray, let me ride behind you then?" she ventured, thinking of her sore back.

"And what will you do with your bundle?" he asked impatiently.

"Put it between us."

"Ha! You do not trust being close to me?"

"Oh, no!" she said quickly. "You said what happened in the night was a mistake, and I believe you."

"You can wager on it. I like my women willing—and certainly more appealing than you are," he said bluntly, eyeing her dirty mantle and snarled long hair.

Brigitte was stung, and her light blue eyes filled rapidly. But she kept still. He had no right to insult her. She had to leave before Druoda changed her mind.

Rowland turned away from her and mounted the big horse, then extended a hand to help Brigitte up. She took it, but caught the angry look in his eyes and let go again.

"If you dislike me so, then why are you taking me?" she asked simply.

"I have no choice."

So that was it, Brigitte thought miserably. Hildegard had lied—he did not want to take her at all. But Druoda was adept at forcing people to her will, even a man like this. She felt more of a burden than ever, but she really had no option but to go.

She took his hand again, and he lifted her effortlessly to the back of the horse. His own provisions were in packs there, slung on each side of the large gray stallion. It made for a very uncomfortable seat, especially with her possessions pressed between them.

She settled herself as comfortably as she could and pulled her skirts down as far as they would go, which was not nearly far enough because she was sitting astride. She straightened herself slowly because of her sore back, ready now. She waited for Rowland to ride out, but he seemed also to be waiting.

"What is it?" she asked hesitantly when he still made no move to leave. "I am ready."

He sighed. "Are you as ignorant as you seem, or do you provoke me intentionally?"

"Provoke you how?"

"You must hold onto me, damosel, or you will find yourself in the dust."

"Oh!" Brigitte's face reddened, and she was thankful that he couldn't see her. "But I cannot reach my arms around you. My sack of clothes hinders me."

"Grab hold of my hauberk," he said cuttingly, then looked over his shoulder and said even more harshly, "And I warn you, do not let go. If you fall from your seat and break any part of your body, I will not be detained to attend you."

"And if my injuries make riding impossible?" she asked, shocked.

"I will put you out of your misery."

She gasped. "I am not an animal, to be destroyed when injured!"

"Do not put it to the test."

Brigitte was too shocked to pursue the subject. With great reluctance, she took hold of his mail shirt. The second she did, he was off. He rode swiftly through the open gate and on through the village. Holding fast, she could not wave at the serfs who waved at her as she galloped by.

Rowland's pace quickened when they reached the road. He seemed to want to leave the area as quickly as she did. Her spirits rose when he turned north toward Orleans, for Maine was north. It was unfor-

tunate that Arnulf was not in Berry, for the less time
she spent with this knight the better. Maine was
many days away, and there was nothing she could
do about that.

Ah, but it would be good to see Arnulf again. The
old knight was truly formidable, but Brigitte was
not intimidated by his brusque manner, for she knew
he had a heart of gold. He would weep over Quintin's
death, and she wished it was not up to her to tell
him, for she knew she would feel Quintin's loss all
over again.

The road took them through a valley which was
rich with crops all during the summer and fall. Cypress trees had been planted as windscreens some
three hundred years before, for the valley was a tree-
less plain. These cypress trees were now bent and
gnarled, and gave the Rhone Valley a bleak and
lonesome look.

While Brigitte anticipated her reunion with Arnulf, Rowland brooded. His anger was mounting
steadily. The unwanted baggage behind him would
cost him, yet she would give nothing in return, for
he wanted nothing from her. There would be food to
buy or hunt on the way, and her passage on the Loire
River between Orleans and Angers to pay for. Worse,
she would delay him, for his horse was burdened by
the extra weight. Rowland's homecoming would be
hard enough, but this delay was going to make it
much more difficult. He sighed with irritation and
bad temper.

The wide road cutting through central France was
much more frequently traveled than were the nu-
merous dirt tracks. There were many people going
south, but only a few traveling to the colder regions

of the north, so Rowland was not slowed by other travelers. But Gui was surely far ahead, having journeyed most of the way by river.

And what of the urgency to reach home? Had Thurston of Mezidon made his move, as Gui feared? Rowland had at least a week of travel before he would find out. As the two galloped toward Rowland's home, he felt his temper growing shorter and shorter.

# Chapter Ten

*I*t was midday when they approached a hostelry on the side of the road. They would not reach Orleans until the next night. The Hun could rest while they went by river, but after that there were more than eighty miles of land yét to cross before they reached Montville. Rowland's horse was his greatest treasure, the best from his father's stable. He was not used to carrying more than Rowland's weight, and Rowland hated to burden him.

There were a few others at the hostelry, which was an inn run by monks. There was a small village beyond the inn. One of the travelers had the look of a merchant, another was an old knight with his squire and a wife and two daughters. The third traveler was a pilgrim. Rowland nodded briefly to the three men before he rode his horse around back to a bubbling stream. He wondered what the others thought of him, traveling alone with a female. She was certainly not his squire, but she would make do in that capacity for the time being.

He dismounted, then reached up to the girl to help her down.

"Do you never wash, girl?"

Her eyes widened, and he noticed that they were

large and a light blue. The tilt of her chin indicated pride, something he would have to break before he reached Montville. An insolent serf would suffer greatly under his stepmother's hands.

"I am accustomed to bathing often," she answered him softly, but her eyes challenged him. "But I fell last night before you stopped me on the road, and I have had no time since then to attend to myself."

"Make use of this stream while you have the chance," he said curtly.

"But there are people nearby," she gasped. "I cannot bathe with strange men nearby."

"You are unlikely to draw their attention," Rowland replied with deliberate sarcasm. "Be quick about it. We leave within the hour."

By God, she would not let him call her filthy again! She started walking upstream, where she might hide from curious eyes, but he shouted, "Stay where I can watch you."

Brigitte bristled. Did he think she would be attacked, or did he think she would run away? She could hardly run away now. She needed his protection until they reached Maine, and Count Arnulf.

She found a reasonably flat rock by the water's edge and knelt down on it. She took off her mantle and rinsed it several times, then slowly and painfully bent to scrub her face in the freezing water until it tingled. Her arms were next, then as much of her legs as she could modestly expose. Last she unbraided her hair, stiff with dried mud, and dunked her head in the water. She could feel many eyes on her, and her face burned with embarrassment. But she had made herself clean, and she decided that if that hulking knight called her filthy again she would spit in his face.

Brigitte opened her bundle of possessions and withdrew first the food she had brought with her and then her spiked comb. Her steel mirror showed her that where she had scratched her face there were no real cuts, only pink marks that would soon go away. She looked like herself again, she decided.

A brisk wind helped to dry her hair, and the bright sun dried out her wet mantle. Brigitte hungrily ate Althea's sweet bread and candied dates, and from time to time looked up at the tall knight in the inn yard who tended his horse and ignored her entirely.

Rowland pretended to be wholly absorbed in rubbing down the Hun, but he watched Brigitte covertly, astounded by her loveliness. Washing had revealed the fine bones in her face, and her drying flaxen hair was a wonder. She had the look of an aristocrat, and he could understand what had made Quintin act the fool over the girl. He would have to be careful, he decided then and there, not to let her see that he was taken with her beauty. It would not do to give the wench the slightest encouragement. She was his serf, and she would never be anything else, Rowland told himself grimly.

He was forced to remind himself of that when the three men approached him, moments later.

"Pardon, sir," one asked. "You have come from the south?" Rowland nodded, and the bearded man went on. "What news of the trouble there? Have the Saracens all been routed?"

"Yes, the pirate dens have all been put to the torch," Rowland replied, turning back to attend his horse, not in the mood for conversation.

"You see, Maynard." The merchant clapped the older knight on the back. "I told you you would not be needed. This is good news you have given us, young man," he told Rowland. "I am Nethard de Lyons, and this is my brother, Sir Maynard. We have come from bringing a shipment of wine to the Bishop of Tours. And this fellow here is—"

"Jonas de Savoy," the pilgrim supplied. "I have also come from Tours, having visited the tombs of St. Martin. Next year I go to the Holy Land."

Manners dictated that Rowland introduce himself. He could not help grinning at the gruff old man who had the look of a habitual pilgrim. There were so many like him, men who made journeys to different shrines every year.

"We could not help admiring your wife, Sir Rowland," Nethard said amiably now. "Not every man is so fortunate."

"You must forgive us, young man," Jonas added. "It does my old eyes good to look on such beauty."

"The wench is not my wife," Rowland explained before turning again to his horse, hoping they would leave.

But they stayed where they were. "Your sister then?"

"No."

"Your companion?" Nethard persisted.

"She is my servant," Rowland said abruptly.

"But she has a noble bearing," Jonas said, surprised.

"Blood does not always tell," Rowland said. "The wench was born a serf."

"A bastard then?"

"I know nothing of her parentage," Rowland replied, becoming annoyed.

"Would you consider selling her services?" Nethard exclaimed.

The man had Rowland's full attention. "I beg your pardon?"

Nethard de Lyons's eyes twinkled. "Would you consider it? I would give you a fair price to have her grace my hall."

Rowland would have dearly loved to be rid of the girl, but he had given his word to Druoda. "I think not. When the wench was given to me, I promised that she would never return to this area."

"*Given* to you! That is unbelievable!" Nethard replied incredulously. "Her owner must have been a woman then, and jealous of her."

"A woman, yes." Rowland took the explanation offered to him and said no more.

"But you do not want her," Nethard said shrewdly. "I can see that. And a girl such as that one should be cherished."

Rowland grunted. "Even if she were Venus, she would be a burden to me. Yet I must take her with me."

Nethard shook his head. "A pity. Ah, that such a gem should not be appreciated." He sighed.

"She is comely." Rowland scowled. "But she is still a burden."

"He is blind," Nethard stated. After the three had offered polite farewells, they left.

Rowland scowled, his eyes boring into the travelers as they walked away. What did these men know? Franks cherished their women and worshiped their beauty. To Rowland, that was foolishness. A woman was only a woman and nothing more. It was ridiculous to give her any importance. She was there to serve and that was all.

# *Chapter Eleven*

$With$ her hair dried and silky, Brigitte braided it into two braids. She tied up her bundle of possessions and reluctantly joined Rowland in the courtyard. He pointed her toward a bench in the shade of the inn and told her to wait for him.

Brigitte was piqued by his curtness. She had expected him to make some comment on her improved appearance and was rankled because he ignored her. But she did as he bid her and waited patiently for him on the bench. The activity at the hostelry did not improve her mood, for too many men stared boldly at her, making her uneasy.

Rowland had gone inside the inn for some food, glad that she had brought her own. It was but a few minutes later that a young man approached her. She would have been thankful for the company, but she learned quickly enough that the young man was a foreigner, English or Irish by the dark looks of him, and she could not understand his language. Still he did not move away, but continued to try to communicate with her, his gaze admiring, his manner pleasant.

Suddenly Rowland appeared out of nowhere to tower above her, legs apart, hands on hips, a furious look on his face. He reached down and yanked Brigitte to her feet. She started to protest his roughness, but thought better of it when she caught his icy glare.

"Do you know this man?"

"No."

"Yet you bid him sit with you, and you spoke to him," Rowland stated darkly, his eyes riveted to her frightened face.

"I did not," Brigitte replied softly. "Though I did not object when he did. I couldn't understand anything he said, so it doesn't matter."

"Are you always this way with strangers?" Rowland demanded harshly, ignoring her last remark.

She answered quickly in defense. "I did nothing wrong. I was in need of a friendly smile."

"That is not what you are in need of," Rowland said ominously.

He did not give Brigitte a chance to reply, but gripped her arm and jerked her away from the inn. She was embarrassed at being dragged behind him like a naughty child, and tried to pull away.

"I want you to release me!" she called to him loudly.

Rowland halted immediately and swung around to face her, a look of disbelief across his face.

*"You* want?"

"You have no reason to treat me this way," she said.

"So your mistress was right. Your audacity is astounding," he growled.

Without another word, Rowland mounted his steed, pulling Brigitte up behind him. They took to the road again, riding as quickly as they had before.

Neither spoke for the rest of the day. When darkness fell, Rowland left the road and entered a forest.

"Why do we go this way?" Brigitte asked timidly after a while, unnerved by the darkness.

"Your silence has been a blessing," Rowland answered curtly. "I must find a place to halt for the night."

Brigitte was aghast. "You mean we will sleep *here?*"

"Do you see a village nearby?" he asked cuttingly, his back stiff.

Brigitte fell silent, all manner of disturbing imaginings coming unbidden to mind.

Rowland stopped where the trees grew so densely that no light shone through at all. There was a small clearing, and he ordered her to gather kindling and place it there for a fire. She complied without question while he secured his horse.

She thought that he had been unable to buy provisions from the poor monks at the hostelry, and she offered. "I have a little food left if you will share it."

"Bring it," he replied before he struck flint to the kindling she had gathered.

She laid out what was left of her food, and he fell to. She studied him warily as they ate, the fire crackling and casting shadows around them, making the rest of the woods seem much darker. She could not help wondering why a man so pleasing to look upon could have such a foul disposition. Were all Normans so gruff, so domineering, and so perpetually angry?

"How soon before we come to Maine?" Brigitte ventured when all the food was gone. "I have never been west of Berry."

"Why do you ask?"

"I only wished to know," she whispered, frightened by his intense glare. "After all, we will part there."

"I will hear nothing about parting, and, I warn you, do not provoke me."

"But you do not care for my company," she pointed out calmly.

"That matters little enough now! You were forced on me, and I am stuck with you."

"Why do you hate me so?"

"Do you not hate me as well?" he asked casually.

She looked at him in surprise. "If you think I hate you simply because of your rough treatment of me since we left Louroux, then you are wrong."

Rowland laughed, and his whole face softened. It was a far more pleasing face with humor in it. "So you think I am rough, do you?"

"Certainly you are," she replied indignantly. "You have threatened me, and you bullied me at the hostelry, as if I had no right to speak to whomever I please."

"You have no rights at all." He was cold again, the laughing lights gone from his eyes. "Let us be clear, girl. You speak to no one without permission."

Brigitte was amused. "You are not serious. I suppose you cannot help the way you are, but you really do overstep your bounds. I am indeed grateful for your protection, but being my escort does not give you leave to dictate to me."

Rowland gasped and then exploded. "By the saints, she was right! She said you would put on haughty airs, but I did not believe you foolish enough to try your tricks with me!"

Rowland had had enough. He knew he had to get

away from the girl. He turned and stalked to his horse and quickly rode off in the direction of the road. A brisk ride might cool his temper.

Brigitte stared after his parting figure in bewilderment that turned quickly to fear as the sounds of his horse became more and more distant.

"What have I done?" she whispered. "Why does he hate me so?"

She moved closer to the fire and drew her mantle tightly about her. He would return, she tried to assure herself. He *would*.

The night sounds became louder, blowing in the wind. Brigitte shivered and curled up in a ball on the cold ground, pulling her mantle up over her head. She prayed for God's protection, and then she prayed to Rowland of Montville.

"Please come back," she whispered anxiously. "I swear I will not raise my voice to you again. I swear I will not argue. I will not speak at all if you will just come back!"

Finally the crackling fire drowned out the other night sounds and lulled her to sleep.

Rowland returned to find her that way. He took a blanket from one of the packs on his horse and stretched out on the ground beside her.

# Chapter Twelve

Rowland woke instantly, sensing imminent danger. He bolted to his feet, automatically drawing his sword and swinging around for sight of an intruder. The dawn sky made the dark shadows difficult to penetrate, and he strained but could see nothing. Tense, he stood utterly still and waited.

It was then Rowland saw the beast sitting on huge haunches not more than five feet away from him. It looked like a dog, but Rowland had never seen one so large before.

Keeping his eyes on the beast, Rowland nudged the sleeping girl with his booted foot. She sat up slowly, and when she moved so did the dog. He started toward her, loping gracefully.

"Get behind me, quickly," Rowland ordered in a harsh whisper.

"Why?" She was alarmed by his tone, and when she saw his raised sword she whispered, "What is it?"

"If you value your life, do as I say!" he snapped.

Brigitte scrambled to her feet and ducked behind Rowland's broad back. She became truly frightened when she heard an animal's threatening growl. Hesitantly, very slowly, she peered around Rowland to see what was growling. Even in the dim light, she could not mistake that form. She dashed around Rowland and stood between the man and the dog. Rowland stared incredulously as she hugged the huge beast, giggling as it licked her face and whined.

"Have you some power over dumb beasts?" Rowland asked, more than a little awed. Was the girl a witch?

Brigitte looked up at him and smiled brightly. "He is my dog. He followed me."

Rowland sheathed the sword and grunted. "I refuse to believe he traced you a full day's ride from Louroux."

"I raised him, and he has been following me for years. He must have escaped from his cage last night at feeding time. He is quite intelligent."

Rowland turned from her without another word. He mounted his horse and without a look in her direction, rode slowly out of the clearing.

"Where are you going?" Brigitte called.

Rowland called over his shoulder, "With luck I will bring back fresh meat. Make use of your time and tend the fire."

And then he was gone. Brigitte sighed. The promises she had made last night were weighing on her heavily. But he had come back.

She caught Wolff's large brown eyes on her and smiled with delight. "Well, my lovely, you must be tired after your long journey." She suddenly threw her arms around him and squeezed tightly. "Oh, Wolff, Wolff, I am so glad you came. I should have brought you with me, but I was afraid to ask. But you found me, and we will not be parted again. I feel so much better now. The Norman will protect me from dangers on the way, and you, my king, will protect me from him!"

Brigitte's fears had receded now that her beloved Wolff was there, and she laughed for the sheer pleasure of it. "Come, we must have the fire burning before he returns, for he is a mean-tempered man who does not like waiting. You must be hungry, Wolff." She gathered sticks and twigs, Wolff trailing by her side. "I imagine you took Leandor by surprise and did not wait for your dinner last night. Or else Leandor let you go. Yes, he would have done that if he thought I needed you."

She continued chattering to Wolff as she had always done, speaking her thoughts aloud. The fire took hold quickly from the coals of the old one, and soon she was warming her hands against the morning chill.

She had just finished combing out and then braiding her long hair when Rowland returned and tossed a fat hare on the ground before her. "Prepare it and save the skin to hold what is left after we have eaten," he told her curtly, then he turned his dark blue eyes on Wolff, who was lying with his head on Brigitte's lap. "And he must go. We don't have enough food to share with him."

"Wolff will not leave me now that he has found me," Brigitte replied confidently. "But you need not worry about feeding him. He is an excellent hunter and can easily catch his own dinner." She took the dog's large head in her hands and gazed into his brown eyes. "Show him, Wolff. Bring back your dinner, and I will cook it for you."

Rowland watched the dog lope out of their camp and shook his head. "You plan to cook for the beast?"

"He is not a beast," she reproached him. "Though his breed is unknown, he is prized for his size and his cunning. And of course I will cook for him. Wolff is tame. He does not eat raw food."

"Neither do I," Rowland retorted. "Get busy."

Before he had finished speaking a poniard landed in the dirt by the hare. Brigitte picked it up and grimaced at the job before her. She had recently learned how to skin animals, but she didn't like it at all.

But *he* obviously was not going to do it. He had sat down before the fire and started cleaning the javelin he had used to kill the hare. She supposed she ought to be grateful to Druoda for making her learn menial tasks.

"What do I call you?" Brigitte said conversationally.

He did not look at her. "Seignior will do."

"Seignior Rowland?"

"Just Seignior."

"That is absurd," she said, keeping her eyes on her task. "I will call you Rowland. And you know my name. I wish you would use it. I do not like being called wench or girl all the time."

Rowland's eyes flashed. "So it begins again." He scowled darkly. "The day has hardly begun, and already you are telling me what *you* will do, what *you* want!"

Brigitte looked up in bewilderment. "What did I say to make you angry again?"

Rowland rose, throwing his javelin down in a sudden burst of anger. "You provoke me intentionally with this pretense at being not what you are. You are a serf, and I am your master, and you will stop pretending otherwise. I gave my word I would keep you, and I am stuck with you till the day you die. But do not press your luck, or that day may arrive sooner than you think."

Brigitte was more stunned than she could let him know. Something was finally becoming clear. "You gave your word to Druoda, is that what you mean?"

"Aye, when she gave you to me."

"She had no right!" Brigitte gasped. "I am not a servant. I have never been a servant!"

"She also told me lies come more readily to you than the truth, and warned me against your flights of fancy."

"You do not understand. Druoda is my guardian, since my family are all dead. She is not my mistress, but my half-brother's aunt. She could not *give* me to you."

"She meant to stone you to death, girl, and would have if I did not agree to take you with me."

"She might have murdered me, for you ruined the plans she had made for me."

"But you admit I saved your life. Give me peace, if for that reason alone."

"You have no right to keep me. I am a lady! My father was a baron!"

He stood so close that his eyes seemed almost black. "It matters not what you were before. What you are now is my servant. You are bound to me, and if I hear you deny it once more, I will take a strap to you. Now get that meat cooked!" he barked. "We have wasted enough time today."

Brigitte moved numbly toward the fire, tears spilling down her cheeks. Hopelessness closed over her like a night sky. She was too weary even to ask him why they hadn't stopped in Maine. She knew why. Druoda had tricked her about that, as she had lied about so many things.

What could she do? If she tried to reason with this obstinate man and tell him how wrong he was, he would beat her. She could not endure another beating, not on top of the one she still suffered from.

Rowland watched her, his temper simmering, until she glanced his way with an expression of such miserable desolation that he looked away, feeling almost remorseful. Almost, but not quite.

Why did she cry and look so dejected? It was not as if her life with him would be harder than it had been before. He had seen the calluses on her hands and knew that she was used to hard work. She would not have to serve a large household anymore, only him. And hadn't he saved her life? Couldn't she at least be grateful for that?

Rowland's musings were disturbed when Wolff trotted back into camp and placed two dead woodcocks at Brigitte's feet. He shook his head, silently conceding that the dog must have come from Louroux after all. One of Brigitte's tasks there was probably to care for the animal. How else would it have done exactly what she said unless it was used to obeying her?

With Wolff's reappearance, Brigitte's silent tears turned to loud sobs, and Rowland jumped to his feet. "Thunderation, woman! You have spent enough tears!"

Wolff started howling with her, and Rowland threw up his arms in exasperation and stalked away from the fire.

Finally she stopped crying, and Wolff licked away

her tears. Drawing a deep sigh, she began to finish her task. Soon, Wolff's food roasting along with the hare, she sat back and looked at her pet mournfully.

"What am I going to do, Wolff?" she asked, as if she expected an answer. "He has made me his servant, and there is no one but me to tell him he has no right to do this.

"Druoda did this to me!" she said vehemently, her eyes bright with anger.

When Rowland returned, the hare was cooked and Wolff had already devoured his food. They ate silently, Brigitte keeping her eyes on the ground.

"I would speak with you, girl, and hope to put your mind at ease," Rowland said gruffly. "You need not fear me as long as you do as I say."

"And if I do not?" she asked after a pause.

"I will treat you no differently from any other serf," he said flatly.

"How many servants do you have?" she ventured.

"I have never had a personal servant other than my squire, who died recently. There are many working in my home, but they are bound to my father. You are the first bound solely to me."

"You are taking me to your home?"

"Yes."

While Brigitte considered this, he went on.

"You will tend my clothes, serve my food, and clean my chamber. You will answer only to me. Is that not less work than you are accustomed to?"

"Much less," she admitted.

He stood up and looked at her. "I expect obedience. As long as you do not anger me, you will fare well. Will you accept your lot and provoke me no more?"

Brigitte hesitated, then spoke quickly, before she

lost courage. "I will not lie to you. I will serve you as long as I must. But if there comes an opportunity for me to leave you, I will."

She expected his temper to flare again, but he only frowned. "No, you will not escape me," he said in a foreign tongue.

"What?"

"I said you had best learn to understand Norse, for there are many at Montville who speak nothing else."

"You said all of that with those few words?" she asked skeptically.

But Rowland did not answer. "Come, we waste time. The dog may come with us. He will make a fine gift for my father."

Brigitte started to protest, but thought better of it. Rowland would find out when the time came that Wolff would not be parted from her.

# Chapter Thirteen

*T*hey did not reach Orleans before nightfall and had to make camp again once the sun set. Brigitte spent the long hours on her uncomfortable perch behind Rowland trying to convince herself that her condition could be endured for a while. After all, she was away from Berry, and from Druoda.

A husband was what she needed, for, once she was safely married, Druoda would have no claim to Louroux and would not profit from her death. But to wed, she needed Arnulf's permission—or that of his liege lord. The King of France was Arnulf's liege, and that was the answer. She could go to court and be married before Druoda knew of it. She need only find someone to take her to the Ile-de-France and Lothair's court. Then she would be free, and Druoda would be forced to leave Louroux.

By the time they camped that night, Brigitte was so satisfied with her reasoning that she looked on her situation as a blessing. And the third day passed quickly, for Rowland began teaching Brigitte the language of his ancestors. It was not easy to grasp, but she learned several words and impressed Rowland.

The days began pleasantly, for Rowland soon found that Wolff was indeed a good hunter. They awoke in the morning to find two plump hares and a wild goose waiting for them.

Rowland was amazed and quite pleased to have the dog do his hunting for him. This put Rowland in so good a mood that he made friends with Wolff, and, to Brigitte's surprise, Wolff liked him. Rowland was not so brusque with Brigitte either. The three of them moved along the road in a happy frame of mind.

Their journey downriver began early on the afternoon after they reached Orleans, and Rowland's disposition improved even more. Brigitte realized that some of his anger had been due to her having delayed him from reaching his home. That evening, after they had both eaten their fill, she questioned him.

"Why are you in such a hurry?"

She was curled up on deck, lying on her side with her head on her arms. Rowland sat by her feet, staring absently at the river.

Rowland explained briefly, telling her that his father had sent a vassal to find him, and that there would soon be war at Montville.

"Unfortunately, it took many months for Gui to find me, since I was in the south of France. The battle may already be finished."

Brigitte's interest was aroused. "So you have only just come from the south?"

"Yes, from fighting the Saracens."

Her eyes brightened. "I hope you killed many!" she said impulsively, knowing it was a Saracen who had killed her brother.

"I did indeed," he grunted. "But why should that interest you? The pirates only threatened the south. You were far from there."

"I did not fear for myself," she explained, her large blue eyes sparkling with hatred for the man who had slain Quintin. "I only hope the Saracens are all dead, every last one of them."

Rowland chuckled. "So my Venus is bloodthirsty. I would not have guessed."

Brigitte lowered her gaze to the fire and sighed. What good would it do to explain how she felt? He didn't care about her feelings.

"I am not bloodthirsty," she said quietly. "The Saracens needed to be destroyed, that is all."

"And so they were."

Brigitte turned from him, putting her back to the fire, but she sensed his eyes were still on her, and she grew uneasy. What did he mean by calling her his Venus? Did it mean he found her more to his liking now? She prayed not.

Feeling certain that Rowland still watched her, Brigitte became more and more nervous, until she remembered that they were not alone on the barge. Wolff lay near her. Her faithful dog would not let the Norman attack her. With that comforting thought, Brigitte slept.

A storm threatened the next day, but did not break. The Loire was already swollen and would surely flood with a heavy rain, so they watched anxiously as dark clouds hid the sun. A strong wind helped to make the river uncomfortably cold. The wind also hindered their progress, and this darkened Rowland's mood so that he was silent most of the day and cross when he did speak.

He was angry with himself for being affected by the cold, for this was mild weather compared to what he had known most of his life. The last six months in the south of France had thinned his blood, and he felt this was a weakness in himself.

That night turned out to be their coldest thus far. Brigitte huddled next to Wolff for warmth, and she did not even mind when Rowland came to lie beside her, for he blocked the wind from her back. What a time to be returning home, in the heart of winter! Warmer clothes would have to be made when he reached home. He hoped the wench could sew an even line, for that task would fall to her.

He turned on his side, toward her, and discerned by her even breathing that she was fast asleep. He picked up one of her long blonde braids and fanned the silky end of it against his cheek. Her lovely features came to him even though he could not see her face, for he had stared at her long enough the night before to have her image forever in his mind.

Rowland had recently felt the first inkling of pride in this girl. She was not only uncommonly beautiful, but she had a quick mind as well and had already grasped an understanding of Norse.

She appeared to have accepted him as her lord and was willing to serve him. This pleased him, for it meant that he would not have to depend on his father's servants. He remembered well that whenever he needed something done, the servants would be busy doing Hedda's bidding.

This girl would serve him well. Because of this,

he was reluctant to take her to his bed. He felt certain that it would be a mistake to change their relationship. Rowland turned away from her and sighed, cursing the girl for being so lovely.

# Chapter Fourteen

*T*he storm had blown south without troubling them, and fair weather followed the barge all the next day. That day they came to the seat of the Count of Tournaine. Brigitte wished she could visit the monastery of St. Michel there, but their barge stopped only long enough to unload passengers and take on two new ones before they were on their way again.

The two newcomers were tall, rough looking Saxons. The Saxon dukes had routed the Eastern kingdom from the Franks, and they now ruled Germany under Otto, a fact that did not please the French. These two had dark, weathered complexions and long, unruly hair the color of dried autumn grass. They wore tunics of thick fur, making them bearlike and menacing. They were armed.

The Saxons kept to themselves, but when their eyes rested on Brigitte with unmistakable interest, she grew uneasy and moved closer to Rowland. He did not look down at her, even when her arm accidentally brushed his. For several days he had seemed to avoid her gaze, and she wondered why.

Late the next afternoon, their sixth day of traveling, they passed the junction where the Maine River joined the Loire, and it was here that Rowland had them put ashore. Brigitte was reluctant to again take her uncomfortable seat on the rear of his horse, but, when she asked if she might walk awhile, she was denied her request. Rowland was determined to cover as much distance as possible before nightfall.

Nightfall came quickly, and they stopped on the left bank of the Maine River, in a small crop of trees. With the river only a few yards away, Brigitte thought of bathing. As soon as Rowland left her and went off to hunt, telling her to prepare a fire, she raced through the area gathering kindling and left it in a pile. Then, yanking a clean tunic from her sack, she ran down to the water's edge, grateful that she possessed some clean clothes.

Directly across the river were deserted marshes, desolate looking in the blue light of dusk. Upriver was a black square shape floating toward Brigitte, and she froze, then quickly scrambled back up the low bank when she realized the shape was a barge. She hid behind a tree, cursing the delay. Wolff came and squatted beside her, and she absently rubbed his ears as she impatiently watched the slow-moving vessel. Finally she looked down at him and frowned.

"You had best go find your own dinner, Wolff. The Norman accepts the meat you bring him, but I doubt he will return the favor and hunt for you." The animal didn't move, so she pushed him gently. "Go on, I will be all right here as soon as that barge passes."

She watched him trot away, then looked back at the river to see that the barge, which carried livestock, was only just then reaching her. It inched along at a maddeningly slow pace. Brigitte knew that she had to be finished and back at the camp before Rowland returned.

Finally the barge diminished in size, and Brigitte quickly stripped herself bare and ran into the water. She gasped at the iciness of it, but submerged herself anyway. Her teeth began to chatter, and she briskly rubbed herself all over while she kept a wary eye out for any more unwelcome vessels. The river was empty now, but it didn't much matter, for the sky had grown black and the moon had not yet risen. She doubted she would be seen even if a vessel passed right by her.

Brigitte finished as quickly as she could and gladly ran from the icy water. She began shaking all over and hastily donned her clean tunic without even drying, tying on the rope belt she had worn before. She was freezing now, and she realized she would probably catch cold for her few moments of luxury. Luxury? No, she would not call bathing a luxury.

Dirt clung to her wet feet so she decided not to put her sandles on yet. She carried them and her other tunic and walked carefully back up to the campsite, cursing herself for not lighting the fire before bathing. It was pitch dark, and she was very cold.

And then she saw the sparks and thought she would die of fright. She held her breath until she made out Rowland's familiar shape hunched down by the fire.

Her breath escaped in a long sigh of relief. "You frightened me terribly," Brigitte said as she came forward and hastily dropped her things. "How long have you been there?"

The look he turned on her made her cringe. "Long enough to wonder why there was no fire here, and no foolhardy woman, either."

"I did not think you would return this quickly."

"You think I have eyes like your dog and can find game in the dark?" he replied caustically. "I waited too long to make camp. There will be no meat unless your Wolff has better luck. I see he is not here."

"I sent him off after you left."

Rowland stood up and faced her. "Come here, girl. Where have you been?"

Brigitte hesitated. She knew that tone. The set of his mouth was hard. And the hair that had grown on his chin recently was surprisingly dark and made him look all the meaner. His eyes were a burning reflection of the fire beside him, and when he reached out to her, Brigitte gasped and jumped back. His hand caught her arm and slid down it, coming away wet.

"So a swim was more important than starting a fire against this chill?"

He hadn't struck her, and she took courage from that. "I did not mean to inconvenience you."

"Me?" he growled. "Look at yourself. Your arm is like ice, and your lips are blue." He shoved her roughly toward the fire. "Warm yourself. If you get sick on me, by God...have you no sense, girl?"

She faced him, her back to the fire, and felt her lips trembling. "I wanted to get clean and I could not bathe completely with you near."

"Why not?"

She looked down, glad that he could not see her blush. "It would not be proper."

"Proper?" he yelled, then stopped, and his eyes traveled down her body slowly. Every line was visible with the soft wool clinging to her wet skin.

When Rowland's eyes finally met hers, his were

smoldering, but not with anger. It was a look she had not seen often in her sheltered life, but which she instinctively recognized. It terrified her.

She started to back away from him, mindless of the fire behind her. But he quickly grabbed one of her braids and yanked her roughly to him. She slammed into his rock-hard body, losing her breath. One of his arms closed around her waist, and she found herself unable to move.

With his free hand he tilted her head up, and his eyes moved slowly over her pale face, possessively covering every inch of it. "Perhaps I can warm you better than the fire, eh?" he said huskily, before his glittering dark blue eyes locked on hers again. He gazed at her hungrily and then said softly, "It will do you no good to fight me, if that is in your mind. You know that."

But she had been so sure he didn't want her. What had made him change his mind?

He pulled her closer, then released her to reach for her belt. At that moment Brigitte bolted. If she could only get outside the firelight, she thought, the darkness beyond would help her to hide. But she didn't get far before his hands caught at her waist and jerked her to a halt. She was turned around and then lifted up into Rowland's arms. "Did you really think you could outrun me?"

His voice was not harsh. In fact, he seemed amused by her. Brigitte glared at him, and he laughed, apparently delighted.

"Where is the wench who fainted in fear the moment I laid her on my bed? I see that you have gained courage since that recent night."

"You praise yourself too much," she said tartly,

enraged by his amused attitude. "I fainted from the pain in my back, not from fear of you."

"What was wrong with your back?"

"I was beaten—thanks to you," she spat, her eyes damning him.

Rowland frowned and gently placed her on his blanket near the fire. Against her murmured protests, he removed her belt and tunic, then raised her clothing and touched the area that no longer bothered her. Then he pushed her back down on the blanket and looked at her sharply.

"Does it still pain you?"

"No, why?"

"You still have bruises. A beating that would leave such violent marks a week later must have been very bad. Of course, you might have expected it, having stolen from your mistress."

"I *told* you I am no thief. What was done to me was done because I tried to run away—"

As soon as she said it, she realized that he wasn't listening.

His mouth came down on hers then, and her chest tightened. She knew she was utterly helpless against his strength, and she was terribly aware that her clothing had been pushed up beyond her breasts.

With both hands she gripped his thick hair and pulled his head back. "You will *not* have me!"

He sat up, moving her hands away easily.

"You think to make it difficult for me?" He grinned. Without waiting for an answer, he chuckled and threw off his heavy mail and tunic. She gasped and sat up, but he pushed her back down and held her there with one hand while his other worked at his trousers.

Brigitte closed her eyes, forcing herself not to cry. Rowland locked his hands on hers and held them by her shoulders. It had been so easy for him, so damnably easy. Her eyes flew open, sparkling with fury. "I hate you!"

He looked at her for a long moment, and she found herself staring boldly back. As she gazed into his deep blue eyes, Brigitte suddenly astonished herself with the understanding that she really cared for Rowland. She could not say that she loved him. That would be going too far. He was, after all, rude and abrupt and sometimes cruel in his remarks. But he was also strong and decisive and fair-minded, and she liked more about him than she had admitted to herself. Besides, she thought, he looks at me with tenderness and, yes, even with love. He pretends he is merely taking what is his, but there's more to this assault than that, much more.

Rowland was thinking how lovely she was, and how much he wanted her. He would never admit as much to Brigitte, but she was special, charming, and he took delight in her strong spirit. No, it would not do to tell her so, but Rowland was beginning to care for her deeply.

He kissed her lovely face, and then moved slowly down her neck to her small breasts. They looked as fragile as porcelain but felt like sun-ripened peaches, and he nuzzled against them for several moments. Then, suddenly impatient for her sweetness, he parted her thighs and entered her.

Rowland gasped. The maiden obstruction was still there! He was stunned, but he said nothing. Gently, he moved back and forth within her, feeling her relax after the first few thrusts. He was very careful to take her gently, and rode her a long time before he shuddered and fell on top of her. Soon he withdrew and moved to lie beside her, gazing down into her face and smiling.

"Why are you smiling at me so smugly?" Brigitte demanded furiously. "You said you would not hurt me, but you did!"

"That was to be expected, since you were still a virgin."

"But..." she began awkwardly, and he chuckled at her confusion.

"You cannot blame me for all the misunderstanding. Had you not fainted, you would have realized."

"But you said you took me."

"I passed out. A man does things when he is drunk that he does not always remember." He shrugged. "I only assumed I took you. But I didn't."

She lay there, her thoughts awhirl, and did not speak.

Rowland ran a finger along the curve of her chin in a soft caress. "What does it matter, little jewel? Then or now, you are still mine."

"But Druoda would not have given me to you if she had known there was no rape."

"But you would have been given to another, so where is the difference?"

Rowland did not give her a chance to answer. His lips closed over hers in a long, tender kiss. When he moved away again, he asked, "Did I hurt you very much?"

"No."

She sounded almost bitter, and he shook his head. "I tried to leave you alone. I wanted you before this, but I did not touch you."

"Then why now?" She seemed as much curious as condemning.

He raised a brow. "You have to ask, when you greet me with your clothes wet and clinging to you, with every curve plain to see? I am not made of stone, damosel."

Brigitte sighed. She had been a fool to relax her guard against him.

"You said I did not appeal to you," she said now. "Are all your statements lies?"

"You were not at your best then. I would have to be blind for you not to appeal to me. And I like knowing that no other man has had you."

He was grinning now, and his arrogance infuriated her. "I wish there had been a hundred before you!"

He only laughed at that, and she pushed at him furiously. "Get away, you overgrown lout!"

He let her up, still chuckling, and watched her grab her tunic and walk stiffly toward the river.

"Where are you going?" he called, but she did not stop.

"To bathe again, now that you have soiled me!" she threw over her shoulder, and his laughter followed her all the way to the river.

# Chapter Fifteen

*B*rigitte lay stiffly by the fire, her hands and feet bound with ribbons from her sack, unable to sleep.

It was bad enough that Rowland of Montville had taken her and then gloated about it. He had been so sure of himself, so pleased with himself, and she began to hate him for it. So when he bedded down and fell asleep almost immediately, she began to think about running away. Yes, she had thought, *that* would show him just how little she cared about Rowland of Montville.

With the moon not yet high, she edged away from Rowland, grabbed her sack, and, waking Wolff to follow, moved quietly away from the campsite. As soon as the fire was a good distance behind her, she stopped long enough to put on her sandals, then began to run.

The sound of her own movement was all Brigitte heard, so she was completely unaware that Rowland had given chase. When his hand reached out and grabbed her arm, she screamed in terror. He dragged her back to camp.

He stood looking down at her, his body rigid with anger and his eyes malevolent. "You can consider yourself fortunate that I neglected to warn you against running away. But I warn you now. If you ever try it again, your back will feel the lash, once for each hour it takes me to find you."

Brigitte felt her flesh crawl, and her back seemed to feel the lash even now. "Then I must be sure you never find me," she whispered so quietly that he could not hear.

Rowland scowled. "I would know what you just said, wench, and the truth!"

Her chin came up a little, and the lie came easily to her. "I said, what if you do not find me?"

"I will find you. I gave my word that you would never escape me, and my word is my life. And if you are foolish enough to try again, wench, let me tell you this. You will not get a beating like the one that left only bruises. My lash draws blood. What marks I give you, you will keep with you always to remind you. You *will* obey me."

Then he had fetched the ribbon and bound her hands and feet, joking grimly, "So I can sleep in peace."

It was a short while later when Brigitte heard movement just outside their camp, and then Wolff's sudden loud barking.

What happened next, Brigitte saw in a blur. Rowland rose quickly, his sword gripped in his hand. But there were two men, and he could face only one at a time. The other struck at Rowland's head from behind, using an ax. Brigitte watched in horror as Rowland crumbled to the ground.

Brigitte screamed, and Wolff attacked the man who had felled Rowland. She had no time to watch though, for the other man ran to her and knelt down beside her.

"Make haste killing the beast," he called over his shoulder. "And then you will have your reward."

Brigitte stared at his grinning face. These were the Saxons from the barge! But they had not left the river when she and Rowland had. How had they come to be here?

"Why did the knight bind you?" the Saxon asked as he cut the ribbons at her hands and feet. "Did he steal you from your master?"

Brigitte was too terrified to say anything, but he did not wait for her answer. "No matter. You are worth leaving our course and killing a man for. Aye, you are well worth it."

She could hardly hear him over Wolff's vicious growls as he attacked the other Saxon, but she understood well enough. They had followed and attacked Rowland in order to steal her. She would go from a Norman's hell to a Saxon's hell.

Brigitte screamed again as the Saxon moved his dagger to the neck of her tunic, meaning to bare his prize. But in the next instant he disappeared, thrown many feet as Wolff charged him. The man did not stand again. Brigitte turned away, unable to watch as her beloved pet reverted to the instincts of his forebears and ripped the Saxon apart. Brigitte was reminded of the baiting of the dog and wolf at Lord Wilhelm's, and she shuddered at the resemblance her pet bore to the wild wolf of the forest. When Wolff was finished, the man was a gory mess, as Lord Wilhelm's tame house dog had been. Both Saxons were hideously dead. The other man's neck and stomach had been ripped open.

When it was quiet again and Brigitte looked around the camp, her stomach heaved and she could not stop the violent spasms. Wolff came and stood by her side, but seeing him covered with the blood of his victims made her even sicker.

Brigitte had never seen a man killed before, yet here she was alone in the forest with three dead men. Three? Tearing away the remnants of ribbons at her hands and feet, she ran to where Rowland lay by the fire. She could see no blood on him, but he was terribly still.

She was free, she realized, free! She could make her way to King Lothair! Rowland was dead! And then the enormity of it struck her. He was really dead. Did she feel anything other than relief?

"I cannot stay here," she told herself aloud.

She stood up and touched Wolff's head to reassure him, but her fingers drew back, smeared with blood. She quickly rubbed them in the dirt and then pointed toward the river.

"Go on, Wolff, and wash. Go swim." He stayed where he was until she stamped her foot angrily. "Do as I say. I will gather my things, and we will leave as soon as you are clean."

He trotted off then, but Brigitte did not move to gather her things. She stood where she was, wrapping her arms about herself and staring at Rowland. The wind rustled the trees, and she felt the cold, but she did not stoop to pick up her mantle. She looked down at the blanket where she had lain with Rowland.

She was shivering when Wolff returned to the camp, but she had not moved. Wolff was dripping wet, but clean, and she smiled weakly at him and called him to her. She picked up the blanket to dry him, but first he shook himself, scattering water all over her and everything else. That was when she heard the moan.

Brigitte froze. One of the men was still alive. But which one? Ah, she didn't want to know, for there was not one of them she wanted to face again.

"Wolff, come! We must go quickly."

She threw the blanket over him, rubbed him only a few quick strokes, and then grabbed her mantle and her sack. She ran to Rowland's horse, but stopped as she reached the stallion. The size of the animal intimidated her, especially without the huge knight standing beside it. And how was she going to mount him without that knight's helping hand?

After many tries she managed to pull herself up into the hard saddle, breathing heavily with the effort, and she looked down for Wolff. But he was still by the camp fire, sniffing Rowland's body. She called him, and then again, sharply, but the dog sat down by the Norman and wouldn't move.

Brigitte sighed in exasperation. So it was *him*. He was the one still alive. She should have known the arrogant bastard was too tough to die that easily. She slid off the horse and moved slowly toward the fire. Giving Wolff a withering look, she bent down to examine Rowland.

There was a large lump on the back of his head. The Saxon's weapon must have turned when he struck, she thought, and only the flat side of the ax hit the mark. As she was considering this, she saw Rowland breathe. He would awake with a sore head, but he was indeed alive.

Brigitte looked at Wolff, who was lying down beside the Norman. She glared at him. "You do not expect me to stay here and help him, do you? I must get away."

Brigitte stood up, but the dog did not rise with her. "I am leaving," she told him flatly. "If I stay here, this man will enslave me. Is that what you want? You want me to suffer at his hands?"

Still the beast did not rise to join her. Brigitte lost her temper and shouted, "I tell you he does not need our help! Now come!"

She began to walk away, but glanced over her shoulder to see if Wolff was following. But he had moved closer to the Norman and lay with his head resting by Rowland's side.

"Damn your hide, stay with him then!" Brigitte cried. "But if you think he will treat you better than I do, you are very much mistaken. You will get his boot for your efforts to please him, for that is the kind of man he is."

She stalked away, determined not to look back. But before she reached the stallion, Wolff suddenly let out the most forlorn howl she had ever heard. It echoed through the forest. She turned back to find him nudging the Norman's side as though trying to turn him over.

"Leave him be, Wolff!" she gasped, afraid Rowland would awaken before she could leave.

She ran back to pull the dog away, and then she saw the puddle of blood seeping out from under the man. He was badly wounded. But how? With great effort, Brigitte managed to turn him over. Then she saw the sword Rowland had dropped before falling. The tip of it had landed on a large stone, pointed just right to slide into Rowland's side when he fell on it.

"It would serve him right to die by his own weapon," Brigitte said coldly.

She could not see how bad the wound was, but there was a great deal of blood on the ground and more soaking his tunic. She turned to Wolff, who was staring at her expectantly, and said stubbornly, "I am not bound to help him after what he has done to me. And do not look at me with those sad eyes, Wolff. If I bind his wound he may awaken, and I will lose my chance to escape. And besides, we do not know for certain that he will die if I do not help him."

Brigitte stopped and looked once more at the unconscious knight. And then her shoulders heaved as she said, "Listen to me. I sound as mean and cold-hearted as he is. I cannot leave a man to die, not even this one."

"I am glad to hear that."

Brigitte gasped as Rowland's dark eyes opened and locked hers. "How long have you been conscious?" she blurted.

"Since you turned me over so ungently," he grunted. "I feel a terrible stabbing in my head."

"Look to your side, Norman, for you are bleeding like a stuck pig," she said bluntly.

Rowland sat up slowly, but he fell back on one elbow, bringing his other hand to his head. "God, my skull is splitting in two." And then he looked at her sharply. "Did you do this to me?"

"If it is hurting you, then I wish I had," she said. "But I did not. A man you did not see struck you from behind."

"I would more easily believe you did it," he said skeptically.

"Then look around you. There are two bodies ready to be buried."

Rowland looked, stunned, and then his eyes fell on Wolff lying beside him. "It seems I underestimated you, dog."

"Remember that the next time you think about attacking me," Brigitte warned him. "If even I had known just how formidable Wolff is, you would have felt his teeth long ago, as those two Saxons did."

"Saxons?"

"They're the two who traveled with us on the river."

Rowland scowled. "They must have been thieves. Why else would they follow us?"

"Oh, yes, they were thieves," she returned bitterly. "But it was me they meant to steal."

"Be damned!" Rowland growled. "I knew you would cause me trouble with that winsome face of yours. I suppose you encouraged those Saxons on the barge?"

"How dare you!" She caught her breath sharply. "I cannot help the way I look, but I tempt no man intentionally. I want no man lusting after me. What you did to me was as vile as I always expected it to be."

"Enough!"

"No, it's not enough," she stormed, wanting to wound him further. "You call yourself my lord, but you did not protect me from those brigands as a lord is bound to protect his serf. I would say you have lost your right to my services, since you did not fulfill your obligations to me."

"Were you hurt?" he demanded.

"Well...no, but no thanks to you."

"If no harm has been done, then I will hear no more talk of rights and obligations. And I did make an effort to protect you. I have wounds to show for it."

Brigitte felt a twinge of remorse for provoking him and was silent.

"I believe you said you would bind my wound?" he reminded her.

"I will do so as long as you understand one thing — I do not feel bound to do it because you call yourself my lord."

"Then do it as a Christian," he said tiredly, his eyes closing wearily. "Get it done."

She turned and went to his horse to rummage through his packs for something to use as a bandage. But Rowland stopped her before she opened them.

"You will find no cloth there."

She faced him. "An old shirt will do."

"The strips from a shirt will not be long enough. You will have to find something in your clothes."

"Mine!" she gasped, coming back to stand over him. "I do not have so many clothes with me that I can spare any for you. I will use one of the blankets."

"We will need the blankets, for the farther north we go, the colder it will get," Rowland told her flatly.

She impatiently grabbed her sack of possessions and withdrew her most worn shift, a yellow linen one, consoling herself with the knowledge that it would not keep her warm in the north anyway. Nor would the blue linen she had brought. That left her only two woolen tunics.

When Brigitte turned back to Rowland, she found he had opened his belt and was trying to remove his tunic. She hesitated a moment, watching his great effort, then pushed his hands away and pulled the garment over his head. He was pale and weak, but he watched her carefully as she cleaned his wound and then bound him tightly with the strips of linen. When she was finished, she helped him into a clean garment, then covered him with the blanket and moved to build up the fire.

"Will you wash the blood from my shirt, damosel?" Rowland asked.

Brigitte nodded quickly, because he asked and did not demand it. She picked up the tunic and went down to the river. When she returned to camp, Brigitte laid Rowland's shirt over a tree limb to dry, then approached him to see if he was asleep.

"Does the lump on your head bother you?" she whispered.

"Yes," he replied with a grimace. "What did he hit me with?"

"An ax," she replied. "You are lucky. The blade was turned away."

"Humph," he grunted. "It feels embedded in my head now."

"It would have been better for me if it were," Brigitte thought, then blushed at her own cruelty.

# Chapter Sixteen

The smell of roasting meat woke Brigitte. A quick glance about the camp showed her that the dead Saxons had been moved away. The clearing was as it had been. Rowland squatted before the fire with Wolff beside him, and she glared at them both.

"My, you have been busy for a man sorely wounded," she remarked caustically.

"Good morn, damosel."

She ignored his greeting. "Pray, did your wound open?"

He chuckled. "No, the Hun did the work," he said, nodding toward his horse.

"And the meat?"

"Your dog provided that."

Brigitte turned a damning look on Wolff. "Traitor! Must you expend yourself to please *him!*"

"Do you always talk to animals?" Rowland asked her with a sidelong look.

"Only to that one," she replied sourly. "Though it seems to do little good of late."

"I hope you do not expect him to answer you."

"Of course not," she said huffily. "I am not addled, Rowland."

He frowned. "I did not give you leave to address me that way."

"I did not ask your leave."

His brows narrowed. "You will address me properly as Seignior."

"I will not. You are not my seignior," Brigitte said firmly. "My father was indeed my seignior, and my brother after him. But now my lord is the Count of Berry. I will call him Seignior, but you are Rowland of Montville and no more. I will call you either Rowland or bastard Norman—it matters not which."

Rowland stood up then and approached her, his eyes glinting.

"I warn you, wench—"

"Wench!" Brigitte burst. "My name is Brigitte—do you hear? *Brigitte!* If you call me wench once more I will scream!"

Rowland's scowl vanished with his surprise at her outburst. "You have a devil in you this morning. What has come over you, girl?"

"You have!" she shouted, near tears. "You have no right being up and about when you were near death a few hours ago. You have the devil in you. You should be weak, but he gives you strength!"

"So that is it." He laughed suddenly. "You still had plans to flee, thinking me too weak to stop you. Well, I am sorry to disappoint you, but I was taught from earliest youth to bear pain and bear it well."

They came to Angers that morning after a few hours of slow progress. Rowland did not push the Hun as hard as he had. Rather than pay their respects to the Count of Anjou, Rowland stopped at the monastery there for provisions and to make arrangements for the two dead Saxons. Then they left the old city.

Brigitte was more than a little put out. "Why could we not stay at least one night? Surely you could use the rest. One more day would not matter."

"I saw no need for it," Rowland replied curtly.

They had both been silent on the way to Angers, but now Brigitte was ready to do battle again. "Why do you avoid towns? Each one we have come to, you have left as quickly as you could."

He did not look back at her. "It's not wise to stay in a place you do not know."

"Of course not. Better to sleep out in the open on the cold ground," she said sarcastically.

"You nag like a wife," Rowland said sharply. "Cease your prattling."

Brigitte was stung, but hardly daunted. They passed vineyards on low lying hills outside Angers, and then entered a marsh. And the farther they rode from Angers, the more irritated Brigitte became. She would not have a warm bed this night, nor would there be company. She would never get any help this way.

"I cannot believe Angers is strange to you. Surely you must know someone there. It's not too late to go back."

"I have no intention of going back, girl. And no, I know no one there."

"But your home is not that far from here, is it?" she ventured.

"A few days more. But that is no reason why I should know people in Angers. I never spent time there. My father always kept me close to home. And when I left home, I went east."

Brigitte giggled at that. "You were kept close to home? What noble's son is kept close to home? A lord's son is sent to another's court for his training. If you were not, then you must come from peasant stock."

Rowland's back stiffened. "My father wished to train me himself," he said icily. "And once we reach Montville, you will no doubt learn that I am a bastard. My mother was a serf, and I am my father's bastard."

"Oh." She could think of nothing to say.

"I admit it freely."

"I might, too, if it were true in my case," she said. "But I am no bastard."

He stopped the Hun and then turned around to look at her. "Your tongue needs a rest, damosel," he said matter-of-factly. "A little walking might help."

And with that he lowered her to the soggy ground, ignoring her cry of rage. He urged his mount on, and Brigitte had no choice but to follow, Wolff trailing her.

# Chapter Seventeen

Rowland halted on a hilltop. Below him was Montville, his home. Brigitte leaned to one side to get a better look at the place she would be living in for a while. It was white, snow thickly covering everything from the fortress on a raised mound to her left to the village alongside it and the pastures, orchard, farmland, and forest beyond.

The snow fell relentlessly, reminding Brigitte uncomfortably of the previous night when the first flakes descended, prompting Rowland to seek her warmth. She would have preferred freezing, but he would not let her, pulling her soft body against his, ignoring her protests. But he did not force himself on her. Whether because of his wound or because of Wolff's low growls she did not know. But he placed warm kisses on her neck until she wiggled away. He did not bother her after that, except to place a heavy hand on her hip and leave it there, as a mark of possession.

Brigitte tried to wipe the memory of last night away as she gazed down on Rowland's home. She thought instead of meeting his father and what she would say to that noble lord. Would he believe her if she told him who she was and what had happened to her? Rowland started down the hill, and Brigitte felt the first twinges of fear. What if no one here believed her? What if she never left this place, but was forced to spend the rest of her life in service here?

A guard motioned them through the open gate, waving a greeting at Rowland. No one came out to greet them. The bailey was windblown and deserted. Not even a groom came out from the stable to take Rowland's horse.

"Is all well here?" Brigitte asked uneasily as Rowland dismounted just outside the stable and helped her down.

"Nothing seems amiss."

"But why has no one come to greet you? The guards must have seen us coming and informed your father," she asked as they left the stables and began walking toward the manor.

"Yes, I am sure he knows I am here."

"And he does not come?" she asked, astonished.

He smiled tolerantly. "Only a fool would leave a warm fire on a day like this."

"But not even a servant has come to tend you," Brigitte persisted.

Rowland shrugged. "You will find Montville is not very hospitable, Brigitte. I do not expect it to be otherwise."

"You said your father had many serfs."

"He does, but they dance to Hedda's tune, and she no doubt sent them off with a hundred tasks when she heard of my approach. That lady goes to great effort to see that I am not made to feel welcome here. I did not think she had changed simply because I have been away these last six years.

"My stepmother is a vicious lady. I would advise you to stay well out of her way, for she will not like you."

"Why? She does not even know me."

"She will not have to." Rowland chuckled. "Hedda will despise you simply because you serve me. She has always taken great pleasure in making my life miserable. She manages to make sure there is never a servant around when I need anything. But now I have you, and she will have no say over you. She will not like that."

"She hates you then?"

"I remind her of her failure to give my father a son. My mother was not of Montville. When she died, Luthor brought me here and placed me above the two daughters Hedda had given him. All that you see here will be mine one day—given to a bastard son rather than Luthor's lawful daughters."

"Then I suppose your sisters hate you as well," Brigitte sighed. "A fine family you have, Rowland. And you have brought me here to live with these disagreeable people."

"Fear not, little jewel," he told her lightly. "I will protect you from their wrath."

The manor house was larger than most, and the great hall was cavernous. Built half of wood, half of stone, it would have dwarfed the Louroux hall. The cooking was done right in the hall, Brigitte saw, for there were two hearths. Cauldrons were bubbling in one, and a large hind of meat roasted. Servants were bustling around the hall, serving dinner to a large company.

Three trestle tables were in the center of the hall. One was raised on a dais and was placed parallel to the longer two below, which were filled now with soldiers, men-at-arms, pages, knights and their squires, and several ladies. The smaller warming hearth had benches before it. To the left, above the cooking fire, was an open arched portal which gave a view from the second story at the rear of the manor and enabled the viewer to see everything going on in the hall.

At the center of the raised table sat an older man of considerable bulk, with hair the color of wheat and cut short in the Norman fashion. He was beardless, as were many of the men, and his face was etched with hard lines. It was a face of strong character. Though he bore little resemblance to Rowland, Brigitte had no doubt that this was Luthor, the lord of Montville.

On either side of him were two women, one of whom was somewhat older than Rowland. The other was older still. Daughter and mother they certainly were. The same plain features marked each: pointed chins, narrow eyes, hawk noses.

With so much noise coming from the crowd, no one took notice of Brigitte and Rowland, and Brigitte was able to study everything in the hall. But she didn't have long to look around. Wolff caught the scent of the hounds running loose in the hall, let out a howl of challenge, and attacked the nearest mongrel before Brigitte could stop him. Other hounds joined in the melee, causing a din.

Brigitte's face turned bright crimson. Her pet was causing such an outrageous commotion that the rest of the hall fell silent. Nervously, she moved to call Wolff off, but Rowland stopped her.

"Leave him be, Brigitte," he chuckled, thoroughly

amused. "This is new territory for him. He is wise to assert himself at the start."

"But he is shaming me."

"How so?" Rowland quirked a brow. "You forget he belongs to me now. And he is only showing my father's hounds that they have a new leader. That is something we at Montville understand very well."

"What? Fighting for dominance?"

"Aye."

"But your father is lord here, is he not?"

"He is indeed." Rowland nodded. "But I am bound to challenge him or he me."

"That is unheard of!"

"Not here, damosel. Luthor would have it no other way. He rules by strength, as did his forefathers. He believes that if he cannot best his men, then he is not fit to lead them. And all must know that he can still beat his heir."

"That is barbaric!" Brigitte gasped, then recovered enough to say, *"You* are barbaric as well!"

Rowland grinned into her light blue eyes. "Have you only just discovered that?"

At that moment a buxom maid ran toward them, her auburn curls flying. Brigitte watched in surprise as the girl threw her arms around Rowland's neck and kissed him soundly.

"What is this?" the girl pouted as he moved away from her embrace. "Why can you not greet me properly, *mon cher?*"

Rowland scowled. "Amelia, what we had once was private, yet you would make it public. Have you no shame, wench, to throw yourself at me before everyone?"

Amelia gasped, and her blue-black eyes widened

angrily. "I have waited all these years for you to return. Luthor knows it, and he does not mind."

"What does he know?" Rowland demanded. "Did you tell him of our dalliance? Have you disgraced your father by proclaiming your wantonness?"

"Why do you attack me?" Amelia cried. "I have told no one about us. Luthor only saw how I pined for you when you left. He thought it amusing."

"And now what will he think, after witnessing this boldness of yours? And your father, who watches us now? Be damned, Amelia!" Rowland growled. "I did not bid you wait for me. For what have you waited? I never promised marriage."

"I thought—"

"You thought wrong!" He cut her short. "And you were silly to wait when your father could have made a match for you. I had no intention of ever returning here, and you knew that."

"Oh, no, Rowland," she said quickly. "I knew you would come back, and you have."

"Enough, Amelia. My father awaits me."

"Nonsense!" She looked from Rowland to Brigitte, who had stepped away from them, embarrassed at hearing their conversation. "Ah! So that is it?" Amelia cried. "You have already taken a wife. Bastard!" she spat, her eyes black with fury. "Unfaithful dog!"

Rowland stiffened, glowering at her in earnest. "Take care, woman, or you will feel the back of my hand, and I will have to kill your father when he challenges me because of it. If you have no thought for yourself, then think of him."

Tears leapt into Amelia's dark eyes. "How could you marry another?"

Rowland sighed in exasperation. "I have not married! Nor will I, for you are all the same with your cursed nagging and whining. You drive a man beyond patience. I will take no woman whom I cannot set aside when the allure is gone and she becomes a shrew."

Rowland walked away then, and Brigitte was left wondering what she should do, for he had completely forgotten her presence. The girl Amelia turned hostile eyes on her, and Brigitte quickly followed Rowland. She did so with her head held high, ignoring the curious stares. She felt totally alone, but she took heart when Wolff joined her, having defeated the last of the Montville hounds. At least Wolff had made a proud showing.

Luthor of Montville rose as Rowland approached, but that was his only acknowledgment of his heir's return. Brigitte was confused by this strange reunion between father and son. Neither man smiled a greeting or spoke. They stood facing each other with stony expressions, more adversaries than kin. They looked one another over thoroughly, noting the changes that had taken place in six years.

Luthor spoke at last. "You are late."

"I was detained."

"So Sir Gui informed me," Luthor replied, his voice marked with displeasure. "You attended some Frenchman's deathbed. You felt that was more important than the future of Montville?"

"The man saved my life. To stay and see if he lived only cost me a few days."

"And did he?"

"Yes."

"Have you paid your debt to him?"

Rowland nodded.

That seemed to pacify Luthor. "Good. I want no loyalties to call you away from here once the trouble begins. You traveled alone with this baggage?" Luthor asked, indicating Brigitte without deigning to glance at her. "Where is your squire?"

"I lost him in the south." Then Rowland grinned. "But this baggage serves well enough."

Luthor guffawed, as did the other men within hearing. Amelia had joined them on the dais, and she said stingingly, "I did not know it was fashionable in France to call a whore a squire."

Rowland turned to Amelia with a ready retort, but his glance fell on Brigitte, and he saw the tears glistening in her eyes.

"I apologize, damosel," he said gently. "There are ladies here who belong in the gutter."

There was more than one gasp in response to this, including Brigitte's. To hear him come to her defense after he had just slurred her himself astonished her.

Before Brigitte could gather her wits and reply, Amelia snapped, "How dare you insult me like that, Rowland?"

He turned an icy look on her now. "If you cannot stand insults, Amelia, then do not give them yourself."

Amelia confronted Luthor then. "Milord, your son has no right to speak to me thusly. And it is not just me he insulted. He *did* say ladies."

"Ha! So he did." Luthor chuckled, not coming to Amelia's defense as she had hoped, or that of his own ladies, who were silently growing indignant with anger. Turning to Brigitte, he said, "Does the wench have a name?"

"The *wench* has a name," Brigitte replied boldly. "I am Brigitte de Louroux, milord."

Rowland's brows narrowed. "She is Brigitte of Montville now—my servant."

*"That* is open to question," Brigitte said flatly. Then she turned and walked stiffly toward the warming fire, calling Wolff to join her.

"Ha!" Luthor chuckled. "I understand why you were detained."

"The girl has yet to adjust to a new master. She has been only trouble so far."

"How came you by such a pretty maid and such a superb animal?"

"The girl was forced on me," Rowland answered briefly, "and the dog followed her."

Luthor gazed hard at Brigitte. "The wench carries herself like a lady. I would swear she is of noble birth, for she has that proud look about her."

Rowland looked hard at his father. "Do not let her hear you say that, sire, for that is just what she would like you to believe."

"Are you saying she claims to be a lady?"

"She will no doubt make every effort to convince you of it."

Luthor frowned. "Are you so sure she is not?"

"Be damned!" Rowland exclaimed. "I am most sure! And I am badgered enough by the girl, so do not plague me about it too, old man."

"Old man, is it?" Luthor grunted. "You meet me in the courtyard at sunrise, and we shall see who is an old man."

Rowland nodded, saying nothing. He wanted no recurrence of their old argument.

After being apprised of Thurston of Mezidon's

preparations for battle and the precautions taken at Montville, Rowland glanced over to the fire where Brigitte sat, her back to the others. Her slim hand rested on Wolff's shaggy head, absently stroking the beast. He wondered what she was thinking as she stared into the dancing flames. What was he going to do with the minx? Why did she still persist in lying about her status? She had done everything but swear to God. But he knew she would not do that, for she had real faith. She proved that when she stayed to tend his wound instead of fleeing. She might have left him to die, but she did not. Perhaps she did not hate him quite so much as she claimed.

Rowland stopped a serving maid who passed near him and whispered to her. He then watched the girl approach Brigitte. The picture Brigitte presented was one of serene reflection, but she simmered inside, near to boiling over with suppressed rage. She could not take much more of Rowland and his arrogance.

Brigitte did not hear the maid's approach, and when she tapped Brigitte on the shoulder, Brigitte jumped.

"What do you want?" she snapped.

The maid's eyes widened in confusion. She did not know what to make of this beautiful French woman whom her lord's son called a servant, but who seemed noble.

"Sir Rowland bids you join him at table and eat before you retire," the maid said nervously.

"Oh, he does, does he?" Brigitte looked to the center of the hall to see Rowland watching her, and her temper flared anew. "Well, you can tell that arrogant cock that I would not lower myself by sitting at table with him!"

The maid's eyes bulged. "I could not say that!"

Brigitte rose. "Then I will."

"Please! Do not do that. I know him and he has the devil's own temper, mistress."

Brigitte stared at the girl curiously. "Why did you call me mistress?"

The maid ducked her head shyly. "It—it seems appropriate."

Brigitte suddenly smiled. She did not know it, but that smile dazzled many onlookers. "You have done me a world of good. What is your name?"

"I am called Goda."

"Goda, I am sorry I snapped at you. I have never been one to take my anger out on a servant, and heaven forbid I should become like Rowland."

"Will you join Sir Rowland then?"

"I will not. But you can show me where I am to sleep. I want nothing more than a little privacy."

"Yes, mistress," Goda said quietly.

Rowland's eyes followed Brigitte as she left the hall with the maid. He thought of the smile she had bestowed on Goda, and he suddenly realized he had a great desire to see that smile again, but only for him.

Listen to me, Rowland thought in amusement. I am wooing a servant!

# Chapter Eighteen

*Brigitte* was taken to a small servants' hut across the bailey. It was not much better than the hovel she had been forced into at Louroux, but at least there was a clean cot and plenty of blankets. After putting her things away in an old chest and sweeping the cobwebs out of the room, she beseeched Goda to take her to the bathhouse and to bring her some food there.

The maid complied without questions, for which Brigitte was grateful. She had taken to dreaming of a hot steaming bath, and she did not even care that she would be using the servants' bath, a tub used by countless others. She had already overstepped herself by asking Goda to bring her food, for servants did not ask other servants to wait on them.

A little while later, Brigitte sat on her cot drying her hair, her feet resting near the brazier of hot coals Goda had kindly brought. Rowland opened her door, unbidden, and it rankled her. She chose to ignore him.

"Does your chamber meet with your approval, damosel?" Rowland asked after a few moments of silence.

"What brings you here, Rowland?" she asked wearily.

"I came to see how you fared," he replied. "And you have yet to answer me."

"What does it matter if the room meets with my approval or not?" she asked bitterly.

"The hut is more sturdily built than the hut I know you used at Louroux."

"You know nothing of that!" she hissed. "You presume because you saw me go there."

"I suppose you will tell me that those were not your quarters at Louroux."

"I would not dream of telling you anything," she replied heavily. "Speaking to you is like speaking to a stone wall."

Rowland ignored the insult. "If those were not your quarters, Brigitte, then why did you go there?"

"Because I am stubborn. Or have you not noticed?"

"Aye, I have indeed noticed." He chuckled.

"It was not amusing, Rowland," she said stiffly. "The very things that made you think I was a servant were conditions I brought about through my own stubbornness."

"What do you mean?"

"You won't believe anything I tell you, and I am weary of being disbelieved."

Rowland strolled into the room and stopped in front of Brigitte. He lifted her chin with a finger, forcing her to meet his penetrating gaze.

"Will you not agree then, that it is time to change your attitude?" he asked softly.

"You toy with me, Rowland, and I do not like it!" she snapped. "I would not consider seducing you even if that were my only recourse."

Rowland grabbed her shoulders and drew her up to him. "Seduce me, little jewel? But you have already done that."

He cupped her face in his hands, and his lips caressed hers in a tender assault. Brigitte was surprised by the pleasing sensation his kiss aroused, and it was several seconds before she stopped him, pushing against his chest until he moved back.

"If you had any decency, you would not subject me to your lust!" she cried.

"Ah, Brigitte, you do not play the game well," he sighed in disappointment.

"I will not play *your* game at all!" she retorted indignantly. "You might call me serf, but you cannot deny I was innocent until you touched me. I will not be your whore!"

"Only I have had you, *cherie,* and only I will. That does not make you a whore."

"To me it does!"

Rowland sighed. "What does it take to make you more agreeable?"

"You jest." She laughed derisively and jerked away from him. She moved to the end of the bed, then turned and faced him with arms akimbo and eyes flashing. "You rob me of my innocence and then say it does not matter. You humiliate me and force me to serve you. Do you suppose I will say thank you?"

"Be damned!" Rowland growled. "I came here to make amends, but I get only shrewishness."

"You can never make amends for what you have done—never!"

"Then I waste my time." He turned and stalked to the door, then stopped and looked back at her darkly. "I give you warning, wench. I can make your life pleasant or intolerable—I care not which. It's up to you to adjust your behavior, for I grow tired of your obstinacy."

He slammed the door shut and was gone. Brigitte sat down on the bed, self-pity taking hold of her. Wolff came over and licked her face.

"What am I to do now, Wolff?" she asked dejectedly. "He expects me to just give up gracefully and serve him with a smile. How can I?"

Tears welled in her eyes. "I hate him! I should have left him to die! Why did I not? We must escape this place, Wolff, we must!"

# Chapter Nineteen

When Rowland met his father in the courtyard for their battle early the next morning, his temper was little improved. Home only one day and already his strength was to be tested. But it was not only that which caused angry lines to crease his face. It was also Amelia.

She had come to his chamber the previous night. Her status as lady's maid warranted her a room near Hedda's, which also placed her near Rowland's chamber. At one time that had been convenient for him, but Rowland had no desire to resume their trysts.

When she had knocked softly at his door, he had believed it was Brigitte, come to admit defeat and make amends. The thought sent a surge of excitement through Rowland, and when he opened the door his face fell.

"Your disappointment is plain, Rowland," Amelia said with just a touch of bitterness. "You hoped I was that yellow-haired wench."

"Be gone, Amelia," Rowland replied angrily. "You were not invited here."

"I will be once you grow tired of her resistance to you," she said confidently. "It is only her resistance that charms you, nothing else."

Amelia giggled. "I know you are a bit rough, *mon cher*. You handle a woman as you do your sword, with a strong grip. But I do not mind. She does, however. Is that right?"

He set his face and said, "You had best start looking for another man to warm you on a cold night, Amelia."

"Because of her?" she hissed.

"She matters not. Amelia and I shared many pleasurable nights, but when I left here that was all ended. I am sorry you thought otherwise." He would not discuss Brigitte with her.

Amelia turned and ran. Rowland slammed the door shut, furious with himself for not taking what was so willingly offered. But the truth was that he desired another, a woman he could not have without forcing her, and he was loathe to force her.

As he faced his father in the cold dawn, he brooded on his encounter with Amelia. His thoughtful scowl did not go unnoticed.

"What troubles you, Rowland?" Luthor asked as he flexed his arms. "Have you grown soft in your absence from Montville, and fear you cannot make a good showing?"

"If anyone is afraid it is you, old man," Rowland answered curtly.

"We shall see." Luthor chuckled, then continued amiably, "I have heard of your many adventures. Aye, you must have grown tired of King Lothair's efforts to regain Lotharingia."

Rowland shrugged. "There was no challenge. A skirmish won, a skirmish lost. A battle must someday reach a conclusion, but I wonder if that one will ever be resolved."

"So you went on to Champagne and then Burgundy?" Luthor added casually.

"You are well informed," Rowland grunted.

"I have many friends who sent me word of your whereabouts now and then. What I taught you was not wasted in Provence. I would have enjoyed that battle myself."

"It was over quickly."

"What route did you travel across central France in coming home?"

Rowland wondered at Luthor's curiosity, but he answered. "I traveled the Loire until Berry. There I delivered the message entrusted to me and was given the girl."

"You then crossed Blois and Maine in a direct route to Montville?"

"No, I traveled the Loire at Orleans until the junction with the Maine River. Then I rode a direct route north."

"You passed Angers then?"

Rowland noted the sudden alarm in Luthor's voice, and he frowned. "Yes, but why should that matter?"

"It does not," Luthor replied, then added curtly, "Let us begin."

Rowland shrugged off Luthor's interrogation and warmed to the challenge at hand. His father thrived on these tests of strength, but only in the last few years before leaving home had Rowland been able to give a good accounting of himself. The will to best his father had always been there, but the means had been long in coming.

The first ringing of metal against metal drew others to the courtyard. The sounds of battle woke Brigitte from sleep, and she hurried to her door, fearing

Montville was under attack. She gasped when she saw Rowland and his father in earnest combat. Brigitte quickly drew on her woolen mantle and ran outside, not even bothering with the hood to cover her unbraided, flowing hair. She stood near two soldiers and watched in fascinated horror as Luthor bore down on Rowland, striking blow after blow with his heavy sword, forcing him to retreat. Rowland was hard-pressed to do anything but counter the blows with sword and shield. This continued the length of the yard, until finally Rowland dodged one powerful downward swing of Luthor's sword and began his own assault, forcing Luthor to retreat.

"How long has this been going on?" Brigitte whispered to the soldiers, her eyes on Rowland.

"Not long," one of them answered.

But it became long. The sun rose and climbed higher, and the battle raged on, neither man giving in. Brigitte grew tired just watching. She knew how heavy a knight's sword was. She could barely lift one with both hands. The strength of body and will it took to last this long awed her.

But the scene became monotonous as the two men crossed the yard back and forth, first one assaulting, then the other. Then suddenly the tempo changed, as if each man were drawing on a new reserve of power. Rowland's sword swung quickly for Luthor's right side, but in a flash it changed direction midway and struck to the left. Luthor was caught off guard. He did not raise his shield quickly enough, and Rowland's weapon sliced through several links of Luthor's mail into his shoulder.

Both men stood still. Brigitte assumed the match was over. Then, to her utter amazement, Luthor began to laugh. What kind of people were these? In the next moment, however, Luthor knocked the sword out of Rowland's hand and his own sword pressed against Rowland's chest.

Rowland threw his shield down, silently admitting defeat, and Luthor lowered his sword.

"Having drawn blood, you should have pressed on, Rowland," Luthor chuckled, "not stopped to see how gravely you had wounded your enemy."

"Were you my real enemy, old man, I would indeed have pressed on," Rowland replied.

"Then perhaps I will take that into consideration and admit to an even match. Yes...for once we have no victor. Do you agree to that?"

Rowland nodded, then grinned. Gesturing to Luthor's shoulder, he said, "You must get that tended."

"I barely feel this scratch," Luthor grunted. "Your own scrapes could use the tender hand of yon pretty maid."

Rowland glanced around and saw Brigitte watching him. She was a vision of loveliness, her hair cascading in disarray over her shoulders like spun gold in the sunlight. She shyly lowered her gaze, and Rowland found himself mesmerized, forgetting his aching muscles.

But the sound of Luthor's rumbling laughter drew him. "You strip the poor wench with your eyes, my boy," he chided. "Can you not wait until you are alone?"

Rowland reddened.

"You do me proud this day, Rowland," his father said. "You are a worthy son. Aye, you were a fine challenge, and I know your wound is not fully healed. You learned all I taught you and more."

Rowland did not know what to say. This was the first time Luthor had ever praised him, let alone so lavishly. Fortunately, Luthor expected no reply. He turned and walked away, leaving Rowland staring after him, wondering. His father had changed. Perhaps he was getting old after all.

Brigitte and Rowland were alone in the courtyard, the others having gone to the hall.

"You have opened your wound," Brigitte scolded.

Rowland grinned apologetically. "It was not intentional. Will you tend it?"

"I suppose I will have to, for I see no one else coming forward to do so," she said severely.

"What troubles you?" he asked hesitantly.

"You!" she snapped, her hands going to her hips in an angry stance. "That foolishness I just witnessed!"

"It was just sport, *cherie*."

"It was not sport. It was madness," she retorted heatedly. "You could have killed each other!"

"We did not fight to kill, Brigitte," Rowland explained patiently. "It was a test of strength, no more. Do French knights not test their skill in sport?"

"Well, yes," she replied reluctantly, "but not so earnestly. You fought as if your honor was at stake."

Rowland chuckled. "In a way it was. We do fight in earnest here. Luthor insists that everyone he teaches be the best. He is a master of war, and, in truth, I have never lasted so long with him before."

"But you were evenly matched," she pointed out. "Even I could see that. In fact, you would have beaten your father if only you had not stopped."

"Do you realize you are praising me, *cherie?*" Rowland teased with a grin.

Brigitte blushed becomingly. "I...I..."

"Come now," he said with mock severity. "Do not spoil the only praise I have heard from your lips with a sharp reply. Be merciful for just this once."

"You jest with me, Rowland. And you have conveniently changed the subject."

"It was a tiring subject," he said evasively. "And besides, we have wasted enough time here. I begin to think you intend to weaken me through loss of blood by keeping me standing here arguing with you."

"That is not such a bad idea," Brigitte said. "But come. My room is near."

"No, I need a change of garments, and I have bandages in my chamber. If you will just help me there."

"You need help walking?" Her eyes widened.

He nodded. "I feel as if I cannot move a muscle," he groaned. "But if you will just give me your hand, *cherie,* I will follow you anywhere."

"My hand, is it?" she snapped. "I don't know about that."

He snatched her hand and started for the manor. "Then you must follow me, I suppose," he said as he pulled her along, mindful for once of his grip.

Rowland's chamber was a cluttered mess, and Brigitte's eyes flew from one opened chest to another, to the scattered clothes, the rumpled bed, and the crumpled rug. Dust thickly covered a marble-topped table and a single high-backed chair, and the walls were blackened with soot.

"Do you actually sleep here?" Brigitte asked distastefully.

He grinned. "The room was left unused for many

years, and I did leave it in a hurry this morn. But it will not take you too long to put it to rights."

"Me?" she gasped and turned on him.

Rowland sighed. "Please, Brigitte, do not start again. Is it too much to ask that you tend a few of my needs?"

Brigitte hesitated. He was asking, not demanding, and that was enough, at least for now.

After she had bandaged him, Brigitte turned toward one of the chests. Rowland grinned. He had Brigitte alone in his room, and for once Wolff was not with her. And she was even in a pleasant mood.

"What color would suit me, *cherie?*"

"Blue definitely, and maybe dark brown. I think you would cut a fine figure in dark brown."

"Then you won't mind making me a new tunic or two, will you? I have so few tunics."

"I am not fooled by that innocent look. I will sew for you, if only to prove that I can. But do not think I mean to be your slave."

The old brown tunic selected and the bandaging finished, Brigitte turned to leave. Rowland called to her. "I do not want you to run away yet."

"Why?" she asked, her voice rising.

"Brigitte, calm yourself and stop edging toward the door. I am not going to rape you." He sighed. "Do you fear me so much?"

"Yes," she answered truthfully.

He frowned. "Was I so rough with you before?"

When she failed to answer, he asked, "Do you think me a harsh man, Brigitte?"

"You have been harsh," she answered truthfully again. "Your manner leaves much to be desired, Rowland, and your temper is too quick."

"So is yours," he pointed out.

She grinned. "I know. I have many faults. I am aware of them. But we were discussing yours, which you seem not to be aware of at all."

He brought his hand up and caressed her cheek with his fingers. "For you I will change."

There was a long, surprised pause, and then she asked, "Why?"

"To see you smile more often."

"I have had little to smile about, Rowland," she told him frankly.

"You will have."

She drew away from him, her eyes darkening. "Are you toying with me?"

"No, I am most sincere," he said softly.

He leaned over and kissed her, softly at first so as not to frighten her, then more intently. She was indeed frightened, and pushed against his chest. Rowland did not release her. His arms pulled her to him even harder. Where her breasts pressed against his chest, he burned. Where she squirmed between his legs, he ached. He was inflamed by her, but she resisted him.

His lips moved to the delicate curve of her neck. "Ah, Brigitte, I want you," he breathed against her ear.

"Rowland, you said you would not rape me," she gasped, straining against him.

"Let me love you," he murmured huskily. "Let me, Brigitte."

He kissed her before she could refuse, but Brigitte finally managed to tear herself away.

"Rowland, you hurt me!" she cried.

He leaned over to look at her and saw her bruised

lips. "Be damned, Brigitte, why are you so frail?" he moaned.

"I cannot help the way I am," she said in a trembling voice. "I was raised with a gentle hand. My skin is sensitive and not used to such treatment."

He lifted her chin, then touched her lips softly with a finger. "I did not mean to hurt you," he said softly.

"I know," she conceded. "But you are trying to force me."

Rowland grinned guiltily. "I could not help myself."

Brigitte's temper rose suddenly. "Do you dare to blame me again? My clothes are not wet and clinging to me this time."

"No."

"Then tell me what I did so that I will be sure not to do it again!" she said hotly.

Rowland laughed heartily. "Ah, little jewel, you are so innocent. Just being near you entices me. Do you not know how very beautiful you are?"

"You must stay away from me."

"Oh, no, Brigitte," he replied, shaking his head slowly but adamantly. "You are every man's dream, but only one man's treasure—mine. I will not stay away from you."

"I am not yours, Rowland." She struggled away and moved backward a couple of feet. "I will never be yours."

Rowland slammed a fist against his thigh. "Why do you hate me so?" he cried in exasperation.

"You know why."

"I have said I will change."

"You said so, and immediately afterward you grabbed me again. I cannot believe what you say."

"You judge me harshly, Brigitte. What happened just now was beyond my control."

"Must I live in continual fear then? I want to know now, Rowland."

He frowned darkly. He could not tell her truthfully that he would never force her again, for, although he did not want it to be that way, he knew now just how little control over himself he had where she was concerned. But, damn, he did not want her to fear him either. And it angered him that she should fear him.

"Well, Rowland?"

He turned away in agitation. "Do not push me, wench!" he barked.

Her eyes pleaded with him. "I must have an answer."

"I will have to think on it. Now let us go," he snapped. "It is time for a meal."

# Chapter Twenty

*The* hall was not as crowded that morning, but Luthor was there and called Rowland to join him.

Brigitte went to the cooking fire. A large room near the hearth was where food was stored and prepared. All the utensils for cooking were kept there; iron and leather cauldrons, salt basins, bread bins. Tankards and silver ewers were stacked on shelves, and a buffet held pots of tin, lead, and iron and plates of wood and lead. Spices were arranged on shelves, and barrels of grain stood in the back of the room. A large table near the entrance was filled with cheese and freshly baked bread just then, beside a huge cauldron of apple cider.

Brigitte brought a large portion of cheese and bread to Rowland without being asked, but quickly left him once she set the food down. She sat by the fire, where a gruel of barley and oats was being ladled for the servants, and accepted a bowl from Goda, along with a chunk of rye bread. It was servants food, but she did not mind. She was in too great a turmoil to care much about food.

As soon as Rowland left the hall, she asked Goda where she would find strong soap and cleaning materials, and she hurried to his chamber. She spent the rest of the day there, cleaning and straightening his things. He had few clothes, but valuable possessions filled his chests: rare glassware, jewels and gold, tapestries of eastern design, and so much fine cloth that she began to wonder if he planned to become a merchant.

His room turned out to be comfortable and attractive once Brigitte finished with it. The skins covering the windows kept out the cold, but still allowed light to enter. The rug on the floor was a novelty of fur pelts which warmed the feet and was far nicer than rushes. The large bed had feather pillows, linen sheets, and a thick eiderdown covering.

Brigitte saved the straightening of that bed for last, reluctant to even go near it. She could not help wondering how long it would be before she slept there. It was what Rowland wanted. He had made that plain enough.

Brigitte grew nervous as the light faded and the time to return to the hall drew near. It had been so much easier contending with Rowland when they were traveling. She had accepted his harshness and took refuge in her anger. But this was a different Rowland, one actually mindful of hurting her. It had thrown her, for she hardly knew how to behave any longer.

Brigitte returned to the great hall with a heavy heart, knowing full well what she would have to do. Even nature was against her, but that could not be helped. She would rather risk freezing to death by fleeing than stay here to await Rowland's pleasure.

Even with the hall crowded, Brigitte saw quickly that Rowland was not there yet. She helped herself to a trencher of food and sat down on an empty bench against the wall, hoping to be finished before he arrived. She could serve him quickly and retire to her room. If what he said was true, and she tempted him by just being near, then she had only this night to worry about, for she would be gone on the morrow.

She saw Wolff by the lord's table. Luthor himself was tossing scraps of meat to him. But when her pet saw her, he bounded over to sit by her, and she greeted him with a smile. Another hound approached, drawn by the smell of her food, but Wolff snapped him away and settled at her feet.

She leaned down and petted him. "I see you are being taken care of by the Lord himself. But do not get too fond of this place, for we will not be staying."

He licked her hand and she frowned. "You will not change my mind this time, Wolff."

Too late Brigitte realized she was speaking aloud, and she glanced up quickly. But she was alone except for Wolff. She looked farther to see if Rowland had entered while she was distracted, but he still had not come in for dinner.

At the lord's table there was a handsome young knight she had not seen before. Her eyes rested on him for a moment, but he sensed her gaze and looked over at her, smiling. He rose and came toward her.

"My lady." He bowed before her. "I am Sir Gui of Falaise. I was not told we had guests."

Brigitte knew who he was. Luthor's vassal, he had been sent to find Rowland and bring him home.

"Has no one told you who I am, Sir Gui?" she asked gently.

"I only just returned from patrol, lady," he explained. Then he grinned. "But this hall has never been graced by such beauty. It was remiss of Lord

Luthor not to mention you." His green eyes twinkled down at her.

"You are kind," Brigitte said shyly.

"Tell me," he smiled, "what is the name of one so lovely?"

Brigitte hesitated. He had called her lady. He thought her a lady. So why should she not tell him the truth?

"I am Lady Brigitte de Louroux," she said quietly.

"Who is your lord? I may know him."

"Count Arnulf of Berry is my lord now," she said easily, as if no one would dare doubt it.

"You are here with him?"

"No."

"Pray, do not tell me you have a husband who brings you here," Gui said in obvious disappointment.

"I have no husband," Brigitte replied, then decided to tell the whole truth. "Sir Rowland brought me here against my will."

Gui's handsome face registered surprise and confusion. "Rowland? I do not understand."

"It is difficult to explain, Sir Gui," Brigitte said, uncomfortable.

He sat down beside her. "You must tell me. If Rowland has abducted you—"

"Rowland is not wholly at fault," she admitted reluctantly. "You see, my father was the Baron de Louroux, and my brother after him." She told Gui her story, and he gazed, in rapt attention, until she had finished.

"But Rowland is no fool," Gui protested. "Surely he could see you are a lady, no matter what Druoda told him."

Brigitte sighed. "There were many things that made him believe Druoda instead of me."

"Rowland must be made to see the wrong he has done," Gui said earnestly.

"I have tried, Sir Gui, truly, but to no avail. Rowland likes me as his servant, and I believe he prefers to ignore the truth because the truth does not suit him." Gui smiled at that, for it was a fine description of his friend's temperament.

The large hardwood door at the front of the hall swung open then, and Rowland entered. Brigitte rose quickly, beginning to doubt now the wisdom of what she had just done. But what really *had* she done but tell the truth? And Sir Gui believed her. He might become her champion.

"Rowland is here," Brigitte said to her new friend. "I must get his food."

Gui rose indignantly. "No, Lady Brigitte. You must not serve like a common serf."

"Oh, but I must," she replied, "or he will beat me."

Gui's face reddened in outrage as she turned and hurried away. She filled a large trencher full of black pudding, sausage, and small game, and quickly looked back just in time to see Rowland greet Gui cheerfully and Gui's cold response.

Brigitte took Rowland's food and ale to the lord's table, sneaking quick looks back at the two men who had begun to have heated words. Others were looking their way too, and she became increasingly nervous. If only she could hear what they were saying! But she did not dare go near them.

"What mischief have you brewed, wench?"

Brigitte caught her breath and turned to Luthor.

"I know not what you mean, milord." She answered him firmly but was unable to meet his gaze.

"I saw you speaking to my vassal, and now he is arguing with my son. Those two are friends, girl. They have never argued before."

"I have done nothing that I regret," Brigitte replied adamantly as she set the food down.

Luthor rose from the large oak table and drew her aside. "Whatever you have done had better not bring about a challenge. I would not care to lose a good man, not when I have a battle brewing."

"Is that all your son is to you, a good man to fight for you?"

"I speak of Sir Gui, wench, for there is no doubt who the victor would be. If I thought my son was in danger because of you, I would have you flayed alive, lady or not."

Brigitte's eyes widened. He knew! Damn him, he knew she was a lady, yet he was going to let Rowland keep her, fully aware that he had no right to.

"You are despicable!" Brigitte hissed furiously. "You know what I am, yet you go along with the injustice your son does me!"

Luthor chuckled. "It matters little to me. Rowland claims you as his servant, and so you are. I will not dispute him over it."

"But he is wrong!" Brigitte cried.

"Understand me, damosel. A man needs a son to follow after him and take his place when he is gone. But besides that, I need my son beside me to fight for my fief. I take pride in what I have made of him. I almost lost him over some foolishness years ago, and only this coming battle with my son-in-law has brought him back. But he is back, and I will not risk losing him again."

"Brigitte!"

She shrank at the thunderous sound and turned to see Rowland coming toward her, his face a black mask of rage. She felt her knees weaken.

"Ah, damosel," Luthor said almost sadly. "I fear now you will regret whatever it is you claim you didn't do."

Her eyes flashed at him. "And you would let him beat me too, wouldn't you?"

"You are not my responsibility, girl," said the older man, turning away.

"Do not hide near my father, wench," Rowland growled. "He will not help you."

Brigitte spoke calmly, desperate to hide her fear. "I did not expect him to. He has already told me he approves anything you do."

"So you *have* asked him for help?"

"No, Rowland," Luthor interjected. "She did not come to me. I spoke to her first."

"Do not defend her, sire," Rowland warned coldly.

Luthor hesitated for only a second, then bowed and left them standing alone on the dais. Rowland grabbed Brigitte's arm and made as if to strike her. She panicked, but instead of moving away, she threw herself at him. Her fingers hooked into his tunic, and she pressed closely enough to feel the heat of his hard, unyielding body.

"If you must beat me, Rowland, use a whip," she whispered. "I could not survive a blow from your fist, not when you are so angry. You will kill me."

"Be damned!" he growled, moving to pry her fingers loose.

But she held tight. "No! You are angry and do not know your own strength. You would kill me with your fists. Is that what you want?"

"Let go, Brigitte," Rowland commanded, though his anger had begun to dissipate.

She heard the change in his tone. And then she felt the change in his body, and saw the gleam in his eye. She pushed away from him, one fear being replaced by another.

"I...I did not mean to throw myself at you," she said lamely.

Rowland sighed. "Get to your room. You have caused enough trouble here today."

"It was not my intention to cause trouble," she offered in a reasonable tone.

But his eyes darkened, and his body grew stiff again. "Get out of my sight, woman, before I change my mind!"

She called Wolff, then left through the door leading to the stable, for the front portal was too heavy for her to open. Once out of the hall, she shivered. How very close she had come to a sound beating! But why was Rowland so angry? What had been said between him and Sir Gui?

She passed through the stable and noticed Rowland's horse there with four others she did not recall seeing before. No doubt those horses belonged to Sir Gui and the others who had been on patrol. But Luthor commanded many men. She wondered where the rest of the horses were kept. But she did not pursue the question. As long as there was at least one horse here she could take with her later, that was all she cared about.

Brigitte pulled her hood up and drew her mantle

closer together before she crossed the bailey to her small hut. It had not snowed that day, but the air was icy. In this weather she would find running away difficult. But she was stubbornly determined, more so now than ever before.

Her room was cold and dark, and there would be no brazier of hot coals for her that night. Without coals or a candle to see by—for those precious items were not wasted on servants—Brigitte had no choice but to go to bed. At least she would be warmer in bed. She did not remove her garments, for she did not want to waste time dressing when the hour to leave arrived.

She heard Wolff moving around in the dark and snapped at him. "Settle down and sleep while you can, for we will not rest once we leave here. And that will be soon, my pet, as soon as all grows quiet."

# Chapter Twenty-one

Several hours later, after donning two extra tunics for warmth and taking all the blankets in the room, she and Wolff went directly to the stable. She would not try to obtain food, for fear someone might see her prowling through the hall. Wolff would provide food for both of them, she had no doubt of that. And she still had a flint Rowland had given her in the forest, a precious flint.

Fortunately, the four extra horses were still in the stable, so she did not have to take Rowland's huge destrier. She was relieved. The Hun was too big for her. Worse, Rowland would never stop looking for her if she had the Hun, for a war horse was far more valuable than any servant.

The other horses were not quite so large, and one, a chestnut-brown gelding, did not shy away when she went to saddle him. With her possessions tied to his saddle and the reins in hand, Brigitte walked cautiously out into the night-blackened courtyard.

Her real worries began there. She knew that most manors had at least one other means of access besides the main gate with its guards, but finding it was a different matter, for a door in the wall would more than likely be concealed. Louroux had a secret tunnel, in case of siege, and it was known by only a few people.

"Come on, Wolff," she whispered. "We must find a way out of this fortress. Help me find a door, Wolff—a door. But quietly."

She began her search to the left of the servants' quarters and worked her way around, past the side of the manor, to the rear. There she found the animal pens and a huge shelter unlike anything she had ever seen before. She wondered if that was where the rest of the horses were kept, but she didn't investigate. She moved slowly along the wall, pulling her horse behind, while Wolff bounded ahead of them.

Brigitte started to worry when they had gone a half circle around with no luck. She began to consider her chances of getting past the gate guards, praying that she wouldn't have to try. She had to hurry. If she did not return to the manor within a few hours, Rowland would be informed and come after her. Her only hope was to not be discovered missing until morning. She needed every hour left of the night in order to be far, far away before Rowland came looking for her.

Wolff barked, and Brigitte sucked in her breath, fearing that the other hounds would begin barking and wake the whole manor. She ran to him quickly before he made more noise, then sighed in relief when she saw the door. It was bolted, but the crossbar lifted after a few shoves, then nearly fell when she lowered it to the ground. The door opened easily.

But then Brigitte's hopes fell again. Below her was at least two feet of stone, for, although the door was level with the ground inside the wall, outside it was not. And that was not even the worst of it. At

the base of the wall on the outside was a tiny ledge
of earth, perhaps a foot wide, followed by a steep
incline of at least ten or twelve feet covered with
snow. A fine exit this! How in heaven's name would
she get the horse down that slope without the poor animal breaking its neck? But she had to try. Damn! She
had to!

Keeping hold of the reins, she stepped down onto
the narrow ledge, then called Wolff to join her. He
looked at her, then down at the ledge, then back at
her again, but made no move to follow.

"If I can do it, you can too," she said sternly. "It's
the horse who will have a difficult time of it."

Cautiously, Wolff moved forward and, after hesitating only a second more, jumped. He landed half
way down the slope, slid a few feet, then found his
footing and ran the rest of the way down.

Seeing Wolff flounder, Brigitte was thoroughly
discouraged. What chance would the horse have? The
jump might break a leg. But she hardened herself.
She needed a horse. She would never make it to the
Ile-de-France without one.

"Come on, my fine steed," she urged sweetly, tug-
ging on his reins. She managed to pull him to the
edge of the portal, but he snorted and backed away.
"Come on now. You will slide most of the way. Let
us see the courage your Normans expect of a fine
war horse like you."

But the animal would not budge, and she wasn't
nearly strong enough to make him. She sank down
on the ledge in despair. What could she do now? If
she left on foot, Rowland would find her quickly.

Wolff bounded back up the slope then and came

to stand beside her, nudging her eagerly. He was excited now, ready to be away.

She sighed. "It's no good, my king. The horse will not move. Maybe he is wiser than I and knows he cannot make the jump." She stood up, but her shoulders slumped dejectedly. "We will have to try and fool the guards. I do not foresee much luck there, but come on, back inside the wall. I must try," she sighed.

Wolff leaped up through the portal with ease. A second later he began snapping at the horse's hind legs, and Brigitte moved out of the way and let go the reins only just in time before the steed jumped forward. She watched in amazement as the huge animal slid down the slope on his rump, Wolff tearing down after him. The horse stood up at the bottom of the incline and simply waited.

Brigitte could not believe what she had seen. She quickly slipped her fingers beneath the door to draw it shut, then slid down the slope. At the bottom, she threw her arms around Wolff and squeezed him with all her might.

"You are wonderful," she whispered. "Absolutely magnificent! Ah, my king, you have saved the day. Now, let us get away from this place!"

Hastily she examined the horse. He seemed fit enough. She took a moment to soothe and praise him before she pulled herself onto his back and urged him forward. Soon the chestnut achieved a full gallop, taking advantage of the open pastureland surrounding Montville. She flew with the wind, exhilarated, and once far enough away from the fortress, she laughed gaily in relief.

She had done it! Rowland would never catch her. It would not matter if he followed her all the way to the Ile-de-France, for, once there, she would have the King's protection. King Lothair would remember her—or, if not her, then her father. And if Rowland dared make a claim on her to Lothair, he would be called to account for everything. No, nothing would stop her now.

The rest of the night seemed to fly by, and before she knew it the sky lightened with dawn. The sun did not come out to help melt the snow, but remained hidden behind thick clouds, as the moon had been. But the pale sunlight was enough to help her see the stark countryside and give wide berth to a fortress she nearly came upon. She skirted it cautiously, knowing she could not trust any Normans.

It would have been easier going south, the way they had come, for she was familiar with that route. But Paris and the King's court were east, and she would get there much sooner if she traveled directly east, even though she did not know the way.

The sun was high before Brigitte stopped in dense woods to let the animals rest. Wolff had kept up with little difficulty, sometimes racing ahead, sometimes lagging behind or running off to amuse himself. But she knew he was tired, and she had to be careful of the horse.

They did not rest long. She tried to light a small fire for a few minutes of warmth but was not able to because all the twigs and sticks she found were damp. She tied sticks together to take with her, hoping they would dry in the wind as she rode.

Brigitte had not considered this obstacle. Nor did she realize until she saw Wolff lapping up snow that she had completely forgotten about bringing water along. She became thankful for the snow and scooped up a handful herself to quench her thirst.

They rode on. Brigitte was already hungry, but that would have to wait until nightfall. She would not take time for Wolff to hunt. Fortunately, the horse had found some grass beneath the snow to munch on. She and Wolff could wait a while longer.

They left the woods and crossed open pastureland. Brigitte was able to skirt around a marsh that would have slowed her down, but she was not so lucky when she came to a thick forest that spread across the land in both directions, leaving her no recourse but to enter it. When night came, she had still not reached the other side of the forest and was forced to make camp there. If she had been in the open she might have ridden for several more hours, but the forest was too dark for riding.

She had better luck with a fire, thanks to the sticks she had carried with her, but they were still damp enough to cause an abundance of smoke. After she had a fire, she felt safe enough to send Wolff off for food. While he was gone, she removed the saddle from the horse and covered him with a blanket, then sat down before the fire.

Her thoughts drifted to Rowland, and she pictured him vividly in her mind. He was such a fine figure of a man, so stalwart, so handsome. Things might have been quite different if only he had believed her when they first left Louroux and had taken her to Count Arnulf, which would have been the honorable thing to do. She might have had a different opinion of him then, might even have liked him a little, despite his roughness.

But that was not the way of it. Hate was new to

Brigitte, and she did not like the feeling. She had never felt so strongly, not even about Druoda. She hated what Druoda had done to her, but not the woman herself. Why did Rowland arouse such strong feeling in her?

Brigitte heard the sound of something approaching and held her breath until Wolff appeared through the underbrush. He had a fine catch, and she quickly prepared their meal, then settled down by the fire. She fell asleep almost instantly, Wolff curled at her feet. But it was not long afterward that his low growl woke her. His ears pointed, and the fur on his back was raised. Then suddenly he charged off into the dark of the forest and out of her sight.

Brigitte called him back, but he did not obey. She sat up, wide awake. The low flames of the fire indicated that she had slept about an hour. Her arms circled her raised knees, and she stared off in the direction Wolff had gone, wondering what sort of wild beast had drawn him away.

Were there wild bears in this black forest? As far as she knew, Wolff had never fought such a formidable foe. How would he fare against a bear, or the more frightening boar?

She worried even more when she could no longer hear Wolff in the distance. There was no sign of him. She called him, and again, louder. She got up and began to pace, then stopped suddenly and chided herself for letting her imagination run wild. He would come back.

Once again she settled by the fire. And, as if to show her how ridiculous her fears had been, Wolff bounded back into camp. She sighed in relief. But her relief was short-lived and her fears revived as she saw that he was not alone. A hound followed, and then a horse.

Brigitte recognized the horse before she saw the rider. Rowland sat stiffly on the Hun, devoid of armor, wearing a thick cloak of fur over his tunic and trousers.

Brigitte was too surprised to speak, too shocked to move, even when Rowland dismounted with a heavy rope clenched tightly in his hand. She watched numbly as he called Wolff to him and that trusting fool obeyed. The dog did not even move away when the rope was tied around his neck. Rowland moved to a far tree and tied the short rope to it. It was happening, but Brigitte could not quite believe it.

The hound that had come with Rowland found the leftover meat Brigitte had wrapped in its own skin and began tearing away the skin to get at the meat. Brigitte stared at the dog for several seconds, and suddenly everything fell into place all at once. That was how Rowland had found her! The hound had tracked them!

Her eyes flew back to Rowland, and she saw that he had Wolff secured to the tree. And the reason he was tying her dog before he had said one word to her became clear. Rowland had something so terrible planned that he could not let Wolff be loose. Before that thought even fully registered, Brigitte ran to her horse as if her life depended on it.

But she had waited too long. Her mantle was caught well before she reached the horse, and the clasp at her throat nearly choked her as she was jerked to a halt and then swung back toward the fire. She fell to the ground, scraping her palms. Wolff began to growl. Brigitte fought the tears already filling her eyes.

She saw Rowland's boots next to her, planted far apart. She looked a little higher, and saw his hands removing his belt. Still higher revealed the set expression on his face, and her own turned white.

Before Brigitte could find the words to plead with him, Rowland's belt descended on her back. She gasped and cried out. He struck her again, and she screamed. Far away she heard Wolff snarling furiously, and then he made a terrible sound as the rope stopped his charge.

By then, she was curled tightly in a ball, cringing as she waited for another lash. It did not come, but she feared to look up at Rowland so she did not know that he had thrown his belt aside and stalked away, disgusted with himself and deeply upset. After taking a few deep breaths to calm himself, he came back and dropped to his knees beside her.

Rowland drew her into his arms and she let him, needing comfort, even from him. Her tears dried, but Rowland continued to hold her, stroking her hair. For a long time neither said anything. At last, she moved away, and he saw accusation in her eyes.

"Be damned!" he growled as he rose to tower over her. "Do you dare to be unrepentant?"

"Repentant?" she threw back. "After what you just did?"

"You led me a merry chase all day, woman. You deserved more than you got for it!"

"To be found by you is my punishment, and more than I can bear," she spat at him. Scrambling to her feet she faced him with flashing blue eyes. "But that means nothing to you. You want to make me suffer!"

"I do not ever want to hurt you!" he said furiously. "You force me to it!"

"Oh, of course, milord," she said, just as furiously. "I am the cause of all my pain. I even beat myself." He stepped toward her menacingly, but she stood her ground. "What? Am I going to beat myself again, milord?"

"You are awfully saucy for a wench who has just been beaten." He frowned.

Her eyes grew larger. "Norman bastard! If I were a man I would kill you!"

Suddenly he laughed. "If you were a man, *cherie,* the drift of my thoughts would be a sin."

She gasped and backed away from him. "I am a woman, and your thoughts are still sinful."

Rowland grinned. "You need not run from me, Brigitte. I have had a hard ride, and only sleep entices me at the moment."

Brigitte watched him warily as he moved to his horse for food and blankets. He returned to the fire and stirred it up before lying down near its warmth.

"Are you hungry?" he asked.

She was amazed. He was behaving as if nothing had happened. "No," she said tautly. "I have eaten very well."

"Ah, provided for by your pet." Rowland turned and looked at Wolff, and his brows knitted thoughtfully. "Do you think if I got rid of that beast, you would not be so quick to run away again? Without him to hunt for you, what would you do?"

"No," she cried, sinking down on her knees beside him. "Wolff is all I have."

"You have me," he reminded her softly.

She shook her head. "You give me only pain and anguish. Only Wolff gives me comfort. I love him."

"And you hate me?"

"What you do to me makes me hate you."

Rowland grunted. "Give me your word that you will not run away again."

"You would take the word of a *servant,* milord?" she asked sarcastically.

"I would take your word."

She raised her chin proudly. "I could give it, but it would be a lie. I will not make promises I cannot keep."

"Be damned!" he rasped, throwing a stick into the fire, sending sparks flying. "Then I cannot promise not to beat you again, and the next time you may not be so heavily clothed."

"I would expect no less of you!" Brigitte snapped.

Rowland stared at her furious face and sighed. "Go to sleep, Brigitte. I can see there is no winning with you, and no reasoning either."

Rowland lay down, but Brigitte stayed where she was, kneeling rigidly. After several moments had passed, she said softly, "There is one thing you could do, Rowland, to assure that I stay with you."

"I am aware of what that is," he replied irritably. "But I cannot keep my distance from you."

"Not that, Rowland."

He sat up quickly, for she had managed to prick his curiosity. "What?"

"Send an inquiry to Count Arnulf for the proof of my claim, and I will be content to wait at Montville for his reply."

"And when his reply comes and you are proved a liar—then what?"

"Are you still so sure I lie, Rowland?" she ventured solemnly.

He grunted. "Very well. I will send the message just to put an end to all this. But I cannot see what you hope to gain."

She smiled, deciding to pretend. Until the message was sent, she needed to keep him believing that he was right. "It's simple. If you send the message, then you are admitting the possibility that you *might* be wrong. I can live with that admission."

"Humph!" he retorted, turning over. "Such logic could only be a woman's."

Brigitte wanted to laugh. How easily he had accepted the lie! She lay down a few feet from him and went to sleep.

# Chapter Twenty-two

Rowland woke with the dawn. He lay stretched out on the ground, staring thoughtfully up through the trees at the pale sky. Brigitte slept on peacefully, unaware of the turmoil she had caused in his mind.

How furious he had been yesterday, not even so much because she had left him but because of the risk she took in setting out alone. The little fool might have fallen prey to thieves or worse. It also rankled that she had run from him, and more so because everyone at Montville was aware of it. His hurt needed assuaging. What had this girl done to him? At one turn he wanted only to master her, at the next, only to protect her. He did not understand the feelings she aroused in him, and he felt confused for the first time in his life. Why, he had even agreed to her ridiculous request.

Rowland frowned, thinking of the message he had agreed to send. Either she really was of noble birth, or Count Arnulf was fond of her and she hoped he would help her. Either way, Rowland stood to lose her, and that made him miserable. He had known her only a brief time, but he knew he did not want to lose her.

"Damn and be damned!" he muttered, as he rolled over to face another day.

It was not all that late when Rowland and Brigitte rode past the gatehouse and into the Montville courtyard. Brigitte was confused when they sighted the fortress soon after sunset, for she had ridden half the night and a day to get away, but it did not take that long to return. She must have gone out of her way somehow, and lost valuable time. She sighed. It was too late to wonder about that now.

As they dismounted and led their horses into the stable, Brigitte asked, "You have not forgotten the message you agreed to send, have you?"

"I have not forgotten," Rowland murmured. He reached out and lowered the hood of her mantle, then pulled her braids out. With one in each hand, he drew her closer to him. "Nor have I forgotten that you could have asked me never to touch you again, but you did not."

"You had already said you would not agree to that," she replied stiffly.

"But you did not even try to bargain, *cherie*," he pointed out, his eyes twinkling.

"I got what I wished, Rowland, and I need only tolerate you for a few weeks more. It makes a difference, knowing my misery will soon end."

"Misery, damosel?"

His lips touched hers ever so lightly, then her cheek, then the sensitive area below her earlobe. When gooseflesh spread down her back, she moaned. He let her go then and grinned devilishly.

"Only a few weeks more? I will have to make the most of them, won't I?"

He did not wait for her answer, but walked toward the passageway leading from the stable to the great hall. Brigitte stared after him in confusion, wondering why she had stood there and let him kiss her. What was the matter with her?

She rubbed her arms briskly and hurried after him, shaking her head. It was his gentleness, she told herself. It always surprised her.

The dinner hour had passed, but the large hall was not empty. There was some drinking going on at the lower tables among the men there. By the warming fire, Luthor was tossing dice with Sir Robert and another knight, while Hedda, Ilse, and their lady's maids worked fine stitchery close by. Hedda was a tall, bony woman whose brown hair had gone to gray, and Ilse looked exactly as her mother had looked thirty years before. Servants were still busy in the cooking area. A young lad was set to keep the dogs away from the meat still roasting, while another fanned the smoke out through a hole above the pit.

Rowland waited for Brigitte to join him before he proceeded into the hall. "Fetch some food for both of us and join me at table." When she started to object, he raised a finger. "I insist. We will weather the storm together."

She stopped in her tracks. "What storm?"

Rowland grinned at the sudden alarm that flashed across her face. "You have committed a grave crime, and my lady stepmother was most upset. She was raving when I rode out after you, and no doubt she ranted all day long about what a terrible example you are to the other servants. Not a single serf has ever run from Montville."

Brigitte paled. "What—what will she do to me?"

"Hedda? Not a thing. You forget, I am your lord, which means that you must answer only to me. For once you will be grateful for my protection." He did not give her a chance to reply, but placed his hand on her back and pushed her toward the food. "Go on. I am a starving man."

Brigitte hurried forward to gather food. The cook grumbled at her tardiness, for she had been in the process of cutting the remaining meat off the bone for pies. But she served up two trenchers while the other servants eyed Brigitte speculatively.

Brigitte began to feel increasingly alarmed. She had actually thought the worst was over, but apparently it was not.

When she started toward the lord's table with a tankard of ale and the two trenchers balanced on her arms, she saw that Luthor and Hedda had joined Rowland and were sitting several seats down the table from him. She slowed her pace, but she could not avoid hearing most of it.

"So?" Hedda demanded of Rowland. "Will you have her stripped and flogged in the courtyard? The horrible example she has set must be corrected."

"This is not your concern, wife." Luthor spoke first.

"It most certainly is," Hedda cried indignantly. "He brought that French bitch here, and her haughtiness has already upset my servants. Now she runs away, and she steals to do it! I demand—"

Brigitte, numb, dropped the trenchers on the table, spilling the ale across the wide boards. She turned wide, frightened blue eyes on Rowland.

"I did not steal."

"You can hardly claim that the horse was yours, damosel," he said lightly, amused.

Brigitte felt her knees go weak, and Rowland grabbed her quickly and lowered her to the chair beside his. What was she being accused of? A hand could be severed for stealing food. But a *horse?* A horse was a knight's lifeblood, the most highly prized of animals, worth far more than a servant, worth even more than land! A free serf would gladly sell his farm for a horse, because a horse was a mark of wealth, setting a man clearly above the peasant class. To steal one was a crime equal to murder, and for a servant to steal one was beyond imagination.

Rowland's amusement vanished when he saw how truly horrified Brigitte was. "Come now, what is done is done."

"I...I did not mean to steal," she murmured brokenly. "I did not think—I mean—I did not consider I was stealing when I took the horse. I have never had to ask for a mount before and...Rowland, help me!"

She began to cry, and Rowland became enraged at himself for letting her fears mount unnecessarily. "Brigitte, calm yourself. You have nothing to fear. You stole a horse, but it was Sir Gui's, and he will not press the matter."

"But—"

"No," he said softly. "I spoke with Gui before I came after you. He was more concerned for you than for his horse. He will not demand retribution."

"Truly?"

"Yes, truly."

"This has been most entertaining," Hedda interjected, her long nose seeming longer than usual and her pale gray eyes riveted on Brigitte. "But hardly to the point. Gui may not demand punishment, but I surely do."

"Who are you to demand anything of me?" Rowland began ominously.

Hedda turned livid, her olive skin mottled with red. "You coddle this bitch!" she accused. "Why? Has she bewitched you?"

"I do not coddle her," Rowland returned. "I have already punished her."

"If you did, it was not enough!" Hedda snapped. "She moves easily, without pain!"

Rowland rose, a threatening gleam in his eyes. "Do you doubt my word, lady? Do you wish to feel what Brigitte suffered?" He reached for his belt. Hedda paled and shifted in her chair, glancing toward Luthor. He did not look at her, but continued to gaze at his son.

"Luthor!"

"Nay, do not look to me, wife. You provoked him after I warned you this was not your concern. You never know when to leave well enough alone."

The second Rowland moved a step toward Hedda, she jumped up and ran from the hall. Luthor chuckled.

"Ah, it does me good to see my shrewish wife turn tail and run." Luthor reached over and slapped Rowland on the back. Taking his chair again, he bellowed for ale. "It has been many a year since she felt my fist—too many."

"With me gone, Hedda has been less bitter?" Rowland suggested.

Luthor shrugged. "Or I simply have not cared."

Rowland fell silent at that and attacked his food. More ale was served, and Luthor leaned back so that he could see Brigitte clearly.

"You do not eat very much damosel," Luthor commented. "Is the food not to your liking?"

"I fear I have lost my appetite, milord," Brigitte replied meekly.

"That will not do." Luthor grinned at her. "Such a frail girl as you will need strength if you plan to withstand my son."

"A point well taken, milord."

Rowland turned a damning look on his father, which delighted Luthor. After taking a long swig of ale, the older man leaned forward and said seriously, "Does my gallant vassal know you have returned, Rowland?"

Rowland would not meet his gaze. "I will leave it for you to inform him."

Luthor's bushy brows came together in a frown. "The wench delayed your meeting when she ran off. Have you had time to reconsider?"

"It is not for me to reconsider. Has he?"

"No," Luthor admitted reluctantly. "I do not understand the boy's stubbornness."

"He is firm in his belief, only that," Rowland offered. "I would expect no less of him."

"But he has always worshiped you. I would not have believed it could ever come to this."

"What would you have me do?" Rowland asked, irritation in his tone. "Ignore a challenge?"

"Of course not. But if further discussion would resolve the matter..."

"Not likely, Luthor."

"But only to avoid bloodshed?"

"Leave it be!" Rowland exploded. "I like it no better than you do, but I have already tried reasoning, and he will not change his stand."

"Will you?"

"No."

Luthor shook his head. *"She* could put a stop to it, you know."

"I will not ask her to."

Brigitte could bear it no more. "Who is 'she'?"

"You, damosel," Luthor replied.

Rowland slammed his hands down on the table. "You had to discuss this in her presence, didn't you?" he accused sharply, glowering at his father.

"You mean she knows nothing of this?" Luthor asked incredulously.

"No."

"Well, then, she should know," Luthor returned huffily.

"Knows what?" Brigitte asked, but both men ignored her.

"It matters not, Luthor, for she is more stubborn than you and I together."

Luthor set down his tankard, rose stiffly, and left them. It was obvious that he was not pleased.

They were alone, and she waited for an explanation, but he said nothing, neither would he look at her. Finally, she leaned forward to prompt him. "Well?"

"Finish your meal, Brigitte, then I will escort you to your room," he said crossly.

"Rowland! Who has challenged you?"

She shrank back from the furious look he turned on her. "If you have finished eating, we will go."

# Chapter Twenty-three

Rowland grabbed Brigitte's arm and dragged her out of the hall and across the courtyard. At her hut, he threw open the door and shoved her inside. He followed after her, noting the hot coals, and saw that her possessions had been brought from the stable. The room was bright. The oil cups attached to the wall had been lit.

"Someone has seen to your needs," he remarked crossly. "It will not go well for that poor soul if Hedda learns that one of her servants is waiting on one of mine."

"I did not ask for this."

"You do not have to," he replied coldly. "Your very manner intimidates less fortunate serfs."

"Fortunate? Me?"

"Yes, of course," he said sharply. "Your back and feet do not ache at the end of the day, and your hands do not bleed at least once a week. You are not seen waiting on many—only on one. You live the life of a lady."

He turned to leave, but Brigitte flew past him and slammed the door shut before he reached for it. "Rowland, wait." She faced him, her hands pressed back against the door, blocking his way.

"You still have not told me who has challenged you. I must know!"

"Why?" he scowled. "So you can gloat?"

"Please, Rowland!" she beseeched him. "Is it Sir Gui?"

"Of course it is Sir Gui!" he stormed. "But then you knew what trouble you caused."

"I swear I never wanted to cause trouble, Rowland," she said earnestly. "I only told him the truth. And I did not seek out Sir Gui. He came to me, assuming I was a guest here, and called me lady, Rowland, without knowing anything about me."

"And of course you took advantage of his mistake." Rowland's eyes glittered. "And you had to tell him I brought you here against your will. You made me a villain, Brigitte!"

"You *are* a villain!"

"Christ!" he exploded. "There is no talking to you."

Rowland reached for the door, but Brigitte grabbed his arm with both hands.

"Rowland! If you had only told me of this sooner, I could have put your mind at ease."

"Do you know some secret about all this?" he asked, his eyes narrowed.

"I know only that there will be no fight," she declared, her chin raised proudly.

Rowland grinned at her arrogance. He could not help himself. "And why not, may I ask?"

"Because I will not allow it."

"You..." He stared at her incredulously.

"What is so astonishing?" she demanded.

*"You* will not allow it?"

"I am serious, Rowland. I will not be the cause of bloodshed!"

Rowland smiled a weary smile. "How unfortunate that you did not consider the matter sooner," he said softly.

"It is not too late."

"Oh, yes, it is, little jewel." He touched her cheek lightly. "You wanted a champion, and you have one in Sir Gui. He believes in you, and so he is honor-bound to fight in your behalf."

Brigitte became alarmed. "But I do not want him to! I will tell him so!"

"Brigitte, I truly wish it were that simple. But Gui is affronted by what he thinks I have done to a fair lady. He is a knight with a gentle heart, as gallant a man as I have ever known. He will not be satisfied with anything less than fighting for your honor."

"But he will listen to me."

"Ah, Brigitte, you are as naive as you are beautiful." Rowland sighed.

"But your father said I could stop the battle," she cried. "Tell me what I must do."

"Can you not guess?" Rowland murmured quietly. It took a moment, but then her eyes widened and she turned away. "Not that!"

"It's the only way, Brigitte. If you do not admit you lied, Gui will fight for your sake, and I may kill my best friend."

"But I did not lie!"

"Can you not swallow your pride for once?"

"Would you?"

"I already have. I am asking you to do this when I was determined to leave you out of it. I grew up with Gui, and it has been my habit to protect him from those who took advantage of him because he is short. I grew to love him as the brother I never had, and I do not want to fight him."

Brigitte squared her shoulders and faced Rowland again. She was desolate, but she could see no other way.

"Very well," she said miserably. "I will do as you ask."

"Just telling him you lied will not do," Rowland warned gently. "You must convince him."

"I will. Now take me to him," she sighed disconsolately.

"I will bring him here."

Brigitte sank down on her bed to wait. She felt numb, drained. She had no choice but to lie. She could not allow Rowland to hurt his friend, perhaps even to kill him.

Quickly she removed her mantle and two of her tunics, for she had not been in her room since Rowland had brought her back. Soon the door opened, and Rowland stepped inside, followed by a confused Sir Gui. Brigitte turned, her hands clasped nervously.

Gui came forward and bowed to her, his green eyes solemn. "Rowland said you wished to see me."

"Urgently," she agreed softly, then looked at Rowland. "Will you leave us? I would speak with Sir Gui alone."

"No," Rowland replied, closing the door, and leaning back against it. "I will stay."

Brigitte glared at Rowland, but she could not risk an argument now. Servants did not question their lords, and for once her attitude had to be properly servile.

She smiled timidly at Sir Gui. "Will you sit?" she

asked, indicating her cot. "I am afraid I cannot offer you a chair."

Gui sat down and glanced around the room. "You sleep in this hovel?" he asked, then shot Rowland a hard look before she could answer.

"This room is quite comfortable," Brigitte said quickly. "I...I am not accustomed to better than this."

"Surely—"

"Sir Gui, listen to me." Brigitte stopped him before he could say more. She sat down beside him, but could not meet his stare. "I fear I have done you a grave injustice by playing out my childish fancies with you."

"What fancies?"

"The other day in the hall, when we spoke ...everything I said to you was a lie. I often play at being a lady, especially with men who know nothing about me. I am truly sorry you thought me serious. My game has never caused any harm before."

Gui frowned. "I can see that Rowland has put you up to this, Lady Brigitte."

"I am simply Brigitte, and you are wrong, Sir Gui," she told him firmly. "Pray, forgive me for being so bold, but I cannot let this misunderstanding continue. I have always been a servant. I was shocked to learn that you have challenged my lord because of my silly pretending. I begged him to bring you here so I could tell you the truth before it is too late. You must not fight over me. I was not telling the truth."

Gui's eyes reflected his doubt. "I am flattered you have gone to so much trouble out of concern for me. You are truly kind, milady."

"You do not believe me?" she gasped.

"Not at all," he said evenly.

"Then you are a fool!"

"There, you see!" He grinned triumphantly. "A mere servant would not dare to speak to me that way."

Brigitte jumped to her feet, looking to Rowland, but he watched without offering help. She took a deep breath, at a loss for a way to convince the young knight, for she knew the battle would end in his death. And then, as she saw the way Rowland's eyes roved over her, she had an inspiration.

She swung around to Gui, her hands on hips and her expression disdainful. "I did not say I was a *mere* servant! Look at me," she demanded haughtily. "Do you think any man could ignore me for long, lord or not?"

"I...I beg your pardon?" Gui stammered.

"If I am bold at times, it is because my last master treated me as an equal. I was the Baron's mistress, Sir Gui." She smiled brazenly. "He was old and lonely, and he spoiled me wonderfully."

"But you said the Baron de Louroux was your father!" Gui exclaimed.

Brigitte wavered. She was hurting terribly, but what choice did she have?

"He was very much *like* a father to me—except in bed, of course. Ask Sir Rowland if you do not believe me. He will tell you I was not a virgin when I came to him."

The implication was that she was Rowland's mistress, but Rowland said nothing, so she added, "You see—he does not deny it. Will you withdraw your ridiculous challenge now?"

Gui was stung. "I did not feel it was ridiculous."

Good heavens, had she not said enough? "Then let me add this. The man who is my lord now is all I could want in a master. He is a strong, robust lover, and I am well pleased with him."

Gui got quickly to his feet. "Then why did you run away from him?"

Brigitte was caught off guard. She hesitated, then said, "Please, Sir Gui, do not make me say it in front of him."

"I insist."

She squeezed her hands and gazed at the floor, pretending acute embarrassment, then leaned forward and whispered so Rowland could not hear her. "I did not know of Amelia when he brought me here. When I learned she had been his mistress and wanted him still, I feared he would cast me aside. I could not bear it. So I left."

"Why do you not want him to know this?" Gui asked skeptically.

"Can you not see I love him? I have already admitted more than I wanted him to know. Where is the challenge if he knows how I feel? He will grow bored with me and find another."

Gui stared hard at her. The suspense was making her nerves jangle. She was exhausted and on the point of screaming that it was all lies. She had done herself a terrible injustice with this farce. Would it be enough to save Sir Gui from his own death?

Gui moved away from her at last, and she turned around in relief. He was not going to make her elaborate. But what did he think of her now? It was all she could do not to burst into tears. Constant humiliation had become a part of her life.

"Meeting you on the field of honor would be pointless now, Rowland. Since you brought me here to listen to this, I assume you will accept my apology?"

Brigitte did not turn to see Rowland nodding agreement. She was too mortified to look at either man. She wanted only for them to leave, and she held her breath, waiting for the door to open and then close.

The moment she heard the door close, she threw herself on her bed and cried out her misery. Such horrible lies! To malign her father like that was unforgivable, even if it had been to save a young man's life. And all those preposterous things she had said about Rowland! Where had those lies come from? Why had they come so quickly to her mind?

"Was it so painful, Brigitte?"

She started, turning to see Rowland standing beside her bed. "Why are you still here?" she asked. "Go away!"

She buried her face in the pillow again and cried harder. Rowland could not stand it. A woman's tears had never bothered him before, but now...He turned to leave, then abruptly changed his mind and sat down on the edge of the bed, and gathered her into his arms.

Brigitte struggled against him. She did not want his comfort. She wanted only to be alone with her misery.

Rowland held her gently, but would not let her go. Brigitte finally gave up resisting him and even rested her cheek against his chest, wetting his tunic with her tears. He rocked her gently, his hands caressing her back, her hair. But she would not stop crying, and the sounds tore at his heart.

"Ah, Brigitte, hush now," he beseeched her softly,

kissing her cheeks. "I cannot bear to hear you cry so."

Brigitte did not know how it happened, but Rowland's lips moved to hers, and she could not find the will to stop him. His mouth was warm, and tasted of her own salty tears. When he began to remove her clothing, she knew it was too late to stop him, and instead of fighting him, her mind fought her own will to resist. Tonight she was his, and they both knew it.

Brigitte entered into a state of wild abandon. Rowland knelt beside the narrow cot, doing magical things to her with his hands and lips, bringing forth passionate responses she never knew herself capable of making. He caressed every part of her, and his touch was gentle, maddeningly so. She had passed the need for tenderness. She wanted to feel his weight on her, to have his lips devour hers, to be bruised by his ardor. More than anything she wanted his hard member to thrust deep inside her, to touch the depths of her.

But when he did finally join his body to hers, he still moved carefully, slowly, and she could not stand it. She raised her hips to force all of him into her. What followed was no less than wondrous. A tight knot formed in her, becoming tighter and tighter until it broke, and the throbbing that followed was exquisite, spreading through her whole body and going on forever.

Rowland quickly followed her to his own fulfillment. A little while later he moved just far enough to her side to take his weight from her slender body. She did not want him to leave her, and he was deeply pleased by that. They fell asleep entwined, smiles lighting their faces.

# Chapter Twenty-four

"It's a good fit, don't you think?"

Brigitte stepped back to admire Rowland in the blue wool tunic she had just finished for him. It clung well to his wide shoulders, emphasizing his fine figure. The deep blue wool brought out the blue of his eyes. She was proud of the way he looked in it and anxious for him to say something, but he was so engrossed in examining the seams and edgings that he seemed not to hear her.

"Well?"

"It's comfortable enough."

"Is that all you can say?" Brigitte exclaimed. "And what of my stitches? They will not break or unravel, you know."

"I have seen better," he replied casually as he studied the hem.

"Oh!" She threw a cord of thread at him, and would have thrown the shears if they had been at hand. "See if I take as much care with the next one I make for you!"

Rowland grinned. "You will have to learn when I am jesting, Brigitte. I am more than pleased with your work. You put all my other clothes to shame. Your stitches are perfect."

Brigitte beamed. She had spent the past six days making Rowland's tunic and a short matching blue woolen mantle, sewing in his room where it was comfortable. A truce had been in effect since the night they had made love. They did not talk about it, but every day since had been different.

More than ever now she noticed his attractiveness, the way his light blond hair curled on his neck, the way his blue eyes crinkled when he laughed, making him look years younger. And he laughed more frequently of late, much more.

Rowland still teased Brigitte, but she no longer took offense. He had already tried to check his roughness, and continued to make every effort at gentleness. She had noticed before that he was willing to change for her, but she had not cared before. Now his efforts pleased her. And more and more she found herself watching Rowland, just looking at him without any particular reason.

The one thing that made their truce so strong was that Rowland made no advances besides a chaste kiss when he escorted her to her room each evening and left her alone there. Brigitte was content to let things continue that way. She was not sure how she would react if Rowland wanted her again. On the one hand was the pleasure of it, on the other was the sinfulness of it. She did not want to decide between the two, and she was grateful that Rowland did not force her. In leaving her alone, he was giving her time.

In fact, time was working against Brigitte, though she didn't realize it. Just yesterday, she had grown nervously excited as the sun lowered and the hour approached when Rowland would take her to the evening meal. And today she had presented the new tunic to him with much anxiety. She did not stop to think why his approval was suddenly so important to her. Nor did she ask herself why she had hurriedly fussed with her hair and straightened her clothing before he entered the room.

"You deserve a day of leisure, Brigitte," Rowland said as he fastened on the short mantle and threw it back over his shoulders. "Would you care for a ride tomorrow? There are a few tame mares in my father's stable, and you can choose a suitable mount from them."

His offer surprised her. "Are you sure your father will not mind?"

"He will not mind at all."

"But is it safe?"

His eyes mirrored confusion for only a moment. "Ah, so you have heard the talk, eh? Thurston has had his men drilling for several weeks, but no one likes to take his army to war in winter. Thurston will wait until the weather warms, or at least until he is assured of some advantage. Right now he has none. In winter, we are always well stocked with food, so a siege will do him no good. And Luthor will not send his men out to fight in the snow. Thurston knows that."

Brigitte's brow creased. "Is there no way to settle this without war?"

"No. Lord Thurston is a greedy man. Greed is what made him marry my stepsister Brenda, for whom he cares nothing at all. He was expecting more land than he got, and now he will not stop until he has it all. He will die. That is the only way to end the quarrel."

Brigitte's frown deepened. "I have never been in

the midst of a war before. My father saw his share, but the only battles fought at Louroux were all fought before I was born. He and my brother both fought in other wars, of course, away from Louroux."

"You never mention your brother," Rowland said, turning to her.

"Because he is dead," she replied softly. "I do not like to talk about him."

Rowland didn't know what to say, so he changed the subject. "You may be in the midst of our war, Brigitte, but you will be safe enough here."

"And what if Montville falls?"

"That is not likely, *cherie*."

"But not impossible either," she pointed out. She drew a deep breath and sighed. "Maybe it's just as well I will not be here." The sharp look he gave her made her stammer, "I mean, I...oh, you know what I meant."

"No, Brigitte, I do not. If you will not be here, where will you be?"

"You sent a messenger to Count Arnulf. Need I explain?" He did not reply, and it was her turn to look sharply at him. "You *did* send a messenger to Count Arnulf?"

Rowland hesitated, but the fear that came suddenly to her eyes made him nod reluctantly. "Yes, I did."

"Well then, you see what I mean."

"Do you really think Count Arnulf can take you away from me?"

"He—he will make you see the truth at last," she said hesitantly.

Rowland moved close to her and ran a finger across that proud chin. There was sorrow in his eyes.

"Must we go through this again, little jewel? I would much rather enjoy the pleasure of your company without an argument ruining your sweet disposition."

She had to smile. He had seen so little of her sweet disposition that his statement was truly ridiculous. But he was right. There was no point in fighting any longer. It would all be over soon enough. The thought caused her smile to disappear, though she could not say why.

When they entered the hall a few minutes later, Brigitte quickly scanned the room, as had become her habit. She was wary of Hedda and Ilse, those two tall, unpleasant women who never ceased sniping at her. She would not usually sit with them, for they were ladies and she was a servant. But Amelia was only a maid, so Brigitte frequently had to sit near her and bear her fierce looks.

Tonight Amelia was not at her usual place at the lower table, but was serving ale to a stranger who sat next to Hedda on Luthor's right.

"Your father has a guest," Brigitte said to Rowland in a low voice.

His eyes followed hers, and then he froze. His expression turned murderous, and his hand went to the hilt of his sword. And then Brigitte jumped back as Rowland rushed forward to the lord's table. She gasped to see him pick the stranger up from his chair and throw him a good distance across the room. Everyone at the lord's table leaped up, and Luthor grabbed Rowland's arm to hold him.

"What is the meaning of this, Rowland?" Luthor demanded, furious. That a guest should be attacked by his son!

Rowland jerked loose and turned to his father in a cold rage. "Did Gui not tell you what happened in Arles when he found me?"

Luthor understood then and tried to pacify Rowland. "Yes, he told me about the fight between you and Roger, but that fight was settled."

"Settled?" Rowland exploded. "How could it be settled when that villainous dog still lives?"

"Rowland!"

"Obviously Gui did not tell you the whole of it. Roger was intent on murder that day. He went for my *back,* Luthor. The Frenchman stopped him, and for that Roger tried to kill him as well."

"That's a lie!"

Father and son turned to the golden-haired man standing just out of Rowland's reach.

"Who claims I went for your back?" Roger of Mezidon demanded indignantly. "You accuse me falsely, Rowland."

"Are you calling me a liar, Roger?" Rowland asked hopefully, desperately wanting an immediate reason to fight him.

"I call you no names," Roger was quick to protest. "I say only that you...were misinformed. I came for you, but I would not have struck you unawares. I was just ready to call your attention to me when some fool Frenchman attacked me. I settled with him first."

"Attacked you?" Rowland cried, incredulous. "He stopped you from killing me, and for that he nearly died."

"You see, you are wrong," Roger said evenly. "There was no murderous intent."

Luthor moved carefully between them. "We have

an argument, and no easy way of settling the dispute. There will be no fight here when the reason is clearly in doubt."

"There is no doubt," Rowland declared adamantly.

"Leave it that *I* have doubts," Luthor replied gruffly. "The argument is at an end, Rowland."

Rowland was livid, but his father had made a pronouncement, and he could not go against him without shaming him. But he could not remain silent either.

"Why is he here? Do we feed our enemy now?"

"Rowland!" Luthor warned in exasperation. "Roger is no enemy of Montville until he declares himself so. I hope I will never hold a man responsible for his brother's actions."

"But he will fight with Thurston against you!" Rowland exclaimed.

Roger shook his head. "I take no sides between Luthor and my brother. Luthor has been like a father to me. Though Thurston is my brother, I do not join him."

"So you say," Rowland scoffed.

"I believe him," Luthor said. "So let us hear no more of it. For many years this was Roger's home. He is welcome here until I have reason not to make him welcome. Now come, let us sit down together and eat."

Rowland grunted.

"At least lighten your mood, Rowland," Luthor chided. "The lovely Brigitte does not know what to make of you."

Rowland turned to see her looking at him, confused and wary. He started toward her, but she backed away, intimidated by his dark scowl. He tried to

reassure her with a smile, but he could not manage
a smile. Brigitte turned to run from the hall.

"Brigitte!"

She stopped, but her heart did not stop its rapid
beat.

"What has come over you, Brigitte? I mean you
no harm," Rowland murmured as he closed the distance between them. "Forgive me for frightening
you."

"I do not understand, Rowland," she said hesitantly. "You changed so—like a madman. Why did
you attack that man without a reason?"

"I had reason, very good reason. But if I speak of
it, I fear I will lose my temper and attack him again.
Roger is an old adversary."

Brigitte looked curiously toward the golden-haired
man who sat next to Hedda at the lord's table. He
was a handsome young man, very darkly bronzed by
the sun, and dressed in grand clothing. He was of
Rowland's height and appeared formidable.

Rowland followed Brigitte's gaze and frowned.
"Roger is impressive. Perhaps you are thinking to
use him against me as you did Gui?"

Her eyes flew back to his. "I have told you that
was never my intent!" she snapped, but he ignored
that argument.

"Women are drawn to Roger despite his black
moods. Stay away from him," Rowland warned
darkly. "He cannot be trusted."

"I have no reason to seek him out," Brigitte replied
huffily.

Rowland's eyes roamed slowly over her before they
locked with hers again. "But he would have every
reason to seek you out, damosel."

Brigitte drew herself up. "I do not like this discussion, Rowland. And we have dallied long enough. I will bring your food to you."

"And your own."

"Not this evening," she said firmly. "I will eat with the servants."

He caught her wrist. "Why?"

"Let go of me, Rowland. There are many watching."

Rowland remained standing where he was, thoughtfully watching Brigitte walk away. He shook his head, wondering at her moods. He had wondered so often if there could really be these two different sides to Brigitte. And the more he thought of it, the more he realized that the vixen he had known might not be a vixen at all, but simply a gentle lady appalled and affronted by her present circumstances. It would explain a great deal—too much, in fact.

Rowland prayed he was wrong, and that the demure, sweet, gentle qualities Brigitte had displayed this last week were entirely false. If they were not false, then he had to face the possibility that she *was* a lady. He did not want to think about that, not at all.

# Chapter Twenty-five

*T*he great hall of Louroux was a nearly empty, somber chamber. The Baron crouched in a gilt-edged chair, drowning his misery in strong wine. There was no one else in the room. Quintin de Louroux was home, but his homecoming had been a thing of great sorrow. The one he had returned for was not there to greet him. And he could not yet understand the reason for her absence. His vibrant, beautiful sister had gone to a nunnery!

It was so unlike Brigitte to want to shut herself away from the world, to sequester herself in a bleak convent. He might understand it better if she had believed him dead. But Druoda had told Brigitte that Quintin was alive, and she had still chosen the austere life. She had left without waiting to see him. Why?

Druoda said that Brigitte had become passionately religious soon after he left for the south of France, and that she had prepared herself for the austere life by moving to the servants' quarters, toiling endlessly about the manor in preparation for the hard life she had chosen.

The worst of it was that Brigitte had told no one which nunnery she planned to enter. It might take years to find her again, and by then, she would be so firmly devoted that he would never be able to convince her to return home with him.

"She bid me tell you not to look for her, Quintin," Druoda said solemnly, her brown eyes sad. "She went so far as to say she would assume a new name, making it impossible for you to find her."

"Did you not try to talk her out of this?" Quintin demanded. The news had hit him hard and he was angry.

"Of course I tried, but you know how stubborn your sister can be. I even offered to find her a fine husband, but she was appalled. If you ask me, the thought of marriage had something to do with her decision. I believe she fears men."

Had Druoda been right? Did Brigitte fear marriage?

"You should never have let the choice of a husband be hers, Quintin," Druoda had added. "You should have insisted Brigitte marry long ago."

Now Quintin was overcome by remorse. If he had found her a good husband before he left, she would be here now, married, perhaps anticipating a child. Now she would never know the joys of motherhood, never know the love of a devoted man.

Was a life devoted to God what she really wanted? Ah, he did not believe it was so. Could Brigitte have changed so much? And it was too terrible to think he might never see again his sister's sweet smile, her gay manner. His sister, the only person he truly cared about, was gone.

Quintin drank from the bottle, no longer bothering with a goblet. Two other bottles lay empty on the table before him. A lavish meal was also there, prepared especially by his aunt, but he had no desire for food and tossed scraps of meat to the three hounds at his feet. He had come home to find the dogs penned, something never done before at Louroux. But that was not the only change. The servants were pleased to see him, but they were not their usual cheerful lot. Many had tried to speak privately with him, but Druoda had shooed them away, for she did not want him disturbed.

Quintin had seen no one but Druoda since his arrival early that afternoon and subsequent discovery that Brigitte was gone. He had locked himself in the hall and growled at anyone who tried to enter. The hour was late, and he was exhausted, yet wide awake. The wine was not helping either, and he began to wonder just how many bottles it would take before sleep was possible.

He had much to do on the morrow and could not afford to be less than alert. He would begin his search for Brigitte immediately. He could have begun today if his men were not so taxed from their encounter with a band of brigands that morning. Two men were wounded, one gravely. But there was no time to think of that. He had to consider which of his men to take with him on the journey to find Brigitte, and what direction to take. There was something missing though, something that would make his search easier, but what it was eluded him. Perhaps he was not as wide awake as he thought.

And then he sat bolt upright as it came to him. Of course! Brigitte would not have left Louroux alone. Someone had to have escorted her. And that man could tell him where she was. Druoda would know who the escort had been! With that thought Quintin shot to his feet. He swayed, falling back in the chair, groaning. His head was throbbing.

"Milord, pray, a word with you?"

Quintin squinted his eyes to try and see into the shadows, but he could not see anyone. "Who is there?"

"Eudora, milord," she said timidly.

"Ah, Althea's daughter." He leaned back in his chair. "Well, where are you, girl? Come forward."

A small form emerged from the stairway, hesitantly, stopping, then coming closer. The tallow candles on the table were stubs and flickered over the girl, making Quintin see two, no, three figures dancing before him.

"Stand still, girl!" Quintin snapped irritably, squinting.

"I...I am, milord."

"What is this?" He frowned. "You sound frightened. Have I ever mistreated you, Eudora? You have no reason to fear me."

Eudora wrung her hands nervously. "I tried to speak to you earlier, milord, but you...you threw a round of cheese at me and told me to get out."

Quintin chuckled at that. "Did I? I am afraid I do not recall it."

"You were understandably distraught, and no wonder, considering what has happened while you were away."

Quintin sighed on hearing those words. "Tell me, Eudora, why did she do it?"

"It is not for me to speak badly of your aunt," Eudora replied uneasily.

"My aunt? I meant my sister. But I suppose you would not know. Where is Mavis? She was closest to

Brigitte. She would know why Brigitte made this decision."

"Were you not told?" Eudora asked in surprise. "Mavis is dead."

Quintin's eyes narrowed. "Mavis? How?"

"She was banished by your aunt and was murdered that very day on the road, by thieves. Though I sometimes wonder if it was really thieves who killed her."

Quintin stared at the girl, sobering quickly. "By what right did my aunt do such a thing?"

"She proclaimed herself mistress of Louroux as soon as we received word of your death."

The news did not disturb Quintin. "You mean she was appointed Brigitte's guardian?"

Eudora grew more uneasy. "Oh, no, milord, not her guardian. The Count of Berry was never informed of your death."

Quintin sat up suddenly. "How is that possible?"

"Druoda kept the news from him. And she would not let Lady Brigitte leave Louroux so that she could go to him. Not even your vassals would help your sister, for they all assumed Druoda and her husband would soon be milady's guardians. They followed only Druoda's orders. Not even Walafrid disputed his wife's actions."

"Do you know what you are telling me, girl?" Quintin's voice was low and angry.

Eudora stepped back nervously. "It is the truth, milord, I swear. I thought surely your aunt would have confessed by now, or I would not have been so brave as to approach you. Everyone here knows how she treated your sister—she could not possibly hope to keep all of that a secret from you."

"My aunt said nothing to me of any of this."

"Then I am sorry. I did not come here to malign Druoda. I came only to see if you could tell me what has happened to Lady Brigitte. I have been so worried. She should have returned before now."

"Returned? What are you saying now, Eudora?" Quintin questioned her slowly. "Perhaps you had best tell me everything you know about my sister."

Eudora did so, hesitantly at first and then all in a rush.

"She tried to run away, and she would have succeeded if that Norman had not found her."

"What Norman?"

"The one who came here seeking the lady of Louroux," Eudora explained.

"Rowland of Montville?"

"Yes...I believe that was his name. She left with the Norman knight."

"That explains everything then," Quintin said. "You see, Rowland of Montville brought the news that I was not dead."

"But we were not told so until a week later," Eudora replied quickly, "and Lady Brigitte did not know at all. I am certain of it." Eudora then asked passionately, "What I do not understand is how your aunt could hope to keep *all* this from—" Eudora paused, staring wide-eyed at the three dogs in front of the Baron. "What ails your hounds, milord?" she whispered.

Quintin turned to see two of the dogs collapsed, trying vainly to rise, and the third just falling, his legs crumpling beneath him. He stared at the dogs and then at the scraps of meat lying beside them. Understanding came slowly, but it came clearly.

Quintin looked at the lavish meal spread before him, prepared especially by his aunt.

"The black hound is unusually still, milord," Eudora said in a quavering voice.

"I fear I have poisoned my own dogs," Quintin said in a quiet voice.

"You?"

"I fed them some of this food prepared for me," he replied grimly. "It would seem I was meant to breathe no more."

"You ate this food?" Eudora gasped, horrified.

"Not a morsel. Only the wine."

"She...she tried—"

"—to kill me," Quintin finished loudly. "My mother's sister. My own blood. And now it's obvious why she did not confess her wickedness and beg my indulgence. If I did not die at supper, she would have tried to poison me again tomorrow. She would have succeeded sometime, since I would not have known what she was about and would have suspected nothing. Eudora, you have saved my life by coming here. Damn! What did my aunt hope to gain by such evil?"

"With your sister gone and you dead, milord, would she not have a claim on Louroux?" Eudora suggested.

Quintin sighed. "I suppose Arnulf would look favorably on her, since she is blood to me. The bitch! My God...where *is* Brigitte? If Druoda could kill me, she could kill Brigitte as well!"

"Milord, I do not think so. Lady Brigitte left with the Norman. She seemed well enough."

"But where has Rowland taken her?" Quintin moaned. "By God, if Druoda cannot tell me where to find Brigitte, I will kill her with my bare hands!"

Quintin strode from the hall, sober now, cold fury having taken over his whole being.

# Chapter Twenty-six

"*T*ake me back!"

The anguished cry caused Brigitte's eyes to fly open, and she turned over in the large bed to stare at Rowland. He was asleep, but he was talking— pleading, in fact.

"Take me back!"

Rowland's head moved from side to side and he thrashed under the covers. A hand struck Brigitte's chest, and she gasped, then sat up.

She nudged his shoulder. "Wake up!" His eyes opened and locked with hers, and she said testily, "I get enough mistreatment from you when you are awake, Rowland. I do not need more when you are asleep."

"Be damned, woman," he sighed irritably. "What have I done now?"

"Your crying out in your sleep woke me and you hit me. Was your dream so upsetting?"

"That dream is always upsetting. I do not understand it and I never have." He frowned into the darkness.

"You have had this dream before?" she asked in surprise.

"Yes. It has haunted me as far back as I can remember." He shook his head. "You said I cried out. What did I say?"

"'Take me back.' You said it so forlornly, Rowland."

Rowland sighed again. "In the dream, there are only faces, that of a young man and a woman, faces I do not recognize. I see them, and when I can see them no more I feel such a terrible loss, as if I am losing everything that is dear to me."

"But you do not know what it is?"

"No. I have never valued anything so much that I feared to lose it." He gave her a strangely tender look. "Until now."

Brigitte blushed and looked away. "You may forget your dream sooner if we do not speak of it anymore."

"It's already forgotten," he smiled, running a finger along her bare arm.

Brigitte moved away. "Rowland—"

"No!" He threw an arm over her waist to keep her beside him, but her eyes widened in panic. He sighed. "Ah, Brigitte, let your feelings guide you."

"I am!" she cried.

Rowland forced her down on the bed and leaned over her, whispering, "You lie, little jewel. You do not at all mind my attentions. If you would only be honest, you would admit you like it when I do this." He kissed her neck. "And this." He gently kneaded a breast beneath the thin linen shift. "And this." His mouth came down on hers, sweetly teasing. "And—"

"No!" She caught his hand before it reached the mound between her legs. "Stop!"

His eyes smoldered with desire as he looked down

at her, and she caught his face between her hands. "Rowland, please. Do not ruin everything."

"Ruin?"

Despite her efforts to hold him back, he kissed her again, passionately this time. But then he released her abruptly and sat up.

"The only thing I would like to ruin is your determination to stay unmoved by me, but I know you wish to keep up that pretense."

Brigitte said nothing to that, for something had stirred within her when his lips seared hers. Did he sense it? Was he aware that, if he had continued to kiss her, she would not have protested again? She was, in fact, disappointed that he had given up so easily. What was wrong with her? Had she turned wanton without realizing it?

"You are not angry with me?" she asked hesitantly, praying he was not.

"Not angry. Disappointed and more than a little frustrated, but not angry. I suppose I must give you time to get used to me."

"You are so generous, milord," she said caustically, now as frustrated as he. "Continue to give me time, and I will be gone before your patience runs out."

Too late she realized what she had said, and she blushed crimson and began to stammer, but his burst of laughter drowned her out.

"So! It seems I spite us both with my patience, eh?"

"No, Rowland," Brigitte denied quickly. "You misunderstood."

"I think not." He smiled knowingly.

He reached for her, but she scrambled off the bed

from the side away from him and ran to quickly don her clothes. Straightening her yellow tunic, she glanced over hesitantly to find him still sitting on the bed, shaking his head.

Reaching for his clothes, he said, "Very well. But one day you will learn that the relationship between man and wife is a most intimate one, and not only once in a while." He paused, then added softly, "We could be just as intimate."

"Do you offer me marriage?"

He stared at her so intently and for such a long time that she grew nervous. "Would you accept?"

"I..."

She frowned in consternation. The impulse to throw caution to the wind and say yes was strong. But she quickly subdued herself.

"Well?"

"Of course I would not accept," she answered adamantly.

Rowland shrugged. "Then there is no need for me to make the offer, is there?"

Brigitte turned away from him, thoroughly hurt. He did not really care. Marriage meant nothing to him. Perhaps *she* meant nothing to him.

She walked stiffly to the door and turned to Wolff, snapping her fingers for him to follow, and then she left the room without waiting for Rowland. Oh, why had she allowed him to talk her into staying in his room?

Damn the man! There was no in-between with him. Either he kept his emotions hidden, or he let them explode in a blind rage. What were his true feelings for her? Would he miss her when she was gone? She hardly dared ask herself what the answer was.

# Chapter Twenty-seven

*R*iding in the crisp morning air with Rowland was invigorating. The weather had not warmed, and Brigitte's cheeks were pink from the cold wind slapping at her face, but she enjoyed the ride and let it lighten her mood.

It was late morning when they returned to the manor. Rowland stayed in the stable for a while, and Brigitte went alone to his room. She sat there sewing, and brooding.

When the door opened, Brigitte was relieved to have her troubled thoughts interrupted. But then she saw that it was not Rowland but Roger of Mezidon who entered the room as if it were his own. Closing the door, he crossed the room and stood a few feet away from where she sat. Brigitte was more than a little surprised and tried to think of some reason for his being there, but there was no reason beyond what Rowland had warned her about. As Roger's blue eyes raked over her, she realized how right Rowland had been.

"You are every bit as lovely as I remembered," he said smoothly.

His flattery made Brigitte uneasy. "You should not be here, Sir Roger."

"Ah, and well I know it."

"Then why—"

"Your name is Brigitte," he interrupted, taking a step closer. "An old Frankish name—it suits you. I have been told much about you."

She did not like his confident attitude or his familiarity. "I am not interested in what you have been told," she said sharply, glad that Wolff was lying under Rowland's bed.

"Your tone wounds me, damosel. I suppose Rowland has warned you against me?"

"He thinks you have set your eye on me and have rape on your mind."

"Ah, damosel, why do you say such a thing? It need not be so."

Brigitte came to her feet instantly, alarmed. "Are you saying Rowland is right?"

Roger was close enough to reach out and run a finger along the soft line of her cheek. "I am here," he grinned in answer, and then chuckled when she flinched. "I searched long for you last night, until I finally realized that Rowland would not let such a prize stay far from his reach. He is indeed lucky, but now it's time I shared some of his luck."

"You will not touch me!" Brigitte snapped.

But Roger was not put off. He reached for her, and she slapped his hand away. Instantly his other hand came around and grabbed her neck. Before she could scream, Roger's mouth covered hers.

Brigitte was stunned and slow to react. Roger's kiss was not unpleasant, but it did not move her, either. If she had felt the trembling in her knees, the rapid swirling in her belly, or even just a little tingling sensation, she might have let the kiss go on, grateful to learn that Rowland was not the only one who could move her. But that was not the case, and at last she tried to push Roger away. He only held her more firmly, both hands gripping her head to keep her lips pressed to his.

Brigitte did not panic. The long needle she still held in her hand, thread attached, was just what she needed. Quickly she jabbed the point into Roger's arm. She had not anticipated such a startled reaction. He jumped back, and the needle tore through the cotton of his long-sleeved tunic and ripped a crimson line down his arm.

They were both mesmerized for a moment by the flow of blood. Then Roger's eyes jerked back to hers, and she cringed at the anger there. In that moment, Brigitte could well imagine Roger using dishonorable means to kill a man. There was something evil about him. She moved back quickly and put the high-backed chair between them.

"There is no need to run from me, damosel." The dark scowl on his face belied his soft tone. "You have only pricked me. Your nails would do far more damage...and I vow I will give you a chance to use them."

"You have made a mistake here, Sir Roger. Rowland will kill you for this."

He quirked a brow at her. "And will you tell him? Will you dare to confess that I have had you? Do you think he will want you after knowing that?"

"Do you think you will be alive to find that out?" she countered. "Rowland will take advantage of the slightest reason to challenge you. Are you not aware of how desperately he wants to kill you? I do not know exactly why, but I am quite sure now that you are deserving of his hate."

"Little bitch!" Roger hissed.

He started around the chair, and, without thinking, Brigitte screamed for Wolff. The great beast scrambled out from under the bed and leaped into the air, knocking Roger flat on his back. Wolff went for Roger's throat, and it was all the big man could do to hold him back.

"Call this monster off! For God's sake, woman! Call him off!"

Brigitte hesitated long enough to terrify Roger, then reluctantly called Wolff to her. He obeyed. She knelt down to praise him, keeping a wary eye on Roger as he rose slowly.

He shot her an incredulous look. "You are mad to set that monster on me. He could have killed me!"

"Oh, yes, he could have easily," Brigitte replied with a bit of malice. "Maybe I should have let him. He has killed men before who have tried to attack me. I have no doubt he enjoyed it, too. He is entirely wild, you see."

"Jesus! You are as pagan as Rowland is!"

"And what are you, noble lord?" she returned contemptuously. "Did you not come in here to assault me? I suppose you see no harm in tumbling a mere servant, eh? Swine!" she spat furiously.

"You dare much, vixen," he growled, his eyes glowing dangerously.

"Do I?" she laughed harshly, no longer afraid of him. "I dare because my breeding demands that I dare. You say you were told about me? Well, you were misinformed, for no one here knows what I am. I am Lady Brigitte de Louroux of Berry, daughter of the late Baron de Louroux, ward now of the Count of Berry, and heir of Louroux and all it encompasses."

"You could not wait to tell him that, could you?"

Roger and Brigitte both turned with a start to see Rowland standing in the open doorway, an unreadable expression on his face.

"If you have been standing there long enough, Rowland, then you know I was simply explaining to Sir Roger why I can be so bold as to call him a swine."

She said this so calmly and so simply that Rowland burst into laughter.

"Does she speak the truth, Rowland?" Roger demanded. "Is she of noble birth?"

Rowland's answer made Brigitte gasp.

"She is all she says she is."

"Then why is she pretending to be a servant? It's outrageous!"

"Are you outraged, Roger?" Rowland asked smoothly as he walked slowly into the room. "Do you wish to challenge me for the lady's honor?"

Roger hesitated, avoiding Rowland's penetrating stare. Brigitte thought he paled a little. Rowland was not as calm as he appeared. He was like a stalking beast. There was no fear in him, only anticipation. He wanted Roger to challenge him—he was desperate for it.

"Roger?"

"I will not challenge you, Rowland, not here in your home. I am aware that you feel you have a moral right to kill me. Rage will give you added strength. Yet you are wrong about me, Rowland."

"I don't believe you."

"Nevertheless, I am not fool enough to fight you

now. I was simply curious to know why the lady is here under false pretenses."

Brigitte spoke up impulsively. "That is none of your concern, Sir Roger."

"Well put, Brigitte," Rowland said, his voice cold. "But should we not enlighten my good friend here? After all, he is entitled to more for his efforts than just that scratch on his arm." Rowland stared intently at Roger, his eyes unyielding. "And how did you come by that scratch, Roger? Can it be my lady was forced to defend herself? Is that why she called you a swine?"

Brigitte moved quickly between the two men. "Rowland, stop it. I know what you are leading up to, but I warned you not to use me this way."

"You were upset when I walked in here," he reminded her sharply. "Why?"

"I was offended by Sir Roger's attitude—it so resembled your own," she said pointedly, and had the satisfaction of seeing him flinch.

Roger drew her attention with an eloquent bow. "If I had known you were a lady, damosel, I would never have offended you."

"That is no excuse, Sir Roger," Brigitte replied coldly.

"Get out, Roger!" Rowland growled, his eyes stormy. "I will deal with you later if my lady has not an innocent explanation for why she drew your blood. For now, I shall only warn you never to come near her again."

Roger left quickly.

Brigitte was furious with Rowland for attempting to use her as an excuse to kill a man. "My lady, is it? Since when am I your lady?" she demanded as soon as Roger closed the door. "Do you at last believe me, or was that simply for his benefit?"

"You will answer my question first, Brigitte!"

"I will not!" she cried, a stubborn tilt to her chin.

Rowland looked away. "Very well. Yes, I said that for his benefit. Would you rather have had me call you a liar in front of him?"

"I would rather your motive was not so loathsome," she replied, disappointed. "You hoped he would challenge you so you could fight him."

"I do not deny that!" he returned crisply, his dark eyes locking with hers. "When I saw him with you, I wanted to tear him apart. Yet I did not want you to feel that you had anything to do with his death. If he had challenged me, he alone would be responsible."

"Rowland, you make too much of this," she said, becoming exasperated. "He simply kissed me, and for that he got what he deserved."

Rowland turned around, heading for the door, and Brigitte called to him, "Rowland! I am glad he kissed me!"

He halted, stood still a moment, and turned slowly to face her. "Did you encourage him?" Rowland asked softly.

"No."

"Yet you welcomed his kiss."

"If I had welcomed it, would I have stopped him?" she cried. "I said only that I was glad it happened. You see, it proved something to me."

"What?"

She lowered her eyes and whispered in a barely audible voice, "It did not move me."

That told Rowland more than a thousand words

would have done. He understood. He alone had the ability to move her. Roger did not. Perhaps no other man could move her. And that she should admit this...

He moved slowly to her, cupped her face in his hands, and gently kissed her. Her knees went weak, the pit of her belly swirled, her body tingled. And when he lifted her in his arms and carried her to his bed, she did not protest. His will and hers were one.

She wanted this man. And as he removed her gown, tearing it in his impatience to press his bare skin to hers, that was all she could think about, how very much she wanted him. A fine, strong man, a gentle man, a violent, vengeful man, he was the only man she wanted to hold in her arms, to caress, to savor. And as he made her move to his rhythm, as he brought her to those glorious ecstatic heights, she wondered fleetingly if she had fallen in love with Rowland of Montville.

# Chapter Twenty-eight

*The* day began with a bright sun, an occasion to cause good cheer these cold days. After Rowland left the hall for the morning exercises and drills in the courtyard, Brigitte sought out Goda and found her in the storeroom, skinning a rabbit for a later meal.

"I could use your help if you are willing, Goda," Brigitte ventured, sitting down on the bench next to the girl. "Rowland insists I quit sewing for him for a while, and make a gown for myself. But I need help in cutting the material."

"I will be happy to, mistress, as soon as I finish here. Lady Hedda set this task for me, and I do not dare leave until I have done."

At the mention of Rowland's stepmother, Brigitte's long-suppressed curiosity rose. "Does Hedda hate Rowland? He has told me so, but I find it hard to believe."

"Oh, to be sure. It has always been so. Sir Rowland has had a hard life here. It's so sad to think of him as a child, and all he suffered here."

"Tell me about him as a child. You were here?"

"I was too young to serve in the manor then, but my mother did. Oh, the stories she would bring home to the village. At the time, I truly thought she in-

233

vented those stories just to frighten me into being good. I was horrified later to learn that they were true."

"What stories?"

"Of how the poor little boy was treated by Lady Hedda," Goda replied, then fell silent as she discarded the skin and reached for a chopping knife.

"Well?" Brigitte asked impatiently. "Do not stop there."

Goda looked about nervously before she answered. "Lady Hedda beat him terribly at every opportunity, and did not even look for a reason when Lord Luthor was not around. Ilse and Lady Brenda were just like their mother, if not worse. One day Lady Brenda was found beating him with a whip, and the boy was bloody and unconscious, yet she continued to beat him."

"Why?" Brigitte gasped.

"He dared to call Lady Brenda sister."

"My God!"

Goda smiled weakly, understanding. "He had a hard life here, and nothing else. Once he grew strong enough to protect himself from the ladies, then he had his father to deal with. And my Lord Luthor is the hardest taskmaster there is. If Rowland did not learn quickly the skills Lord Luthor taught him, he would receive terrible blows for his failure. And then there were the older boys here to contend with."

Brigitte fell silent as she watched Goda working. A sadness overcame her as she considered Rowland's terrible life. Her heart went out to the little boy who had been so mistreated. She could appreciate all the more now the gentle side of Rowland that she had come to know. It was remarkable that he had learned any tenderness at all.

A little later Brigitte moved across the hall with Goda beside her, looking forward to cutting the material for her new clothes. Brigitte was so lost in her thoughts that she and Goda reached the stairs leading to the second floor without realizing it. But the strident voice that cut into those thoughts halted their steps.

"Where do you think you are off to?"

Goda, at Brigitte's side, had a look of dread on her face. Brigitte turned to see Hedda stomping toward the stairs. Ilse was behind her, as were Amelia and Ilse's lady's maid.

"Well?" Hedda demanded as she reached them. She placed her hands on her bony hips and eyed Goda harshly. "Answer me, girl!"

Goda blanched, well aware of the consequences of being singled out by Hedda. "I...I..."

She could not finish. Brigitte felt her temper rising at seeing her friend so cowed. "She was accompanying me to my lord's chamber," Brigitte told Hedda curtly, not bothering to hide her dislike for the woman.

"Why? He does not need my servant. He has his own servant now."

The woman's scorn was not lost on Brigitte, and the tittering of the other three women standing behind Hedda made her furious. But she fought the urge to let her temper loose.

"It is not Sir Rowland who has need of Goda but I who requested her help." Brigitte spoke calmly.

But she was stunned by Hedda's reaction. "You!" the woman exploded. "By the saints! By God—"

"Madame, you need not carry on as if a crime has been committed," Brigitte interrupted sharply. "I

merely asked Goda for a moment of her time. Her
task was finished. I was not taking her away from
her duties."

"Silence!" Hedda shouted furiously. "Goda's duties are never finished. Her time is not her own. She
serves me and those I bid her serve—but certainly
no bastard's whore!"

Brigitte gasped. She could not have been more
surprised if Hedda had slapped her. The snickers of
the other women grew louder and louder inside her
head, and she saw that they were thoroughly enjoy-
ing the scene.

"Goda!" Hedda snapped. "Get back to the work-
room. I will deal with you later."

Tears welling in her eyes, Goda hurried away.
Brigitte watched her leave, knowing that if the girl
was punished, it would be her fault. Yet what had
she done that was so terrible? Hedda had been
watching for an excuse to inflict her cruelty.

"And you!" Hedda turned her attention back to
Brigitte. "Get out of this hall. I am forced to tolerate
your presence when the bastard is around, but not
otherwise."

Brigitte drew herself up proudly, wanting desperately to strike the old witch. Keeping her voice
level, she said, "You, madame, have the manners of
a cow." Hedda turned a shade darker, and began
sputtering, but Brigitte added, "And anyone who calls
you lady does so only to mock you!"

Brigitte turned her back, but before she reached
the first stair step, Hedda's clawlike hand bit into
her shoulder and swung her around. The woman
slapped her, hard, and Brigitte's head snapped to the
side. Her cheek burned with the imprint of that cruel

hand, but she did not move. She stood still, smoldering, and defied Hedda with the contempt in her eyes.

Brigitte's disdain brought a cry from Hedda, who was used to servants cowering at her feet when the rage was upon her. She turned livid and raised her hand again, but her hand was suddenly caught in a grip from behind. Then Hedda was yanked off her feet and thrown into her group of ladies. All four women fell back into the rushes from the impact of Hedda's falling body.

Sprawling on the floor, astonished, Amelia was the first to rise and back away. Ilse and her maid scrambled to their feet next and ran from the hall without looking back. Hedda rose laboriously and tottered to her feet to face Rowland, in a towering rage.

"If you ever lay a hand on her again I will kill you, old hag!" Rowland said in a voice that turned her blood cold. "I will choke that putrid life from your body with my bare hands! Is that clear?"

In answer Hedda began to scream her loudest. In moments knights, squires, and pages came running in from the yard, and servants appeared from every corner of the hall. Brigitte backed nervously up the stairs and hid in the shadows, terrified. Was this happening because of her?

No one came near the two combatants once they saw who was standing over their mistress. If it had been anyone else, they would have protected their lord's lady with their lives. But they would not go against the lord's son. All knew on whom the lord's favor fell.

"What in the devil's name?" Luthor pushed his

way through the crowd and came forward, scowling
when he saw Hedda and Rowland glaring at one
another.

"Luthor!" Hedda whined. "He tried to kill me!"

Luthor looked at Rowland and met his furious
gaze. "If I had tried to kill the hag she would be
dead," Rowland growled. "I have warned her that I
will kill her if she ever lays a hand on Brigitte again.
No one touches what is mine, no one! Not even you,"
he told Luthor firmly.

The silence in the hall was complete. Everyone
waited tensely to see how the lord would react. Rowland's statement would have brought a blow from
Luthor not too many years before.

"He is not lord here," Hedda spoke up. "By what
right does he tell *you* what you can and cannot do?"

"Shut up, woman!" Luthor turned cold eyes on his
wife and then roared. "Out! Everyone out!"

There was a rush for the doors, and Hedda, too,
made to flee until Luthor growled, "Not you, woman!"

The cavernous hall was quickly emptied except
for Luthor, Hedda, Rowland, and Brigitte, who was
forgotten on the stairs, too afraid to move. She held
her breath. Would Rowland be banished? How dare
he speak to his father that way before everyone?

But Luthor's fury was not for his son. He caught
Hedda a vicious blow that sent her sprawling into
the rushes once again, then came to stand over her,
his face crimson.

"You forced Rowland to make that statement,
woman. He was within his bounds, for I have nothing
to do with that girl. She belongs only to him!"

Luthor turned away in disgust, then continued
coldly. "You were warned, Hedda, that the girl was

none of your affair. She is bound to Rowland and he is sworn to protect her. You think because you are my lady you need not heed his warnings? Wife, if he kills you because of the girl, I will do nothing about it. He will be ridding me of a cankerous sore I should have rid myself of years ago." At Hedda's gasp, he added, "You can be thankful I did not shame you with these words before the others. But this is the last consideration I will give you, Hedda."

With that, Luthor left the hall.

# Chapter Twenty-nine

Two days had passed since Brigitte had crossed words with Hedda. They were calmer days, as Hedda and her maid did not venture into the hall while Brigitte was there. She had not seen either of them since and was grateful for that.

They were dour days, however, with purple-tinged clouds ever present. Another storm was brewing. The last snow had yet to melt, and a new storm would soon thicken the white carpet that stretched as far as the eye could see.

Brigitte did not mind the dark days, though. She was happy. She didn't understand it and she didn't try to. She just felt gloriously happy. Everyone noticed the change. Her soft, bubbling laughter was heard frequently. Her smiles brought comment, at times shy, secretive smiles, as did the way her eyes met and held Rowland's.

The old lord saw it and was pleased. The young rascals are in love, he thought wistfully, remembering his own first love, lost to him before he had met and married the shrew who was now his wife. Luthor had never forgotten his Gerda. Nor had he ever loved another woman. If she had lived, Gerda would have given him sons.

Sons. A mist always gathered in Luthor's eyes when he thought of sons. A man of his bearing, a man of his strength, had to have sons. But Luthor had daughters, damned daughters just like their damned mother. Hedda had conceived no more after Ilse, nor did any of his other bedmates.

But Luthor had Rowland, and Rowland was a man to be proud of, the answer to his prayers. What Rowland did not know of his birth could not hurt him. No, the secret would die with Luthor, and Montville would have a strong lord after Luthor died. He had seen to that.

Rowland quickly brushed Brigitte's cheek with a feathery kiss. They had just finished the morning meal, and he laughed at her embarrassment before he sauntered out of the hall, leaving her smiling after him, embarrassed yet pleased by his parting display of affection.

Rowland walked briskly to the stable, where the Hun was saddled and waiting for his morning exercise, which Rowland rarely denied his prized steed. The darker clouds to the north still hovered low over the horizon, moving east, then west, then east again, as if undecided in which direction to unleash their storm. Rowland hoped those dark clouds stayed north. He could do without being bound in, and this storm promised to be a violent one.

The Hun greeted Rowland, blowing a cloud of steam in his face, and Rowland talked to the animal cheerfully as he led him out of the stable. The horse was jittery.

Sir Gui met Rowland at the entrance, as he was returning his own mount to the stable. They both stopped to speak, but there was an uncomfortable silence between the two old friends.

"You are the early one, eh?" Rowland remarked casually, hoping Gui would respond genially for a change.

He was disappointed by Gui's curt "Yes."

Rowland stared at Gui's back, shrugged irritably, and began to mount the Hun, then changed his mind abruptly and followed Gui back into the stable.

"What is wrong, old friend?" Rowland demanded. "Did you not believe Brigitte that night?"

Gui did not want to answer, but as he saw Rowland's pain and confusion, he relented. "If it had been between you then as it is now, then I might have believed her. But I was not fooled, Rowland. She did a noble thing, lying to prevent the death of one of us—my death," he conceded. "I am well aware that my skills cannot compare to yours."

"Be damned!" Rowland said in exasperation. "Then why did you not challenge me again?"

"And have the lady's efforts go for nothing?" Gui asked, astonished.

Rowland was most uncomfortable, for Gui was bitter. "I do not mistreat her, Gui. You can see she is happy. Can you not see that I damn myself and our love if I admit she is who she claims to be? But you do not know the circumstances. I took her from Louroux, and no one stayed me. She was *given* to me, forced on me. If she were truly a baron's daughter, do you think that would have happened? Be damned, the whole of Berry would be here demanding I release her!"

Gui's eyes narrowed angrily. "Who is to say that will not still happen? And who is to say the lady's happiness is not because she is sure that *will* happen soon. She is, you know, under the misconception that you sent a messenger to Berry. But I know you did not!"

Rowland gasped. "How do you know that?"

Gui shrugged, delighted to see Rowland upset. "Knowing the way servants gossip, it's a wonder the lady herself has not learned of your deception. I wonder how she will react when she finds out. Do you think she will still be so happy?"

"She has no wish to leave me now," Rowland said stiffly.

"Are you so sure?"

For a moment, Rowland wanted to connect his fist with Gui's taunting mouth. The urge was strong, but he let out a low growl of anger and threw himself onto the Hun, desperate to put as much distance as he could between him and the man who voiced his own doubts.

He charged out into the bailey, causing a knight and page who had been practicing with swords to leap out of the way and fall, sprawling, into the snow. Rowland spurred the Hun cruelly, heading for open fields.

But, for the first time in his life, Rowland lost control of the Hun. The stallion swerved sharply and Rowland could not turn him back. The steed passed the servants' huts, spewing mud over rough plankings, galloped back into the yard, disrupting the exercise there as warrior and servant alike fought to get out of the path of the huge animal, and then tore crazily across the yard, pulling left and then right in an erratic path.

Rowland was beside himself. He could not stop

the animal, and the horse seemed blind to its path as it charged straight for the stone wall at the side of the manor, turning only at the last moment to gallop madly toward the rear yard. As soon as the Hun burst into the open yard behind the manor, he began to buck wildly in a desperate attempt to unseat his rider. And unseat him he did. Rowland went flying over the Hun's head, landing on his side in the mud. He then rolled as fast as he could out of the animal's path, as the Hun's forelegs came close to shattering his shoulder.

Rowland sat up slowly, aching, and stared after his horse as the animal continued to buck wildly for several more minutes before it finally slowed to a halt. Rowland felt no anger at being so shamefully unseated. He felt only a terrible loss as he realized that the Hun was crazed and would have to be destroyed. The notion tore at Rowland's gut. That horse was his pride, the finest steed ever sired at Montville. There would never be another like him.

Men came running from the front and side yards and gathered around Rowland as he eased himself to his feet. Grooms warily approached the Hun, but Rowland barked them away. A knife would have to be taken to the Hun's neck, but he himself would be the one to do it, no other.

Sir Gui came to his side and offered him a cloth to wipe the mud from his face and hands. "Are you injured?"

Rowland shook his head. "A little sore is all."

"My God, what could have caused this? I have never seen the horse so possessed. Dogs and wolves, but never a horse and never this one!"

Rowland's bewilderment equalled Gui's. "He is possessed."

The pain in Rowland's eyes told Gui what had to be done. "Rowland, I am sorry. Would you like me to—?"

"No." Rowland stopped him. He drew the dagger from his own belt and, with a heavy step, walked toward the Hun.

Gui followed. "At least let me help. You may not be able to hold him still."

Rowland nodded, and together they approached the skittish animal. The Hun shied away, his eyes rolling wildly, his feet churning the mud, but finally Rowland's soothing voice calmed him enough that he could grab the reins.

"I will remove the trappings," Gui offered. "The saddle will be difficult to remove...afterward."

Rowland glared at him. "To hell with the trappings! The horse...ah," he cried, his shoulders slumping in defeat. "Do it, then. I will hold him."

Carefully Gui unstrapped the saddle and pulled it off, handing it to a nearby groom. There was silence in the yard as everyone solemnly watched Rowland brace himself to cut the throat of his beloved horse. In the silence, Sir Gui's sharp cry was like a thunderclap.

When Rowland saw the blood and all the thorns embedded in the Hun's back, thorns that had been pushed in deeply by his own heavy weight, relief flooded his being. But the relief was tinged with horror, for he had come too close to killing the Hun. If not for Gui removing the saddle, he would have discovered the thorns too late.

"Roger," Rowland hissed.

Gui, standing near Rowland, felt his flesh crawl. "Rowland, you do not know for sure."

But Rowland did not even seem to have heard. He turned on his heel and started for the manor, Gui running to catch up.

"Rowland, listen to me," Gui said anxiously. "You have no proof!"

Rowland stopped and turned to Gui, barely managing to check himself. There was so much hate to be unleashed, but not on Gui.

"I have no doubts."

"And if you are wrong?"

"Twice now you have tried to defend that blackguard. You waste your efforts, Gui," Rowland said darkly. "I was meant to break my neck or to kill the horse I prize. All my life I have suffered at the hands of others, and I am through with it."

"But if you *are* wrong?" Gui persisted.

"Truly, I do not care. I should have torn Roger apart long ago."

Gui did not run after him as Rowland continued to the hall with an unwavering determination. Gui sighed. Even if Roger were not guilty of this terrible deed, he was guilty of so many others.

# Chapter Thirty

*W*ith her arms piled high with clothing, Brigitte left Rowland's chamber, closing the door with her foot, and started down the corridor. She stopped short when she saw Roger of Mezidon sitting in the arched window that looked down on the hall. He wasn't looking down at the hall but directly at her, as if he had been perched there waiting for her.

Quickly she looked behind her, then groaned when she realized that Wolff had not followed her out of the room but was shut inside. She wanted to drop the bundle in her arms and run when Roger rose and started toward her, but she reminded herself that Roger had been warned to leave her alone. He would surely not be so foolish as to ignore the warning.

"So, Lady Brigitte," Roger said in a belittling voice. "You not only pretend to be a servant, but you play the part very well. I wonder why?"

"Let me pass."

"Do not brush me aside, *lady,* when I have so diligently waited for you. I had begun to despair of ever finding you without one of your beasts at your heel. The wolf and the lion guard you well."

"I am sure Rowland will be amused by your description of him," she replied. "I can just hear his roar of laughter."

"You toy with me, lady," Roger said darkly. "You think I fear that lout?"

She raised a brow. "You do not? But I see you do not, since you have not heeded Rowland's warning. You live very dangerously, milord. They will someday sing ballads of your bravery."

"Your derision is misplaced, damosel." Roger did not try to hide his anger. "Save it for Rowland, for he grows soft in your taming of him."

He reached for her, but she stepped quickly back, a warning in her eyes. "I will scream if you touch me. You are despicable!"

"So I may be, but at least *I* would make you my wife."

"Your wife?"

"You seem surprised. Rowland does not think highly enough of you to offer marriage?"

"He does not know—"

Brigitte stopped, amazed at herself for defending Rowland's treatment of her. Did Rowland not respect her? She had given in to him completely. Was his opinion of her low because she had?

She gave Roger a look of pure loathing for the doubts he had raised in her mind and said, "I have said all—"

A voice they both recognized bellowed Roger's name from the hall, drowning out Brigitte's words. She stared at Roger and could almost smell the fear in him. Rowland had come to her rescue once again. But then, he could not know that Roger had detained her. Was there another reason for the sound of death in Rowland's voice?

Rowland appeared at the end of the corridor, the arched window at his back. He charged forward with a cry of rage. Brigitte stood frozen, her breath caught in her throat as Rowland's large hands closed around Roger's neck. She was knocked backward by Roger's struggle and fell to the floor, the clothes she had been clasping spilling around her. When she looked at the two men again, Roger was choking to death. He could not tear loose Rowland's fingers. The realization that she was witnessing a death made her stomach lurch. She couldn't bear to think that Rowland could really kill Roger.

"Stop!" she screamed, unable to stand it anymore.

Rowland looked up, giving Roger the chance to bring both arms up between Rowland's and break his hold. He threw a blow to Rowland's jaw, but Rowland was not moved, not even a little. Roger was terrified. He had not fazed Rowland. In a panic, Roger doubled his legs up and kicked out blindly. His booted feet caught Rowland's chest, and Rowland was thrown back, stumbling toward the arched window. Brigitte screamed as the window ledge, less than two feet from the floor, caught the back of Rowland's knees and he fell through the opening.

Brigitte closed her eyes, her mind refusing to accept that Rowland was gone. How many times had she stopped at that window to look down on the hall before descending the stairs next to it? It was a killing height, with the hard stone floor of the hall many feet below. And Roger had pushed him! Roger!

She opened her eyes, but Roger was no longer beside her. He was at the window, gloating. Watching him peer down through the window, she was struck suddenly by a desire alien to her, the desire to kill. It made her rise and move forward slowly, carefully. She could actually see her desire in her mind. As she inched forward, she had time to consider that this was murder, and still she did not stop. Her hands reached out.

Roger, still standing at the window, looking down, had not moved. She steeled herself. Her hands were inches from Roger's back. She had only to lean forward. But Roger bent over at that moment and began hammering on the window ledge with his fists. And then she saw fingers clinging to the ledge. Rowland's fingers! He had managed to catch the ledge, and now Roger was trying to beat him off and break his grasp.

Brigitte would always wonder where she got the strength to pull Roger away from that window and shove him the several feet to the stairs, where he tumbled down the stone steps, giving Rowland the chance he needed to climb through the window to safety. Roger, unhurt, ran the rest of the way down the steps and fled, Rowland tearing down the stairs after him.

Rowland caught up to Roger in the stable and quickly Roger flew through the open doors and slid several feet into the muddy yard. Rowland leaped on him. A crowd soon gathered, and Brigitte arrived just as Sir Gui got there. Luthor was there, watching his son kill with only his hands. Sir Gui stood next to him, also watching, and Brigitte ran to them and dug her fingers into Luthor's arm. He turned his inscrutable eyes on her. "Will you stop them?" she pleaded earnestly.

"No, damosel," Luthor said curtly, before he turned back to the bloody scene.

"Please, Luthor!"

If he had heard her, he gave no sign. She looked once more at the two men on the ground. Roger was no longer moving, but Rowland's fists still pounded him.

Brigitte turned away, tears burning her eyes as she ran back to the hall. She did not see Rowland stop the assault, did not see him leave the courtyard in disgust. Roger was badly beaten, but still alive.

# Chapter Thirty-one

*B*rigitte spent the remainder of that day shut up in Rowland's chamber, brooding and crying and cursing Rowland. It was not until late that evening that she learned Rowland had not killed Roger after all.

It was Goda who told her the news. Rowland had sent the girl up to summon Brigitte to the hall. He had always come himself to escort her to the evening meal. But tonight he had sent Goda. She quickly learned why.

"Sir Rowland is drunk, mistress," Goda informed Brigitte reluctantly. "He took to the ale as soon as Lord Roger was led through the gate by his squire. I say good riddance to that one."

"He was all right, though?"

"He is cursing one and all, and in a black mood," Goda replied. "But it's the drink. I doubt he even knows what he is saying."

"I meant Roger. Was he all right?"

"He was as right as could be expected," Goda answered. "His face is terribly swollen, and he has some broken bones—a finger and a few ribs, I think. But he will mend well enough—more's the pity."

"That is cruel, Goda," Brigitte snapped, then sighed

dismally. "Forgive me. I am a fine one to pass judgment, when I almost killed Roger myself."

"When did you do that?" Goda's eyes grew round with wonder.

"This morning," Brigitte admitted. "When the fight first began."

"But Sir Rowland is not dead. So why are you so upset?"

"Why?" Brigitte's voice rose. "How can you ask me why? Roger is an evil man, but still, he was terrified of Rowland. It was not a fair fight, that is what sickens me. Rowland was too enraged for it to be a fair fight. He wanted blood, and he got blood. He meant to kill Roger with his bare hands."

Goda placed a hand gently on Brigitte's shoulder. "Did you not mean to do the same?"

"That was altogether different," Brigitte replied stonily. "I thought Rowland was dead."

Goda left quietly a little later, and Brigitte sank down in her chair. No, she did not want to join Rowland in the hall, not if he was drunk.

Rowland was not so drunk that he could not sense something wrong. Goda returned to the hall alone. Why would Brigitte not join him? He scowled darkly. The answer came readily enough. It was the very reason he kept refilling his tankard, the reason he had stayed in the hall all day, afraid to face Brigitte. She knew of his deception. Someone must have told her. Perhaps Roger had done so. Why else would the snake seek her out after he had been warned to stay away from her? Yes, that was it. Brigitte knew he had not honored their bargain, had not sent the message to Count Arnulf after all.

He rested his head on his arms and heaved a great sigh. Damn this for happening when everything was going so well. He wished this day to hell. Well, there was nothing else he could do but face her. She knew he had lied, and she would be furious. He would just have to get the confrontation over with. Rowland left the hall. A few moments later he entered his chamber to find Brigitte tying up her bundle of possessions, the few articles that she had moved to his room when she began sleeping there.

Finding her doing this had a startling effect on him. He saw himself losing Brigitte. He saw them growing apart again, and he couldn't bear the idea.

"Is that necessary?" Rowland asked softly, when he could think of nothing else to say.

Brigitte deigned to glance at him briefly before she looked away. "Of course it is. Roger is gone. There is no reason for me to stay in this room anymore. You wanted me here only because of him, didn't you?"

"And if I ask you to stay? I know Roger was the reason you first began staying here, but—"

"You can insist I stay in this room, but I do not want to be here, not after today."

Her voice was of ice, and that further unnerved him.

"Brigitte, I know you are angry—"

"Angry is putting it mildly," she snapped.

"Then curse me. But get it over with. If I could take back the lie I would."

"Lie?" she asked, bewildered.

Rowland saw her surprise and could have bitten his tongue. But if it was not the deception that had her riled, then...

"Why are you angry?"

She ignored that. "What lie, Rowland?"

He feigned innocence. "What are you talking about?"

"You...oh!" she exclaimed. "I refuse to talk to you when you are drunk!"

Brigitte moved to the door, forgetting her bundle, but Rowland stepped quickly in front of her. "Why are you so angry?" He tried a cajoling tone. "Because I have drunk a bit too much?"

"You can drown in ale for all I care," she hissed, her blue eyes flashing. "Your brutality is what appalls me. You were bestial today in your thirst for blood. You nearly killed Roger!"

"But I did not kill him, Brigitte," he replied softly. He was trying to understand her anger, but he could not.

Rowland raised a hand to caress her cheek, but she cringed. "I cannot bear to have you touch me after I witnessed such cruelty."

Rowland's temper finally exploded. "You dare to take that vermin's side against me! My touch revolts you, does it? Damn you, wench, it's my protection you enjoy. You are a serf, yet I treat you like a queen. I am your lord, yet you condemn me!"

"I did not ask for your protection," Brigitte countered hastily.

"By God, then I will withdraw it, and see how well you fare without it!"

"Rowland!"

"Your disloyalty sickens me. Be damned!" he stormed. "I suffered worse beatings from Roger when I was younger. Now that I finally gave back what he deserved, you condemn me and cannot bear my touch."

"Rowland, please," Brigitte cried. "I did not mean to seem disloyal."

"You change your tune now out of fear, but I know your true feelings!" Rowland's fury was boundless. "Get out of here, Brigitte. I shall give you what you want. You are free now, free of me!"

Brigitte could not speak for the lump in her throat. She grabbed her bundle of clothes and ran from the room without looking back, closing the door. Once shut away from him she burst into tears. What had she done? What in heaven's name had she done?

# Chapter Thirty-two

"So, Rowland has broken his bond to you?"

Brigitte stirred her breakfast absently, uncomfortable under Luthor's scrutiny. She could not look at him. She was sitting on a bench where the servants ate, which proclaimed to all that something was amiss between her and Rowland. Rowland was apparently oblivious to her presence, which confirmed it. Luthor knew all about the matter, for Rowland had told him.

"Were you not a bit hard on him?" Luthor continued, as he stood by the servants' bench looking down at her.

Brigitte kept her head bowed, unwilling to face him. "Yes, I was."

"Why, damosel?" Luthor asked gently. "He had done nothing to be ashamed of."

"I realize that now," she confessed. "Too many disturbing things happened too quickly yesterday, and I was upset and angry."

"And now he is in a fine temper. Perhaps if you told him what you just told me, he would understand."

She finally looked at Luthor. "You do not believe

that any more than I do. I hurt him, and now he wants me to suffer for it."

"Rowland will relent," Luthor said gruffly.

"Maybe," she said wistfully, her blue eyes clouding, "but I will not be here when he does."

Luthor looked sternly at her. "And where will you be, damosel?"

"I cannot stay here any longer. I will leave today."

"On foot?"

"Milord, I do not own a horse."

Luthor shook his head adamantly. "You will not be allowed to leave here on foot."

"Everyone here accepted Rowland's claim on me, and you must now accept that I am without a lord because he has given me my freedom. No one here can stop me from going where I will."

"I can." Luthor was irritated. "As lord here, I cannot let you do anything so foolish as to try to walk from here to the next fief."

"I asked you once for help, milord, but you did not give it. Now you offer it when I do not want it."

"Before, you asked me to go against my son," Luthor reminded her.

"Ah! You are not worried about my safety. Rowland is your concern. You would keep me here because you think he will change his mind about me."

"I know he will."

"Am I to understand then that you are offering me your protection?"

"Yes."

"Rowland will not thank you for interfering, milord. He expects me to go."

"Nonsense," Luthor scoffed. "My son will come to his senses."

Brigitte shrugged. "Very well, I will stay for a while. It will not be long before my lord sends for me. You will have to let me go then, or risk war with the Count of Berry."

"What the devil do you mean?" Luthor demanded, angered by yet another new turn.

Brigitte smiled. "Rowland sent a messenger to Berry to inquire about my claim. He will learn that I am daughter of the late Lord of Louroux. When Count Arnulf sends for me, Rowland will know at last that I have not lied to him and that all this has been a mistake."

"A messenger, eh?" Luthor said, more to himself. "Rowland told you he sent someone?"

"Yes," she answered. "He agreed to, if I promised not to run away again."

"I see." Luthor grew thoughtful.

"You realize what proof of your claim would do to Rowland? He is a man of honor, damosel, and he will accept whatever retribution Count Arnulf demands. If combat to the death with a champion of Berry is demanded, Rowland will agree. He could die."

"No!" Brigitte said emphatically. "I will not allow it to come to that. This was not his fault at all. Someone else is guilty. And I...I bear no malice toward Rowland."

"Well, we will just have to wait and see what the future brings." Luthor chuckled. "Perhaps you will leave us, or perhaps you will stay here so you and my son can be as you were before."

"We will not be as we were before."

"As I said, we will see. Truth is, it will take only a few days for Rowland to relent," Luthor prophesied, shaking a finger at her. "Mark my words, damosel."

Brigitte frowned. Just a moment before he had been afraid of the consequences of Count Arnulf's anger, and now he was unruffled. To be sure, the man was strange.

As he began to move away, she said suddenly, "I will accept your protection, milord, but I will not serve you."

Luthor turned back, stared at her briefly, and then bellowed with laughter. "I do not expect you to, damosel. You are free to do as you will. Just do not attempt to leave Montville alone."

"And the lady Hedda? Will you keep her from me?"

"She will not bother you." Inclining his head in a mock bow, Luthor left her.

Brigitte was much relieved. She had not wanted to leave Montville without a horse. Now she could wait for Count Arnulf or his emissary to take her home.

She left the hall shortly thereafter, to return to the hut. She had spent a miserable night there, alone. Rowland was in the courtyard as she passed around it. He saw her, and she stopped, but he quickly turned away. She darted a glance at him and hurried on her way.

With a heavy heart, she closed the door to her little room. She was thoroughly miserable. Sitting on the cot, she moaned, "I should not care. But I...do...I do care!"

She cried for most of the morning, lying on the little bed. At about midday she dragged herself from the cot and went to the old chest where she had dropped her bundle of possessions the night before. Examining her gowns, she decided to wash them all, even the blue linen, which she had not worn since the night she met Rowland. She fingered the glittering sapphires on the bodice and wondered how Rowland would react if she walked into the hall that evening wearing such a gown. She sighed. It would cause trouble. She might be accused of stealing it. But she would wash it.

She draped the gowns over her arm and started for the door, but just as she opened it, Amelia arrived and stood staring at Brigitte, her eyes alight with malice.

"What do you want?"

Amelia laughed deeply, tossing her red-brown hair, crossing her arms across her ample chest, and leaning against the door frame to block Brigitte's way. "Still the high and mighty little whore, eh? I suppose you believe he will take you back to his bed?"

Brigitte blushed, trying not to show how shocked she was. She would never get used to Amelia's brash ways. But she would not let Amelia know she was shocked by her vulgarity.

"How should I answer you?" Brigitte replied calmly. "I could of course have him back if I wanted him, but I do not."

Amelia's eyes widened, then narrowed. "Liar! He is finished with you. And it did not take long for him to tire of you." She laughed. "He was mine for much longer than he was yours, and he will be mine again. He will wed me, not some frigid French whore who cannot possibly know how to please him. You see how quickly he tired of you."

Brigitte's cheeks burned. Amelia had cut her, despite her efforts to remain aloof.

"I have known only one man, Amelia," she rushed

on, unable to stop herself. "You would like to think he was not pleased with me, but I know differently. Rowland knows I came to him innocent of other men. You could not say the same, could you?"

"Bitch!"

Brigitte laughed humorlessly. "Well, perhaps a bitch is what I am, but of the two of us, you are the whore. I have heard the gossip about you, and surely Rowland has, too."

"Lies! They tell lies about me!" Amelia snapped, her brown eyes darkening to black.

"Oh, I believe Rowland knows a great deal about you, Amelia," Brigitte purred.

"Well, here is something *you* do not know," Amelia screeched, infuriated. "He lied to you, but he has never lied to me!" She grinned delightedly at Brigitte's obvious confusion. "You are a fool! Everyone knows of the bargain you struck with him. Little Goda has nothing better to do than gossip. Everyone knows Rowland did not honor that bargain. He cares so little for you that he simply didn't bother."

Brigitte's hands clenched into fists, her nails biting into her palms. "Are you saying he did not send a messenger to Berry?"

"Of course not. Whatever for?" Amelia smirked. "How silly you are."

"It's not true!" Brigitte shouted. She threw her gowns on the cot and then, striding past Amelia, ran into the courtyard in search of Rowland.

He sat on a horse at the end of the courtyard, near the stables. It was not the Hun, for he was not yet healed.

Brigitte ran to him and cried, without preamble,

"Did you honor our bargain? Did you send to Count Arnulf?"

"I did not," he said flatly, his eyes flickering briefly.

There was a stunned silence, and then she gave an anguished cry. "Why not?"

"It was a foolish request," he said simply, trying not to sound as ashamed as he felt.

"You thought so little of me that you lied to me?"

Rowland leaned forward, his blue eyes dark as midnight, but before he could respond, she went on.

"You are a bastard! I will never forgive you!"

He turned his horse around and rode away without answering. His apparent indifference inflamed her beyond control, and she screamed at his departing figure, "I hate you, Rowland! I hope the devil waits impatiently for you! Damn you, damn you, *damn you!*"

Hands led her back to her hut, but she did not feel them. For a long time, she felt nothing at all.

Rowland paced the yard that night like a caged cat. He moved to Brigitte's hut once, twice, three times, then abruptly turned away. Each time, he heard her tears and retreated. It would do no good to ask her forgiveness now. She needed time.

That night, Rowland dreamed his same old haunting dream. But this time, when he awoke, he felt close to understanding the dream. This time, he really had lost what was dearest to him.

# Chapter Thirty-three

*T*hree days had passed, and Brigitte was bone weary when she reached her destination. She had ridden relentlessly for the first two days and would have reached Angers that morning but for a snowstorm. Fortunately the weather had passed her by late afternoon. It was slow going after that, trudging through three- and four-foot snow drifts, losing sight of Wolff again and again. But the worst part of her journey was over.

Brigitte found a warm bed at the monastery, though not a private room, for she was taken for a poor traveler and put in the large dormitory. It was still a bed, and she was too tired to protest. She had no coins to pay for better, and she was, in fact, a beggar. But in the morning she would be on her way to an audience with the Count of Anjou. She did not know him, but she had no doubt he would help her once she told her story. She slept, confident that the morning would see her in safe hands at last.

She regretted tricking kind Sir Gui out of a horse, but he would not have let her take one if he had known she planned her escape, and she had not known any way of obtaining a horse except by ruse.

Morning came soon enough. Brigitte begged a private room and water for washing, which the young priest frowned on but brought her just the same. She spent two hours on her toilet, grooming with special care, and dressed in her blue linen gowns.

Bedecked in her finery, the sapphires turning her eyes a darker blue, the hood of her mantle covering her tightly wound golden braids, Brigitte seemed to be royal. Avoiding the young priest so as not to cause alarm at her transformation, she left the monastery for the Count's palace.

She had no problem getting through the gates there, even unescorted. A groom took her mount and gave her the directions to the great hall where the Count of Anjou held his court. Brigitte grew nervous at the sight of so many nobles hurrying through corridors. The Count of Anjou was a very powerful man. Would he have time to hear her plea? An escort was all she meant to ask for, a few men to take her to Berry. She would pay the Count with her sapphires if necessary.

The chamber was cavernous, at least as large as the great hall of Montville. Hundreds of people were milling about, all richly garbed nobles and their fine ladies. It was the most impressive she had ever seen, and Brigitte was awed and terrified. Which of these grandly dressed men was the Count of Anjou? His court was an informal one, and, as there was no dais, there was no way of knowing which of the men was the Count.

"You are here to see the Count, milady?"

She turned to the portly bald man beside her and smiled uneasily. "Is he here?"

The man smirked, his gray eyes glinting. "His highness is most definitely present, milady."

Brigitte grew uneasy at the man's frank disdain. An enemy of the Count's? A jealous lord? Thank God she had never been involved in court intrigues. Druoda would be happy here, but she was not.

"I do not know him, milord," Brigitte said, hoping the man would not ask too many questions.

"Why, you will know him by all his splendor. There." The man pointed to the middle of the room. "In the red velvet, with an emerald as large as his nose around his neck. That jewel was mine, given in payment for a favor I never received."

Brigitte felt her spirits fall. Would the Count treat her callously, then? Would he agree to help her, take her sapphires, and then forget her?

As she studied the man in red velvet, her eyes fell on a tall man beside him. She froze.

Rowland! It was not possible! But there he stood, dressed grandly in a black jeweled tunic of a glossy material, with fine hose and black velvet cape. She was not even aware he possessed such finery. Obviously he had lied to her about not knowing anyone in Angers, for the Count was speaking to him as if they were old friends. Brigitte was further stunned to see that a young woman hung on Rowland's arm, a beautiful young woman. Someone else he did not know?

Oh God! She ducked behind a large pillar before he saw her. What was he telling the Count? To expect a petition from a serf claiming to be a lady, and to deliver her directly to him? Damn him! He *would* tell the Count that, of course he would! The sly bas-

tard. Damn him for getting here first! How had he
done it?

She turned and left the hall unobtrusively, her
hood pulled closely around her face. But as soon as
she reached the corridor she started to run and did
not stop until she reached the stable. She nearly
pounced on the young groom who had taken her horse
away.

"Where is my mare? Where? Quickly!"

"There...lady," the boy stammered, pointing to
a stall several feet away.

Brigitte rushed to it and quickly led the mare out
of the stable.

Mounting without help, she forced herself to set
a sedate pace until she got beyond the castle gates.
It took every effort of will to walk the mare across
the courtyard. She feared that Rowland would come
running after her at any moment. She kept looking
back, unable to stop herself.

At last Brigitte was outside the walls. No one
was following. At least not yet. She started south
at a gallop but stopped suddenly, nearly unseating
herself. Wolff! She had left him at the monastery.
She turned around quickly and rode back to the
monastery, careful now not to ride too fast and draw
attention. As she rode, worrying over her new di-
lemma, she continued to look back over her shoulder again and again for Rowland. Every little sound
she heard was Rowland galloping up behind her.

And then, suddenly, there he was, coming toward
her down the road. She drew up, too astonished to
wonder why he was ahead of her, coming from the
north, instead of behind her, coming from the castle.
She shook her head, terribly confused. He was get-

ting closer and closer, his black cape billowing in the wind behind him. Panicking, she swung her horse around and set her heels to the mare. But Rowland was quickly right behind her. He could not reach the reins of her horse because she veered away from him, so he reached for her instead, pulling her across the space of the two horses and onto his lap. She squirmed away, making it nearly impossible for him to manage his horse.

"Brigitte, stop, or we will both fall," he said.

"Then let us fall!" she cried.

He managed to draw her into one arm and halt his horse. "There. Now, if you do not stop screeching I will turn you over my lap and give you a beating that will draw a crowd."

Rowland spoke softly, close to her ear, and she quieted immediately. "You would, too, brute that you are," she said more quietly.

He chuckled then. "You have led me a merry chase once again, little jewel."

"You had no right to chase me down," she snapped. "Have you forgotten that you released me?"

"Ah, well, I have changed my mind about that," he said slowly.

She was furious. "Insufferable lout! The bonds do not work that way and you know it. You cannot cast me aside and take me back as you please! You were never my lord in the first place. I did not swear fealty to you."

"I swore it. That was enough. Now come, we should not be arguing out here. Stop your fussing. I have you, and you know you cannot fight me."

She fell silent, and Rowland moved ahead to retrieve her mare. He had her back again. She was

enraged, and she was exhilarated. He had come for
her, had followed her all this way.

"Where are you taking me?" she asked calmly.

"Home."

"To Berry?" she asked quickly.

"To Montville. That is your home now, and it will
always be. I swore you would never return to Berry,
and that was a promise I had forgotten when I set
you free."

Brigitte went rigid. "So that is why you came after
me! Only because of that! I hate you!"

"Brigitte," Rowland growled, tightening his hold
on her. "What do you want to hear from me? That I
could not bear to see you go? That if you are not near
me I feel as if a part of myself is gone? I am a man
of war, Brigitte. I know nothing of tender words. So
do not expect them from me."

"You just said them, Rowland," she whispered
softly.

They both fell silent. Brigitte relaxed in Rowland's strong arms, contentment flowing through her.
She did not try to fight herself, but let the warm
feeling take over. Then suddenly she remembered
Wolff.

"Wait!" She sat upright, bumping Rowland's chin
with her head and hearing him swear. She explained, and Rowland followed her directions.

At the monastery Wolff could not be found. He
had run off with a pack of hounds soon after Brigitte
left, the priest informed them, and had not returned. There was nothing to do but wait until he
did.

Rowland paid for a private room, telling the priest
quite shamelessly that Brigitte was his wife. Whether

or not the priest believed him, the young man allowed nothing to show on his face. But Brigitte was not amused.

"You have told everyone else we meet that I am your servant," Brigitte said as soon as they were alone. "Why not the priest?"

He reached for her, but she neatly ducked under his arm and away. "Just what are you doing?"

"Come now, *cherie,* you know exactly what I have in mind. It has been seven days since I have held you in my arms, and that is too long."

"I was in your arms on the way here," she reminded him tartly.

"Be damned, you know what I meant."

"You be damned, I am not sure I want to be with you."

"Liar. You could fit no other arms as well as mine. Now come here."

"Rowland," she protested. "This is a holy place. Have you no shame?"

"Not where you are concerned."

He caught her shoulder and jerked her to him, and her body molded to his hard frame. After a few moments, she felt as if her body were a part of his. She saw the fire in his eyes before his mouth came down to claim hers. Her lips parted under his gentle onslaught. His warm breath was intoxicating. Had he not been holding her firmly, she would have fallen to the floor. Fit in his arms? She was made for his arms alone.

He released her lips and picked her up. She was in a dream, a dream of his eyes loving her, burning with his need for her. But when she felt the bed under her and Rowland's hands upon her, she knew she was not really dreaming.

He undressed her slowly and unbraided her hair so he could run his fingers through it. She reveled in his tingling touch and could not help but touch him at every opportunity. A hand, an arm, his cheek, she thrilled to the feel of him.

When Rowland was as naked as she was, Brigitte stroked the hard muscles on his chest, leaning up to kiss his shoulders. Then she forced him to lie down. She wanted to make love to him, wanted to show him how glad she was to be with him again.

She leaned over him, her flaxen hair falling down over his chest like a silken caress. She kissed his lips teasingly, tenderly, darting her small tongue into his mouth playfully. She nibbled his ear, then trailed her lips and tongue down his neck to his chest. She licked and teased the nipples there as his hands caressed her breasts. She wanted to kiss him all over as he had done to her so many times. But when she moved lower, Rowland caught her shoulders and pulled her up to him.

"Witch," he breathed huskily. "You have already set a fire in me. I have never wanted you more than I do now. Any lower and I would spill my seed too soon."

"Then take me now, lover." She grinned. "Take me."

He rolled on top of her and took her passionately, wildly, and she delighted in his every thrust. They reached the heights together, and it was over quickly, in a long, magnificent cresting.

Rowland moved away and pulled Brigitte close.

She snuggled against his shoulder, one leg curled up over his, her hand resting possessively on his chest. She had never felt more at peace as she drifted off to sleep, secure, the future far, far away.

# Chapter Thirty-four

"Brigitte."

The hand resting on her hip shook her gently, and she stirred with a smile before she opened her eyes. Rowland leaned over the bed and placed a soft kiss on her cheek. He was dressed and grinning down at her.

"You slept an hour, little jewel. Now come. We can be far from here before the sun sets."

Brigitte grinned and stretched languidly. "Are you certain you wish to leave now?" she asked, her eyes gleaming.

"Ah, damosel, do not tempt me," he groaned, turning away to find her clothes. She giggled, and he threw her clothes at her for punishment. "You will pay for that tonight, I promise you," he growled.

"I will look forward to it," she teased.

She was in a jubilant mood. She could not have been happier.

"Has Wolff returned then?" she asked as she slipped on her clothing.

"Yes."

Rowland sat down on the bed to watch her. Then his hand circled her waist, and he pulled her to him to stand between his legs. She was surprised and

touched when his arms went around her and he laid
his head against her breasts. He just held her like
that for several moments. She was deeply moved.
She wrapped her arms around his head to hold him
closer, for she understood what he was telling her.

"Do you love me, Brigitte?"

The question made her want to cry, for she truly
did not know. "I have known much love in my life.
The love of my mother and father, of my brother, of
servants and friends. But what I feel for you is different from all of the others. I am not sure if what
I feel for you is love, Rowland. I have never loved a
man before, so I cannot say."

"Not even—" He could not say it. He would not
remind her of her lord at Louroux, the one who had
loved and pampered her, the one who had probably
given her the sapphire-studded tunic.

She gripped his head between her hands and forced
him to look at her. "Not even who?"

"I only thought there must have been someone in
Berry," he said evasively. "Someone you had hoped
to marry, perhaps, or someone you spent much time
with?"

She smiled. "There was no one. And I can tell you
this, Rowland. I am happy being with you. I was
desolate when you set me aside. And it devastated
me to think you cared so little for me that you would
not honor our bargain. Will you tell me why you lied
to me?"

"I was afraid someone would come and take you
from me," he said simply, his eyes on her face. She
squeezed him tighter.

"Do you still want me to send someone to Berry?"
he whispered.

"No," she whispered in return. "Not anymore." She did not wish to think about it anymore.

He crushed her to him once again, then released her and whacked her behind. "Get dressed, wench."

He resumed his rough exterior, feeling awkward with the tender feelings she stirred in him. He had a need for her that went beyond the joining of their bodies. And if she did not love him, did he love her? Could he answer that any better than she? He had never known love at all, any kind of love. He knew nothing of it. But he knew he wanted Brigitte's love. Perhaps one day she would know for sure and tell him so. For the present it was enough to know that she was happy, that there would be no more threats from Berry, and that she would not leave him again.

"This gown is too thin for traveling," she broke into his thoughts. "I see you changed your clothes," she added, noticing the brown woolen tunic he wore under his black cape.

He looked down. "I did not change, *cherie*. I brought no other clothes with me. There was no time."

"Rowland, that is an outright lie," Brigitte said, surprised.

"A lie?"

"That you brought no other clothes with you. I saw you this morning at the palace, and you were wearing a bejeweled tunic."

Rowland laughed. "You were mistaken. I had only just arrived in Angers when I found you in the street."

"But I tell you I saw you talking with the Count," she insisted.

"No, you did not," he replied firmly. "Someone must have looked like me."

"I know you when I see you, Rowland," she said

curtly. "I was shocked to find you there—with a woman hanging on your arm—speaking to the Count as if you were old friends. You had told me you knew no one in Angers."

"I did not lie to you, Brigitte. I was not at the palace. I have never met the Count of Anjou. I can swear to it."

She frowned, gazing at him in bewilderment. Why would he lie about this? She thought back to when she had seen him riding toward her. She had known then that it was impossible for him to be there after she left him at the palace, yet he was there. And she could not recall seeing the black bejeweled tunic on him then. When they had come to this room, she had not noticed his clothes at all.

"I do not understand, Rowland," she said slowly, mystified. "The man I saw at the palace was you. He had your face...your build. And he was your height. How many men do you know as tall as you? His hair was the same color." She stopped, her eyes widening. "Perhaps he was not as broad of chest? No, I think not."

Rowland was as mystified as she was. "Who was this man who looked so like me in every other way?"

"He seemed a noble lord. And the woman with him was richly garbed in velvet and jewels. The Count spoke with him in a friendly way. Rowland, I cannot explain it. There was not just a resemblance. What I saw is what you would see if you looked in a mirror. He could have been your twin."

Rowland grunted. "Twins indeed. If two sons had been born to Luthor, you can stake your life that he would have brought them both home. I would like to see this man for myself," Rowland said suddenly. "Dress yourself in your finery, Brigitte. We are going to the Count's court."

# Chapter Thirty-five

"*E*varard de Martel. You should be ashamed!"

Rowland looked dumbfounded at the plump woman who glared at him before she gave Brigitte a withering look and moved abruptly away. They had just entered the palace where the Count was receiving in his private chamber. Scores of men and women were waiting in the great hall, hoping to see him. It was midafternoon, and many would have to come back another day.

"Was that woman speaking to me?" Rowland whispered to Brigitte. An arm crooked in his, she stood very close to him.

"She certainly was, and didn't like me."

"She called me Evarard de Martel."

Brigitte nodded. "She has obviously made the mistake I did, the other way around. Evarard must be the man's name."

"How do we find him?" Rowland said, uneasy at that point.

He had never liked court life. During the years he had spent in service to the King of France, he had stayed well away from the King's court.

"Do you see him?" Rowland asked.

Brigitte had already scanned the hall twice. "He is not here."

"Ah, Lord Evarard, you are back again. Playing the field this time, eh?" The portly man Brigitte had spoken to that morning approached them. "Have you grown tired of your new bride so soon?" he added with a sly wink before he turned to Brigitte. "Milady, did you have your audience with the Count?"

"No, I fear I left rather quickly," she said smoothly.

"Enough," Rowland said roughly, pulling Brigitte across the room away from the talkative lord. "I know you were here this morning, but why? You came to see the Count. Why?" he demanded.

"There is no reason to be upset, Rowland," Brigitte said as she pried his fingers from her arm. "I came to request an escort to Berry. You did not think I planned to go all the way alone, did you?"

"Forgive me," he sighed, running his fingers through his hair. "This matter of Evarard de Martel has upset me." Then he grinned. "I suppose I have him to thank that you did not get the Count's protection, but ran from here straight into my arms?"

"I suppose you do."

"Well then, let us find him so I can thank him. Wait here and I will find out where his home is."

Brigitte caught his arm as he turned away. "You cannot do that, Rowland. Everyone will think you are mad, for they think you *are* Lord Evarard. Let me question someone. I will find out where the man lives and as much about him as I can."

Rowland nodded reluctantly. Brigitte spoke with two ladies before she found one who knew Lord Evarard. That matron, cousin to the Count of Anjou, was most informative.

"I hope you have not set your eye on dear Evarard, for he is newly married and quite enamored of his bride," Lady Anne remarked in a confidential manner. "I fear you will be very disappointed."

"Oh, no, milady," Brigitte assured her. "I was only curious. He is such a handsome young lord. His wife is truly fortunate."

"Yes, a fine match they are," Lady Anne replied. "The marriage was arranged by the Count himself, as a favor to Baron Goddard de Cernay."

"Baron Goddard?"

"Evarard's father. The Baron and my cousin are close friends, you see."

"Cernay is quite far from here, is it not?" Brigitte groped, having never even heard of Cernay.

"Not so very far. Just across the Loire and to the west. Cernay is in Poitou."

Brigitte knew that an old Roman road led directly from Berry to Poitou on the west coast.

"But Lord Evarard lives here in Anjou, does he not?" Brigitte asked.

"He lives in Poitou near his father, my dear," the tall lady said. "He and his family are guests here. The wedding was held here, and then the cold weather set in early, and my cousin insisted the family stay for the winter."

"They are a large family? Lord Evarard has brothers and sisters?"

"My, but you *are* inquisitive. He was an only child. I understand Lady Eleonore had a difficult time with the birth. She never conceived again, the poor woman. I have seven children myself and thirty-four grandchildren. And every one of them is a joy to me."

"You are most fortunate, lady. And you have been very patient with me. My dear mother always said I had more curiosity than was good for me. I do thank you."

Brigitte moved away quickly, before the woman could question her. She left the hall, knowing Rowland was watching her. He followed, meeting her in the corridor outside the great hall.

"Well?"

"He is here in the palace with his family. They are guests of the Count."

"His family?"

"His wife, father, and mother. His father is the Baron de Cernay and a close friend of the Count."

"I have never heard of him."

"Nor have I," Brigitte replied.

"Well?" Rowland asked impatiently. "I know you would have asked, Brigitte, so out with it."

"He is an only child," she admitted, smiling guiltily. He knew her too well. He knew what she had suspected.

"I would still like to meet the man," Rowland said.

"So would I." Brigitte grinned mischievously. "Too bad he is married. I might find him more to my liking than you."

"You think so, eh?" he said, reaching for her.

"Rowland," she laughed, holding him off, then growing more serious. "I will find a page to take me to his rooms. You follow at a discreet distance.

And be sure not to let the page see you," she warned sternly. "Or he will think you are de Martel."

The Baron de Cernay's suite of rooms was on the east side of the palace. The page did not question Brigitte's request, and soon left her in the corridor outside a closed door. After a few moments, Rowland joined her.

Brigitte waited for him to knock, but he just stared at the closed door, frowning, as if he were afraid to discover what lay on the other side. She understood then that Rowland was not going to knock, that he would rather not know after all.

"This is absurd," he said gruffly. "We have no business disturbing these people."

He started to leave, and she whispered, "There is no reason why we cannot meet them, Rowland."

"And tell them what?" he asked. "That we are curious?"

"I suspect there will be no need to tell them anything," Brigitte replied quietly, her gaze on the door as though she were able to see straight through it.

She knocked on the door before Rowland could stop her, and then she had to keep him there until the door opened. Just before it did, Rowland pulled away from her and stomped off down the corridor.

"Rowland, come back," Brigitte called softly, agitated. "You will have to come back, for I will not leave here until you do."

He turned, scowling darkly at her just as the door opened. He stopped and did not approach the door. A tall woman stood there, looking at Brigitte, who seemed to be alone in the hallway. The woman was about forty years old, and quite beautiful, regal

looking, with pale blonde hair and the bluest of
eyes, eyes like sapphires, eyes like Rowland's.

"Yes? What can I do for you?" the woman asked
softly in a musical voice.

"I have come to see Evarard de Martel, milady.
Would it be possible to have a few words with
him?"

"My son is here and will be pleased to see you,"
the lady replied genially. "May I ask why you wish
to see him?"

"You are the Baroness de Cernay?"

"I am."

"Baroness, my lord, Rowland of Montville, would
like very much to meet your son." Brigitte turned
to Rowland. "Please, Rowland," she beseeched him.

He stepped forward reluctantly from out of the
shadows, dragging his feet like a man on the way to
his execution. At last he stood beside Brigitte. Brigitte clasped his hand to hold him there. She was
not sure what she expected.

A frown creased the woman's brow. "Evarard, what
trick is this?" the Baroness asked sternly.

Rowland did not answer. He was staring at the
face from his dream, a face older by many years, but
the same face that had haunted him since he was a
small child. He could not find words.

Deep, resounding laughter sounded from a room
beyond, and then a man's voice was heard chiding,
teasing his companion. The Baroness paled. She
took a step back and wavered, as though about to
faint. Rowland stepped forward to catch her, but
she gasped and stiffened, her eyes widening, so he
did not touch her. He could not take his eyes from

her face, nor she from his. And then she reached
out a trembling hand to touch his face, very softly.

"Raoul." The whisper tore from her with a sob.
She stepped farther back and screamed. "Goddard!
Goddard, come quickly!" A man rushed through a
doorway behind her, and she demanded brokenly,
"Tell me...tell me I am not dreaming. Tell me he
is real, Goddard!"

The man stopped, shocked to an ashen color as
he saw Rowland. Rowland moved back into the
doorway, beside Brigitte. This was the man from
his dream. He had stepped into his own nightmare.

"Raoul?"

The man spoke. Rowland looked from Brigitte to
him, confusion prompting anger.

"I am Rowland of Montville," he said emphatically. "My name is not Raoul!"

The young woman Brigitte had seen that morning
with Evarard de Martel appeared in the room then
and gasped when she saw Rowland. Evarard quickly
followed his wife into the room.

"Emma?" Evarard asked, then followed her horrified expression until his eyes fell on Rowland.

"My God!" Rowland barely got the words out. Moving past the Baron and Baroness, he walked slowly
toward Evarard, drawn to him inexorably. He was
looking into a mirror, seeing himself, every bit of
himself, in another man.

He and Evarard stood eye to eye, of an exact
height. Evarard lifted a hand and touched Rowland's cheek in a soft gesture, disbelievingly. Rowland stood utterly still, his eyes riveted on the other
man.

"Brother!" Evarard cried.

Pain grew in Rowland's eyes, for there was truth to that cry. The horror of his life, his empty life, flashed through his mind all at once, and he turned on the Baron and Baroness.

"Did you have to give me away?" he whispered in anguish. "Were two sons too many? Did you have cause to dislike me?"

"My God, Raoul, you are wrong!" Goddard exclaimed, horrified. "You were taken from us—stolen!"

Rowland glared at him furiously, disbelievingly, and started toward the door.

Brigitte, knowing he was going to leave these people without hearing what they had to say, quickly closed the door and stood before it, barring his way. But he caught her wrist, threw open the door, and pulled her out of the room and down the corridor. She tried to stop him, crying, "You cannot leave, Rowland."

There was such anguish in his eyes, such torment as he looked down at her. And then he crushed her to him, and she felt his body shaking.

"I cannot allow myself to believe them, Brigitte. I would have to kill Luthor!"

"No, Rowland! No. You must consider Luthor's reason. A man so desperate for a son that he must steal one—"

"My life has been hell with him!"

Evarard had run after them, but he stopped and watched them cling to each other and heard what they were saying.

"You must go back in there, Rowland," Brigitte said in a firm tone. "You cannot deny them. And your brother, Rowland, are you not curious about him? Do you not want to know him?"

She wiped at his eyes with her mantle, amazed to see that he could cry.

"Ah, *cherie.*" Rowland kissed her tenderly. "What would I do if you were not here to talk sense to me?"

"You would have to fight me." Evarard interrupted at last. "For I will not let you go."

Rowland turned to face his brother. He grinned suddenly, eyeing Evarard's thin frame and courtier's clothes. "You would have had a difficult time of it— brother. I can see you are not a man of war."

"And I can see that you are," Evarard countered, grinning just as broadly.

There was silence then as the two men stared at each other. Brigitte shook her head. Rowland needed a little prodding.

"Go on, damn you." She pushed him forward. "Greet your brother properly. He is too intimidated by your mean face to do so."

Rowland moved forward very slowly, and then clasped Evarard's neck and pulled him into a bear hug, embracing his brother fiercely. Evarard laughed, and Brigitte cried.

When the three young people re-entered the room, Eleonore was crying in Goddard's arms. He shook her gently to let her know that Rowland had returned, and when she saw him, she cried all the harder. She moved to embrace the son who had been denied her all these years. Eleonore took Rowland's face in her hands, her eyes glistening with tears. Rowland suddenly went cold, then warm again. He could barely breathe, but did not look

away from her. This was his mother, his own mother.
With a moan from deep within him, he gathered
her in his arms and buried his face in her neck,
murmuring something meant only for her ears.

"My Raoul," she whispered, holding him close.
"I thought I had lost you a second time when you
walked out that door. I could not bear it, to lose
you again. But you came back, my baby, you came
back to me."

Rowland cried. His mother. How he had needed
this mother when he was small. How he had yearned
for her, and now she was overflowing with the love
he had always wanted so desperately.

Goddard came forward and embraced his son
wordlessly. Rowland held back a little. A mother and
brother were all new, but he had a father. Yet Luthor
was not his father, and had never really seemed to
be his father.

At last Rowland returned his father's embrace,
and then he laughed suddenly and caught Brigitte's
hand to pull her to him. "Do you realize, *cherie,* that
I am no longer a bastard?"

She grinned up at his glowing face.

"Oh, Raoul." Eleonore gasped. "Is that what you
thought?"

"I was told so, lady, by the man who claims to be
my father."

"Who is the man who took you from us?" Goddard
asked Rowland.

"Luthor of Montville."

"He will pay dearly!" Evarard said angrily.

"I will tend to him, brother," Rowland replied
coldly, then added in a lighter tone, "but I do not
wish to talk of him. You are French?" At Goddard's

nod, Rowland chuckled. "Then I am French. Ha!" He winked at Brigitte. "No longer can you call me Norman as an insult."

"Rowland!" she cried, embarrassed.

"You were raised in Normandy?" Goddard asked now. "That is where he took you?"

"Yes."

"No wonder we could not find you. We searched all of Anjou and the surrounding borders, but we never thought to search as far away as Normandy."

"But what brought you to Angers?" Evarard asked.

"Chasing this little one," Rowland said. Pulling Brigitte closer, he chuckled. "I have you to thank for finding her, and her to thank for finding you. She saw you this morning when she came to see the Count. But she thought you were me, and she ran from the palace. If she had not run when she did, I would never have found her."

At their looks of bewilderment he added, "It is all a very long story, and best saved for another time."

"Tell me what happened all those years ago," Rowland said to his parents. "How was Luthor able to take me from you?"

Eleonore answered. "We were here in Angers for the celebration of St. Remi's Day. The Count had such a fine harvest that year that there was a huge banquet, with nobles from all over the land. We had taken both you and Evarard down to the great hall, to show you off, I fear. We were so proud of our twins. You were so small then, still in swaddling, and so dear." Rowland reddened, but Evarard laughed, used to his mother's coddling. "Later that night my lady's maid took you back to this very room. And that was the last ever we saw of you, Raoul."

"Rowland, my love," Goddard corrected her gently. "He has been called Rowland most of his life. We will have to let go of the name we gave him at birth."

"For me he will always be Raoul." Eleonore shook her head stubbornly.

"Your mother is a sentimental woman, Rowland," Goddard explained. "We were both heartbroken when we returned to our rooms and found the maid unconscious and only Evarard in his bed. You were gone. I had enemies. What man does not? I feared one of them had taken you, and I feared you were dead. But your mother never gave up hope. In all these years, she never gave up hope."

"Was this man, Luthor, good to you?" Eleonore ventured softly.

"Good?" Rowland frowned, his gaze reflective.

There were things he would never tell these people. Who could truly understand the harshness of his life? How could he explain that life to them?

"Luthor is a hardened warlord," Rowland began. "He is well respected in Normandy. Nobles wait years to send their sons to him for training, rather than sending boys to another lord. My own training began as soon as I could hold a sword. Luthor took special care with me. He was...a hard taskmaster. He taught me not only the skills of war, but the strategies as well. He made me strive for perfection." Rowland grinned to make light of it. "I was prepared from an early age to take over Montville and be able to keep it against all odds, for though Luthor has two daughters by a wife, Montville comes to me. Now that I know I am not blood kin to Luthor, I suppose Montville does not belong to me."

"There can be no question of that, of course, since there are daughters," Goddard pointed out. "But you—"

Rowland interrupted in an overly harsh tone. "I could take Montville even without the right to it. There is no question of that."

That told his family more about him than anything else could have done. He was a man of war, a hardened man, a forceful man who was prepared to take what he wanted. These gentle people would have a difficult time understanding such a strong force.

"Rowland is short with words," Brigitte said lightly, breaking the silence. "He did not mean that he intends to take Montville by force, only that he could if he wanted to do so."

Rowland frowned at her, for he did not feel his words needed explaining. She pinched him in answer and got an even blacker scowl.

"You should not feel you have lost anything because you are not the man's son," Goddard said. "I know nothing of Montville, but you have a large estate in Poitou, given you at birth by my liege, the Count of Poitou. Evarard has managed your lands there with the same care he has given his own. Like your mother, he never gave up hope of your returning to us one day."

"Well, brother." Rowland grinned. "Am I a rich man then?"

Evarard was delighted to answer. "You are quite richer than I, since your rents have accumulated over the years whereas I have had to live from my rents. I must admit I live in a grand manner."

Rowland laughed. "Well then, for the trouble you have gone to on my behalf, I insist you take my rents, those that have accumulated, and keep them for yourself."

"I cannot!" Evarard protested, surprised.

"You can," Rowland insisted. "I want nothing that I have not earned. And I would be grateful if you will continue to look after my lands until I claim them."

"You will not claim them now?"

"Now," Rowland said darkly, "I must return to Montville."

"I will go with you to Normandy," Evarard offered.

But Rowland shook his head adamantly. "I must confront Luthor alone. He will have the devil's own loathing for you, brother, for were it not for your face, I would never have learned about my family, or known of his sin. Your life would be in danger at Montville."

"And what of yours?"

"Luthor and I are equally matched. I have no fear of him. It is he who must reckon with me."

"Rowland," Evarard began hesitantly, frowning. "Perhaps it would be wisest not to see this man again. Could you live with yourself if you killed him?"

"I could not live with myself if I do not hear from him why he did what he did," Rowland said softly, his voice calm but his eyes hard.

They talked on through the night, moving to a comfortable room and eating as a family for the first time in twenty-three years. Rowland listened quietly to his family reminiscing, and Brigitte wondered if hearing these things did not add to his sorrow over not having been a part of it all. He was enthralled, and could not take his eyes from them.

# Chapter Thirty-six

"Do you realize, Brigitte, that if you had not run off to Angers, I might never have found my family? For years Luthor protested my going there, knowing what I might find. I never asked myself what he had against the town of Angers. This time he failed to keep me from Angers, and he failed because of you."

They were on the south hill overlooking Montville. Brigitte was worried about the confrontation at hand, for it had been a silent Rowland who had ridden beside her for three days.

He grinned at her. "Each time you have run from me, something good has come of it."

"What good came of the first time?"

"Were you not mine after that?"

She blushed. "Will you confront Luthor in private?" Brigitte asked, getting back to her immediate fears.

"It matters not."

"It matters terribly, Rowland. Please, you must speak to him alone. No one else here need know what has happened. I know there is a rage in you, Rowland, but do not let it blind you. Luthor has called you his son all these years. You share a bond with

Luthor, a bond of years that weighs as heavily as
kinship. Remember that when you face him."

Rowland did not answer her, but moved slowly on
down the hill, leaving Brigitte with her fears unre-
lieved.

Luthor was in the great hall when they entered.
As he watched them approach, there was a wariness
about him, as if he already knew.

"So you brought her back once more," Luthor said
jovially, rising from his seat before the fire.

"I brought her back."

Luthor looked at Brigitte. "Did I not tell you he
would relent, damosel?"

"You did, milord," Brigitte answered softly.

"You were gone a week," Luthor said to Rowland
now. "I suppose she reached Angers?"

"She did."

There was long silence, and then Luthor sighed
the sigh of a broken man. "You know?"

Rowland did not answer. There was no need. "I
wish to talk to you alone, Luthor," he said. "Will you
ride with me?"

Luthor nodded and followed Rowland from the hall.
As Brigitte watched them go, she was filled with
terrible pity for the older man. She had seen Luthor's
shoulders slump, had seen the weary resignation in
his face.

Rowland drew up and dismounted on the crest of
the hill where he and Brigitte had stopped only a
while earlier. He remembered her warning. But there
was a rage in him that fought to be released, the
rage of a little boy begging for love, the rage of a
little boy beaten, scorned, humiliated cruelly. All of
it, his rage reminded him, need not have been.

Luthor dismounted, and as he faced his son, Rowland demanded, half in fury, half in anguish, "Damn you, Luthor! Why?"

"I will tell you, Rowland," Luthor said quietly. "I will tell you of the shame of a man with no sons."

"There is no shame in that," Rowland cried.

"You cannot know, Rowland," Luthor said earnestly. "You cannot know how much I wanted a son until you want one of your own. Daughters I have— dozens of daughters, all over Normandy. But not one son, not one! I am an old man, nearly sixty years old. I became desperate for a son to take my lands. I nearly killed Hedda when she gave me another daughter. That is why she never conceived again, and why she hated you so."

"But why me, Luthor? Why not some peasant's son—a child who would be grateful for what you could give him?"

"You are not grateful? I made you a man to be reckoned with, a great warrior. You are not grateful for that?"

"You brought me here to be raised by that harridan, to suffer at her hands. You took me from a loving mother...and gave me to Hedda!"

"I made a strong man of you, Rowland."

"My brother is a strong man, yet he was raised by loving parents. You denied me everything, Luthor!"

"I have loved you."

"You do not know love!"

"You are wrong," Luthor replied softly after a shocked silence, his eyes reflecting pain. "I just do not know how to show love. But I do love you, Row-

land. I have loved you as if you were my son. I made
you my son."

Rowland steeled himself against pity and said
harshly, "But why me?"

"They had two sons, two sons born at one time,
when I had none. I was in Angers with Duke Richard.
When I saw the Baron and his wife with their twin
boys, I was overcome by the injustice of it. I had not
planned to take you. Impulse ruled me, an idea came
to me suddenly. I felt no remorse, Rowland. I will
not say I did. They had twins. One would be gone,
but they would still have one. They would still have
a son, and I would have a son. I rode for two days,
killing my horse, to bring you straight here. You
were mine."

"God!" Rowland shouted to the heavens. "You had
no right, Luthor!"

"I know that. I changed your life from what it
would have been. But I will tell you this. I will not
ask your forgiveness, for if I had to do it again, I
would do what I did. Montville needs you," he said
in a different voice, straightening a little.

"Montville will have another lord after you, but
that will not be me," Rowland said bitterly.

"No, Rowland, you do not mean that. I have devoted nearly half my life preparing you to be lord
here. You are not my blood, but I would trust Montville to no one but you."

"I do not want it."

"Will you let Thurston have it then?" Luthor demanded angrily. "He cares nothing for the people
here, or the land, or the horses we both love. He
wants only more property, then more after that. He
will bring down Duke Richard's wrath with his petty

wars for more land, and Montville will be crushed between them. Is that what you want to happen here?"

"Enough!"

"Rowland—"

"I said enough!" Rowland shouted, throwing himself toward his horse. "I must think, Luthor. I do not know if I can tolerate you now, knowing what I know. I must think."

Rowland entered his chamber a little while later. The warmth of it was like a balm, soothing the raw edges of his anger. The room had never before been a warm place to come to, but with Brigitte in it...

She was watching him anxiously. Rowland sighed, dropping his shoulders and sinking down in a chair, avoiding her probing eyes.

"I do not know, Brigitte," he said quietly. "I cannot forgive him, but I am not sure what to do."

"Did you fight?"

"Only with words."

"And his reason?"

"As you guessed, he was desperate for a son." Rowland rested his head in her hands and then quickly looked up at her. "I wish to God it had not been me!"

Drawn by his anguished cry, Brigitte went down on her knees in front of him and wrapped her arms around him. She did not say anything.

Rowland stroked her hair tenderly, moved. "Ah, my little jewel. What would I do without you?"

# Chapter Thirty-seven

*T*he tightly drawn skins over the windows glowed faintly with the dawn's first light as Rowland's pacing woke Brigitte. A tiny flame in an oil cup cast dim shadows around the room. The tallow wick was nearly gone.

Brigitte leaned on an elbow, her hair falling over her shoulders in golden disarray. "You could not sleep?"

He was startled. "No." He went on pacing.

"Is it so difficult, Rowland? Can I help?"

Rowland came over to the bed and sat down on the edge, his back to her. "I must decide this for myself. It's Montville that is in question, not Luthor. He still wants me to have it."

"Why does that displease you? Have you not always known you would be lord here one day?"

"When I left here six years ago, I gave it up. I planned never to return. And now I have given it up all over again."

"You came home when you were needed. You are still needed. Montville is still under threat. This is what troubles you. You cannot leave, knowing you are needed here."

"I swear you are a witch," Rowland said, looking over his shoulder at her.

"You cannot separate Montville from Luthor, Rowland, that is the problem. But they are separate. And Montville will always need a strong lord."

He stretched out on the bed beside her. "But Luthor is still here. If I go now, when Montville faces war, I will have no right to claim it later. But if I stay, I must stay here with Luthor. That I am not sure I can do. I wanted to kill him, Brigitte. I wanted to challenge him for the last test of strength—a battle to the death. I do not know what held me back— you, perhaps, and what you said to me. But, if I stay, I may still challenge him."

"Who can say what we will or will not do?" Brigitte spoke softly and laid her head on his chest. "You can let time resolve your problem, Rowland. You can stay and see what happens. If it comes to the point where your bitterness is stronger than anything else and you must kill Luthor or leave—then leave. For now, let the matter rest. Control your resentment and stay here. Is that not what you really want to do?"

Rowland tilted her face so that his lips could gently caress hers. "As I said, you are a witch."

It was several hours later, when Brigitte and Rowland were below in the great hall, that a knight ran through the hall to Luthor with the news of an approaching army. "Thurston of Mezidon has not waited for the end of winter. He comes now!"

Rowland and Luthor both stood, glancing quickly at one another. "What can he be thinking of?" Rowland demanded. "He knows we can withstand a siege. His army will die from the cold."

"Is he sure he can draw us out?" Sir Gui suggested.

"Perhaps he is confident of a way in," Luthor said darkly, looking at his daughter Ilse, who looked down at her lap. "Where did your husband, Geoffrey, really go when he left here three days ago? Did he go to Thurston?"

"No!" Lady Ilse was ashen in the face of her father's accusation. "Geoffrey went to Rouen to visit his family there as he told you!"

"If I see him outside these walls with Thurston I swear I will kill you, woman. Daughter or not, no one betrays Montville and lives."

Ilse burst into tears at her father's heartless words and ran from the hall. Outside, the villagers were pouring into the courtyard, having been warned. The gates were closing, the walls manned.

Rowland turned to Luthor. "We will know about Geoffrey when we see what Thurston does. How close is the army?" he asked the knight.

"Some—probably half of the army—were sighted just over the south hill. The rest have not been seen yet."

"They will be," Rowland said ominously. "Thurston undoubtedly plans on making a good showing by surrounding us. To the walls then."

They ran from the hall. Rowland ordered Brigitte to stay there and not to leave the hall for any reason. "I will bring you news when I have a chance."

She watched him go with a tightness in her chest. How quickly his problem had been solved. He and Luthor had not spoken that morning. The icy silence between them had caused whispered comments. Yet here was a threat to Montville, and they were instantly joined.

From his position on the high wall, Rowland looked out across the snow-covered hills. Luthor, Gui, and Sir Robert stood beside him. No one could see a soul moving out there, not to the north, west, or south.

"He is mad," Rowland said confidently. "Look at all that snow. The last storm left several feet. He must be mad."

"Aye," Luthor replied. "Or very clever. Yet I cannot imagine his plan. I do not see how he thinks he can have victory now."

Rowland frowned. "How large was the army?"

Sir Robert summoned the knight who had seen the army on his patrol.

"I counted more than a hundred riders, and at least half of them were knights," the man answered. "There were two wagons as well."

Rowland was stunned. "Where in hell would he get so many horses?"

"Stolen, no doubt," Gui suggested. "From the Bretons he has raided."

"Yet that is only half his army, or even less, for all we can know now," Sir Robert pointed out.

"How many men on foot?" Rowland questioned.

"None."

"None at all?"

"That is right," the knight said soberly.

"But so many horsemen! We have not half that many trained to ride," Luthor cried.

"Thurston knows that. It could be the advantage he thinks he has."

"Look there!" Gui was staring at the top of the hill.

A single rider came into view and stopped, looking down at Montville. He was a knight and in full armor, that much was clear even at such a long distance.

"Is it Thurston?" Gui asked.

"I cannot tell," Luthor replied. "Rowland?"

Rowland shaded his eyes against the glare of snow, then shook his head. "He is too far away."

At last the knight on the hill was joined by another and then many more, until a very long line of horsemen was spread out across the southern hill. But these were not all of Thurston's men. Even so, the horsemen were terrible to look upon. Nearly all of them were knights, and one knight was worth ten men on foot.

"Now we will see what he has in mind," Luthor said levelly as the first knight started down the hill toward Montville.

He came alone, and Rowland watched, amazed at Thurston's boldness. What did he expect, coming alone? A single arrow would put an end to it all.

Rowland began to frown as the knight drew nearer. He was not Thurston.

The knight was directly below. He looked up at the high walls of Montville, and Rowland saw his face clearly. He gasped. It could not be. But it was.

"Be damned!" Rowland growled, his body stiffening.

"What is it, Rowland?" Luthor demanded.

"The devil sent here to vex me!" Rowland rasped.

"Will you make sense!"

"That is not Thurston's army out there, Luthor. Montville will have to face Thurston another time. That army of knights is from Berry!"

"Rowland of Montville! Will you come out and face me?" the knight cried from below.

Rowland took a deep breath before he shouted down from the parapet, "I am coming!"

Luthor caught his arm. "Who the devil is that?"

"That is the Baron de Louroux, the man who saved my life in Arles, the man who sent me to Louroux with the message that delayed my coming here."

"Louroux? The wench is from Louroux!"

"You do understand. That is why he is here." Rowland might have laughed if he were not so furious. "Can you credit this? He marched an army across France during winter for a servant! For a servant!"

"Then maybe not a servant," Luthor ventured, murmuring.

"I do not give a damn what she is!" Rowland stormed. "He cannot have her."

"You will fight a man who saved your life?"

"If I must I will fight his whole army."

"Rowland, then there is no need for you to go out there," Luthor said rapidly. "They cannot take the wench if we do not open the gates for them."

Luthor was willing to back Rowland when this was not his fight. Rowland did not fail to understand that.

"I will still go down," Rowland said in a calmer tone. "I owe him that courtesy."

"Very well," Luthor agreed. "But at the first sign of trouble an arrow will pierce his heart."

Rowland rode through the gates at a swift gallop. Quintin had moved back to a distance halfway between Montville and his army. So much for Luthor's arrow, Rowland thought with dark humor. He was angry, furiously so. Lady Druoda had lied to him.

There was no way Quintin could have known where to find Brigitte unless Druoda had told him. But his anger came not so much from that as from jealousy. Another man wanted his Brigitte enough to bring an army to take her away. Was Quintin de Louroux so in love with her still?

Quintin watched the approach of Rowland of Montville with narrowed eyes. He was burning with a violent, bitter rage, rage that had stayed with him since leaving Louroux more than a fortnight before. His rage had festered and grown since then.

Druoda had confessed everything, confessed to scheming and conniving to obtain Louroux for herself, confessed to forcing Brigitte into betrothal to Wilhelm d'Arsnay, confessed to keeping Brigitte from Arnulf, confessed to beating her.

Rowland of Montville had raped Brigitte. Knowing who she was, Druoda said, the man had still raped her. In doing this he had ruined Druoda's plans. Druoda confessed to panicking when Quintin came home, trying to poison him. She had begged his mercy. He was merciful in that, wanting to kill her, he had only banished her.

It was Rowland he now wanted to kill, Rowland, whom he had sent in good faith to Louroux, who had repaid the debt he owed Quintin by raping Brigitte and taking her from her home.

The two warhorses came face to face in the open field, the Hun outflanking the French horse by half a foot. As the horses were unmatched, so too were the riders. Rowland had disdained his helm and shield, wearing only a sword strapped to his hip, while Quintin was in full armor. Still, Rowland was the bigger of the two, the stronger, and perhaps the more skilled.

"Is she here, Norman?" Quintin demanded.

"She is here."

"Then I must kill you."

"If you want to see me dead, Baron, you will have to send a dozen of your strongest men to challenge me."

"Your arrogance does not move me," Quintin replied. "Nor do I send others to fight in my stead, Sir Rowland. I will be the one to kill you. And then Lady Brigitte will be taken home."

Rowland took the truth without showing that his worst fear had been realized. *Lady Brigitte. Lady!* So, it was true.

"This is Brigitte's home now," Rowland said evenly. "She will be my wife."

Now Quintin laughed unpleasantly. "Do you think I would allow her to marry the likes of you?"

"If you are dead, you will have little indeed to say of it," Rowland said evenly.

"My lord Arnulf knows my wishes in this regard. If I die, he will be Brigitte's lord, and he is here now to see that she is taken from you."

"So, you brought the whole of Berry to her rescue, eh? You will need a greater army than that to break through the walls of Montville."

"If that is what it will take, so be it. But if you cared anything at all for Brigitte, you would let her go. You and I will still battle, but she must not be made to feel that she brought about deaths. And there will be many deaths here."

"I will not give her up," Rowland said in a quiet voice.

"Then defend yourself," Quintin replied harshly, and drew his sword.

The clang of steel brought men running to the top of Montville's walls. Brigitte, having grown impatient waiting in the hall, quickly followed the others to the walls.

She recognized Rowland and his warhorse right away, caught her breath, and held it. He was waging a furious assault against his opponent, yet he was without armor. The fool! He could die so easily!

She saw Luthor several feet away and went to him. "Why are they fighting?" she demanded, her fear for Rowland making her tone harsh. "Will there be no war—only this battle?"

Luthor looked down at her solemnly. "You should not be up here, damosel."

"Tell me!" Her voice rose to a high pitch. "What does this mean? Why does Thurston fight Rowland?"

"It is not Thurston. But if you fear for Rowland, you need not," Luthor replied with pride. "The Frenchman is an easy prey."

"Frenchman? A French army?"

Brigitte stared out over the wall at the army lining the long crest of the hill. She saw many banners, some she recognized. And then she saw Arnulf's and gasped. He had come for her after all! And beside his banner was—oh God! Her eyes flew to the knight on the field with Rowland, and she screamed.

Quintin heard Brigitte screaming his name. What he heard was her plea for rescue. Rowland heard her, but what he heard in her voice was joy. The effect on each man was the same, however. Each now wanted more than ever to draw the other's blood.

Quintin was struck from his horse, and they fought

on the ground. Already the mighty blows Quintin was fending off were telling on him. He knew as well as any man could that he was going to die. But he would not die until he had made every effort and used all of his strength.

It was no good. Rowland was just too strong for Quintin, and too skilled. Without even a shield, he blocked Quintin. Rowland kept him on the defensive for many minutes, and then Quintin felt that sword breaking through the chain links of his mail and slip smoothly into his shoulder.

The pain! Quintin dropped to his knees. He did not mean to, but his legs gave way. He tried to hold on to his sword, but he had lost his grip as well as the use of his legs. And in that moment Rowland's sword was at his throat.

"It would be easy. You know that, eh?" Rowland said coldly, putting just enough pressure on the sword that a trickle of blood ran down Quintin's neck.

Quintin disdained to answer. His shoulder throbbed. He had failed. Oh, Brigitte!

The sword fell abruptly away. "I give you your life, Quintin de Louroux," Rowland pronounced. "I give it to you only because I owe it to you. Thus we are even now. My debt is paid."

Rowland mounted and rode back to Montville as four French knights rode down the southern hill to collect their fallen lord. Brigitte. She knew—she knew! She had seen Quintin. And she *was* Lady Brigitte, Quintin's ward. No wonder he meant to marry her. A lady, not a serf. Druoda had lied to him! But she had not lied about what Brigitte and Quintin felt for each other. That was obvious. And obvious too was the realization that Brigitte would never stay willingly with him. Rowland had heard the joy in her voice as she cried out to Quintin, her love.

# Chapter Thirty-eight

"What the hell was Brigitte doing up on the wall?" Rowland demanded when Luthor met him in the stable.

"She came up with the others to witness a splendid fight," Luthor replied in good humor. "You showed those French what they are up against, by God!"

"Where is she now?" Rowland snapped irritably.

"Ah, well, the wench is not as strong as I supposed. She fainted dead away when you bested the French knight. I had her taken to your room."

Rowland ran from the stable into the hall, charged up the stairs, and threw open the door to his room.

Brigitte lay on his bed, unconscious. The noise stirred her, and she began to moan. But she was still not quite conscious, lost in some torment deep within her.

Rowland sat down beside her and smoothed the hair back from her face. "Brigitte? Brigitte!" he said more firmly, patting her cheek.

Her eyes opened, and then widened when they fell on Rowland. A sob tore from her throat, and she began pounding her fists on his chest until he grabbed them.

"You killed him!" Brigitte screamed shrilly. *"You killed him!"*

Rowland's eyes narrowed with anger. "He is not dead," he said curtly, "he is wounded."

He watched the play of emotions that swiftly crossed Brigitte's face. She sat up.

"I must go to him."

But he held her firmly on the bed. "You will not go to him, Brigitte."

"I must!"

"No!" he said harshly, and then, "I know who he is, Brigitte."

This statement shocked her. "You know? You know and yet you fought him! Oh, God, I hate you!" she sobbed. "I thought you cared a little for me. But you have no heart. You are made of stone!"

Rowland was surprised by the depth of his own hurt. "I could do nothing else but fight him!" he told her furiously. "I will *not* let him have you! The only way you will marry him is if I am dead, Brigitte!"

"Marry him?" she cried brokenly. "Marry my brother?"

Rowland fell back, staring at her stupidly. "Brother?"

"How dare you pretend? You know Quintin is my brother! You said so!"

Rowland shook his head, stunned. "I thought him your lord. Quintin de Louroux is your brother? Why did you not tell me?"

Brigitte heard his denial through her sobbing. "I thought he was dead, and it was too painful to speak of."

"Then who is Druoda if not his sister? She told me he meant to marry you, but that she would pre-

vent it. She said she would kill you before he returned to Louroux unless I agreed to take you with
me."

"Lies, all lies!" Brigitte stormed. "She is Quintin's
aunt. I told you, and told you that she had lied about
me. *Why* could you not believe...?" Brigitte gasped.
"Before Quintin returned to Louroux? You knew he
would return? You knew he was alive, and you did
not tell me?"

Rowland could not meet her gaze. "I thought you
loved him, that you would try to return to him," he
began.

But Brigitte was too enraged to listen. "Loved him?
Of course I love him! He is my brother. He is the
only family I have. And I am going to him—now!"

She scrambled from the bed, but Rowland caught
her around the waist before she reached the door.
"Brigitte, I cannot allow it. If I let you go to him, he
will stop you from coming back to me."

She stared at him, aghast. "Do you think I want
to come back? I never want to see your face again!
You fought my brother, and you nearly killed him!"

"You are not leaving here, Brigitte," Rowland said
with stony finality.

"I hate you, Rowland!" she hissed. "You can keep
me here, but you will never have me again. I will
kill myself if you do!"

She collapsed on the floor in broken sobs. Rowland
stood staring at her, and then left the room.

It was late night. The French army had with-
drawn that day, but not far. Smoke spiraling over
the hilltop from many camp fires gave evidence that

the French knights were only just beyond the hill.
They intended to stay.

Rowland had not gone back to his room for the
rest of the day. He didn't know what to say to Brigitte. Each time he thought of what he might say to
her, he imagined her reply, and he realized he could
not face her.

He had stubbornly refused to believe her all those
many weeks, when all along she had told the truth.
He had raped a gentlebred lady. He had forced her
to serve him. He had treated her very badly. She
had forgiven him for all of that. Miraculously, she
had forgiven him. But she would not forgive him for
fighting her brother. She would never forgive him
for that, or for failing to tell her that Quintin was
alive. He had no right to keep her, but he could not
bear the thought of losing her. And Quintin would
never let Rowland have her in marriage.

Perhaps when Quintin realized he would never
see his sister again unless he agreed to the marriage,
then the Frenchman might relent. Brigitte would
not be willing, but a woman could be married without her consent. Only the guardian's permission was
necessary.

Perhaps if he told her, if she knew how sorry he
was for every wrong he had done her, then she would
hate him less. He had to see her. He could not stand
imagining her hatred any longer.

Rowland opened the door to his room with a small
degree of hope, more than he had felt all day. But
the room was empty. Brigitte's possessions were still
there, but she was not. A search of the manor only
wasted time. Neither Brigitte nor her dog could be
found. What was found at last was that the door in

the rear wall had been unbolted from within and left unbolted.

Rowland ran and saddled the Hun. Brigitte had to have left after dark, or someone would have seen her crossing the field. Perhaps she had not yet reached the French camp. Maybe, maybe he could catch her before she did. He had to hope.

At last, his heart beating wildly, he crested the top of the southern hill. There was no army beyond it now, nothing but empty pasture and the remains of many camp fires, cold now, ashes blowing over trampled snow.

"Brigitte! Brigitte!" It was a passionate, hopeless cry that no one heard except the wind.

# Chapter Thirty-nine

*B*rigitte huddled in the wagon next to her brother. They were in no real hurry, for the knights of Berry would have welcomed pursuit. It was slow traveling, but each hour took them farther and farther from Montville.

Brigitte leaned her head back wearily and stared up at the starless sky. Quintin slept fitfully. He was burning with fever and in pain, moaning in his sleep, and she could not help him. She had even worsened his condition, for they had argued terribly, just as terribly as she had fought with Rowland.

Quintin had not wanted to leave. He was fierce about staying. He wanted to attack Montville, to reduce the walled fief to rubble. What he wanted most was Rowland's head. She had paled when she heard that. She didn't know exactly how it had happened, but suddenly she was defending Rowland.

"He spared *your* life! He let you live when he could have killed you!" she had cried.

But Quintin's black rage had not cooled. It had even grown. "He must die for what he has done to you!"

"But Rowland is not at fault for what happened," Brigitte insisted. "Druoda is."

"No, Brigitte. The Norman convinced Druoda to let him take you away."

Brigitte considered the idea and then laughed bitterly at the absurdity of it. "Did she tell you that? Ah, Quintin, do you not know yet how skillfully she lies? Rowland did not want me. He was furious that he had to take me with him. He may want me now, but he did not then. Druoda told him she would kill me if he did not take me. And because of what he had done to me, he agreed."

*"That* is another reason he must die!"

*"That* did not even happen at Louroux!" Brigitte had countered.

"You—you are saying he did not rape you?"

"No. He was drunk, and I was too terrified to speak. We both thought it had happened, but the truth is that he passed out, and I fainted. In the morning, we both assumed the deed had been done, and so did Druoda. But it was all a mistake."

"He still took you away, knowing you were my sister, knowing Druoda had no right to give you to him!"

"Is this more of Druoda's lying? Rowland thought me a servant. He would not believe me when I told him otherwise because that is what Druoda convinced him I was. Even today, when you came, he thought you were my lord. He did not know I was your sister. He thought Druoda was your sister."

"Why would Druoda still lie to me, after she had admitted everything else she had done?"

"Can you not guess?" Brigitte asked. "The answer comes easily to me, for I know her, having lived with her. She made her own deeds seem less terrible by lying about Rowland's. Did you kill her?"

"No, I banished her.

"You see? She has been let off lightly, but you came here to kill Rowland. You still want to kill him, even when he spared your life.

"But Rowland knew you lived, and he never told me," Brigitte said then, more to herself than to him. "I thought you dead until today."

"You cannot defend him for that, Brigitte, for I sent him to Louroux to tell you I lived."

"He told Druoda, thinking her your sister. He did do as you bid him, Quintin."

"You make excuses for him," Quintin accused. "Why do you defend him?"

Brigitte cast her eyes down before admitting softly, "I have been happy here, Quintin. I was not at first, but then I became happy. I do not want you to kill Rowland any more than I want him to kill you. And one of you will certainly die if we do not leave here. I want to go home now. No more need be done. I do not need to be avenged, for I have not been harmed."

"You are saying he never touched you in all this time?" Quintin asked doubtfully.

"He did not," Brigitte replied firmly, hoping the lie would put an end to it.

It did. Quintin agreed to leave. No more was said.

She would never see Rowland again. She would bury her feelings for him, never to remember them ever again. Somehow she would manage to forget everything that had passed between her and Rowland of Montville.

# Chapter Forty

*T*he warming breath of spring thawed the land and brought Thurston of Mezidon to Montville. The Norman army was not so impressive, not after Montville had been threatened by a much greater army only months before. There were at least two hundred fighting men with Thurston, but no more than a dozen trained knights.

Rowland looked with disdain at the gathering of men come to take Montville from him. Mercenaries, most of them, perhaps a few good fighting men, but mostly peasants trying to better their lot. There was no loyalty there. Men for hire would not fight to the bitter end.

Four knights rode up to Montville's gates, Thurston in the lead. Rowland recognized another of the four and sneered. Roger. He had joined his brother, perhaps using the battle as a chance to kill Rowland. Roger would have reported the strength of Montville to Thurston, yet his brother was foolish enough to make war. Rowland was sure Geoffrey was down there somewhere, too.

"Luthor!" Thurston bellowed from below. "I challenge you for Montville!"

"By what right?" Luthor demanded.

"By the sacred right of marriage to your eldest daughter. Montville will come to me upon your death. I do not choose to wait."

"Little dog." Luthor laughed contemptuously. "You have no rights here. My son, Rowland, will have Montville. You? Never!"

"He is a bastard! You cannot favor him over your legitimate daughter."

"I can, and I have!" Luthor shouted down. "I raised him to take my place, and so he shall."

"Then I challenge your bastard!"

Rowland had listened impatiently to this exchange. He was burning for a fight. The despair he had sunk into after Brigitte's leaving had recently turned to uncontrollable anger. This was the opportunity he needed to release his fury.

But Luthor had other plans. He gripped Rowland's arm, warning him to silence.

"Lord of jackals!" Luthor threw at Thurston. "My son would not lower himself to a contest with the likes of you. He does not waste his skill on peasants."

"Cowards!" Thurston blustered. "Hide behind your walls then. You will yet face me!"

The knights rode back to join their army on the field in front of Montville. Rowland watched them go, then turned on Luthor furiously.

"Why? I could have made short work of this by meeting him."

"Oh, yes," said Luthor shrewdly, "you would have—in a fair contest. But use your wits, Rowland. Thurston came to me in his youth, but he was always lazy, contemptuous of learning. A sorrier knight never rode through these walls. Consider what chance he would have against you or me. Thurston knows full well he could not win, yet he still made the challenge. Why? He would never have done so if he did not have some foul plan to assure his winning."

"Do you intend to hide behind these walls, then?"

"Of course not," Luthor roared. "He may have expected to avoid a war by killing me, but a war he will get. A battle will be joined on the field, but it will be when I choose."

"In the meantime you will let him lay waste to Montville?" Rowland asked, watching Thurston's divide, many with torches lit, and head for the village.

Luthor's eyes blazed as he saw what Rowland was looking at. "The bastard! So be it," he growled. "We ride out now and finish this matter quickly."

Rowland tried to stop Luthor from a rash move, but it was too late. Luthor would not listen. He was not thinking clearly but letting his anger dictate to him, and that was something a warrior could not afford to do. Yet Rowland had no choice but to follow. Forty of the finest warhorses in the land were soon mounted, and Luthor gave the order. The knights and soldiers of Montville charged through the gates to meet the Lord of Mezidon and his men.

Rowland led half of the Montville defenders after the torch bearers. The village was already in flames, every hut, every shelter toppling in black smoke and orange fire. Thurston's men had left the fires to circle around the manor and join their comrades once more. Rowland doubled back after them.

When he reached the field of battle, his blood chilled at sight of the slaughter there. And then horror struck, pain tore him as he saw Luthor fall. It happened before Rowland could reach Luthor, and he saw that they had been tricked. Thirty more horsemen had come over the southern hill to attack Luthor and his men. An old ploy, but it had worked. Luthor was down. Half the men with him were down.

Rowland was no longer thinking clearly. As Luthor had reacted through his emotions, so did Rowland. A madman, he charged into battle, his twenty warriors charging behind him. He broke the flank, his sword cutting left and right, until he reached the center. There he found Luthor. Thurston's blade had gone clear through him.

Lord Thurston of Mezidon froze when he saw Rowland's eyes. Death was in them. The Hun bearing down on him, Rowland's bloody sword raised, Thurston was trapped. There was no escape for him, and he became transfixed by Rowland's bloodcurdling cry of rage.

Thurston fought wildly, carelessly, and was quickly dispatched. But as Rowland pulled his sword from Thurston's body, a blade entered his back. His eyes widened in surprise, but he reacted instantly, swinging backward with his sword arm. He hit something, but he didn't see what it was. It hurt too much to turn and see. The bloodlust was still in him, the din of battle still rang in his head, but he was nearly blinded, and confused as well, for all he could see was Luthor falling, strong, undefeatable Luthor falling to another's sword.

A horse collided with the Hun, and Rowland fell, hitting the ground with a great shock of pain. He heard nothing after that.

* * *

"He is dead!" Hedda exclaimed over Rowland as he was carried into the hall by two knights. "Oh, finally!"

Gui glared at her as he gestured for Rowland to be placed next to the other wounded men, then told the knights to leave. He turned to her and said coldly, "He is not dead, Lady Hedda, not yet."

Her brown eyes widened in disappointment. "But will he die?"

The hopeful plea in her voice disgusted Gui, and he permitted himself to forget her position at Mont-ville. "Be gone from here! You have lost your hus-band. Have you no tears?"

Hedda's eyes blazed. "I will shed tears for my lord when his bastard is dead!" she hissed. "This one should have died long ago. His horse should have killed him. I was so sure! It should have been finished then!"

"Lady?" Gui demanded, afraid to voice the ques-tion.

She backed away, shaking her head. "I said noth-ing. It was not I! It was not I!"

Hedda ran to Luthor. His body had been placed in the rushes. She threw herself over him and her mournful wails filled the great hall. But Gui knew they were false tears.

"So, I was wrong about Roger."

Gui looked down to find Rowland's eyes open.

"You heard her?" he asked Rowland.

"I heard her."

Gui knelt down beside Rowland. His voice held bitterness when he said, "You were wrong about Roger on that score, but only that one. You are lying here now because of Roger."

Rowland tried to rise, but fell back with a grimace of pain. "How bad is it?"

"Bad," Gui admitted. "But you are strong."

"Luthor was strong," Rowland said, and then the bloody scene ran through his mind all over again. "Luthor?"

"I am sorry, Rowland. He is dead."

Rowland closed his eyes. Of course. He had known when he saw Luthor fall. Luthor. Not his father, yet his father still. The bond of years made it so, just as Brigitte had said. The bond was stronger than Rowland had ever guessed. He began to feel pain deep inside him that was worse than he might have imagined.

"He will rest in peace," Rowland said at last. "He is avenged."

"I saw," Gui replied quietly. "I saw you avenge yourself as well."

Rowland frowned. "Meaning?"

"Do you not know who put the blade to your back?" Gui asked. "Roger. Your own blade cut into him deeply, and he fell even before you did. Roger is dead."

"Are you sure?"

"Yes. And Thurston's men scattered. But Roger's treachery was unmistakable. I am sorry I doubted you about him. I did not think it possible that even Roger could attack from behind. But you knew him better than I did."

Rowland did not hear Gui's last words because blessed unconsciousness had overtaken him. He could no longer feel the pain of loss or the pain of his wound.

\* \* \*

As Rowland fought to hold on to life, Brigitte greeted the blossoming of spring with a saddened heart. Her secret could no longer be hidden. Quintin was livid when she gave up making excuses for her weight and admitted the truth.

"A child?" he exploded. "You are going to bear that Norman's child?"

"My child."

"You lied to me, Brigitte!" Quintin stormed.

That was the root of his rage, that she had lied to him for the first time ever. She had kept the news of her condition from him ever since they had returned to Louroux, though she had known then. And he was aware she had known, for she was four months into her pregnancy.

"Why? Why did you lie to me?" Quintin demanded.

Brigitte hardened herself to the pain in his voice. "If I had told you the truth, would you have left Montville?"

"Of course not." He was shocked.

"There is your answer, Quintin," Brigitte replied stonily. "I was not going to have men fight for my honor when it was I who gave up that honor. There was no reason for a battle."

"But what else did you lie about?"

She lowered her eyes, unable to meet his accusing gaze. "I kept my true feelings from you," she admitted at last. "I was furious that day. I hated Rowland for fighting you. I was so hurt by it that I wanted to die."

"Yet still you defended him to me."

"Yes," she breathed softly.

Quintin walked away, leaving Brigitte in tears.

He was so disappointed in her, and her heart was torn. Only she knew how much she longed for Rowland. She prayed each day that he would come for her. But how could she explain that to Quintin?

# Chapter Forty-one

Rowland stretched, then groaned. It seemed as if the stiffness of his wound would never leave him. He looked sideways at his brother to find him grinning at him.

"I wager you have no scars, or you would not find my pain so amusing, brother," Rowland growled.

"You win that wager," Evarard chuckled. "I have not made war a way of life. I have little sympathy for those who do when their wounds act up and they groan in their cups."

"Groan in their cups indeed," Rowland grunted, not amused in the least. "You will not find me groaning in my cups over a little pain!"

"Oh, no, only over her."

Rowland scowled. "We will not talk of her. I told you more than I should have last evening."

"When you were groaning in your cups," Evarard laughed.

Rowland jumped to his feet, then winced at the stab of pain. His wound was only two months old and still decidedly tender. "I can do without your amusement," he said brusquely.

Evarard was not disturbed by Rowland's temper.

"Where is your humor, man? Did it take flight along with your lady?"

"Evarard, I swear if you were anyone but my brother, I would tear you apart!" Rowland growled, his fists clenched. "Do not mention her to me again."

"It is because I am your brother that I can speak my mind," Evarard said seriously. "You would think twice before laying a fist to this face, for that would be the same as hitting your own self."

"Do not be so sure, brother."

"You see?" Evarard grew solemn. "You are much too serious, when I am only jesting. You have an anger in you, Rowland. You let it live in you instead of ridding yourself of it."

"You presume too much."

"Do I?" Evarard ventured. "She left you. She chose to go with her brother rather than stay with you. You took that lightly?"

"Enough, Evarard!"

"You will never see the lady again. This means nothing to you, eh?"

"Enough!" Rowland exploded.

"You do not call that anger?" Evarard continued at risk, for Rowland's face was a mask of rage. "Look at yourself, brother. You are ready to thrash me for pointing out what eats at you. Why do you not just end your life? You obviously cannot live without this woman, yet you make no efforts to win her back."

"Damn you, Evarard. Tell me how I am to win her back when she despises me now? Tell me how to get near her, when her brother would kill me on sight?"

"Ah, Rowland, these are only obstacles you make

more important than they are. You do not even try. You fear failure. To fail would really be the end. Yet you do not know if you would fail, nor will you know until you make an attempt."

When Rowland remained silent, Evarard pressed his advantage. "What if the lady is as desolate as you are? What if her brother's temper has cooled? I will not hold my tongue. Whatever you did wrong is between you and the lady. You must make amends to her. She may understand better than you think. But how will you ever know until you see her? Go. Go to Berry, Rowland. Talk to her brother. Then see her and tell her what is in your heart. You have nothing to lose, and if you do not go at all then all is lost."

Rowland thought back on his talk with Evarard as he rode closer and closer to Louroux. It had taken his brother's good sense to show him what a pigheaded fool he was.

It was the beginning of summer. For too long he had accepted his misery and done nothing. For too long he had been separated from Brigitte, churning with the anger of it. He should have come for her sooner. He should never have let her go to begin with.

"Lord Rowland of Montville, milord," Leandor announced uneasily.

Quintin shot to his feet as Rowland followed the bailiff into the hall, and his hand went to the hilt of his sword.

"If you challenge me, Baron, I will not accept," Rowland said immediately, putting Quintin at a disadvantage. Quintin was speechless, amazed by Rowland's appearance. Not once, not even in his wildest dreams, would he have thought the Norman so reckless as to come to Louroux. Why, if he wished, Quintin could have him clapped in irons and never released. He was lord here.

"Either you are a man who has no wish to live out the rest of his life, or you are the biggest fool in Christendom," Quintin said when he had found his voice. "I had not taken you for a fool, Norman, but then I was wrong about you from the start as well. I put my trust in you, but you taught me a valuable lesson."

"I did not come here to fight with you, milord," Rowland replied. "I came to make peace."

"Peace?" Quintin shouted, enraged by Rowland's calm. Without hesitation, he struck a blow to the bigger man's face. But Rowland appeared not to have noticed. He held his temper.

"Damn you!" Quintin exploded. "How dare you come here?"

"Because I love her," Rowland replied simply, with a firmness that could not be denied. The words sounded right. He said them with ease, and he said them again. "I love Brigitte. I want her for my wife."

Quintin nearly choked. "You wanted her in lust as well and did not hesitate to violate her! You took her violently!"

"Did she tell you that?"

"You took her, and that speaks for itself!"

"I was never violent with Brigitte." Rowland replied. "I was not gentle at first, I admit that, for I was a hardened man. But it did not take long for your sister to change me, because I wanted desperately to please her."

"That matters not."

Rowland lost his patience. "Be damned! Put yourself in my place. Brigitte was given to me by Druoda. I thought Druoda was your sister. Brigitte was bound to me as a servant. Traveling alone with her to Montville was a torment, as it would be to any man faced with such beauty. I thought, as did she, that I had already deflowered her here at Louroux. If I had known she was still a virgin, then perhaps I would have let her be—I cannot say. But that was not the case. Have you never taken a woman to your bed without asking her consent?"

"We are speaking of my *sister,* not some servant who can expect no less, who is conditioned from birth to serve her lord. Brigitte is a gentlebred lady, and no lady should have suffered what you put her through!"

"She forgave me," Rowland insisted quietly.

"Did she indeed? I know nothing of this, for she never speaks of you at all."

"My fight with you is what turned her against me," Rowland returned.

"Just as well, for she will never see you again."

"Be reasonable. I offer marriage. I am Lord of Montville now, and I have a large estate in Cernay as well. As my wife, she would never want for anything, especially devotion. I would make up all the days of her life for the wrong I did her. The past cannot be changed. I can, however, swear to you that I will never again cause her pain."

"There is no way you can make amends for what you did to Brigitte," Quintin said coldly.

"What does Brigitte say?"

"That has no bearing."

Rowland was losing patience again. "Will you at least allow me to see her?"

"I have told you she will never see you again! Now be gone from here, Norman, while I am willing to let you go freely. You forget where you are."

"I do not forget, Baron," Rowland replied quietly, his gaze unwavering. "Brigitte means more to me than my life."

Quintin watched silently as Rowland turned and left the hall. But he had no time to ponder those last heartfelt words before Brigitte came into the room. Damn! The last thing Brigitte needed was to see that man and be upset. She was utterly miserable and snappish recently.

"Leandor says we have a visitor," Brigitte said as she came forward.

"Leandor was mistaken," Quintin replied more curtly than he meant to.

"Mistaken?"

"It was only a messenger," he replied. One had come that morning whom his sister knew nothing about. "Arnulf is making a celebration next month. The occasion is a niece's marriage. I am to attend."

"Then you may not be here when—"

"No." He cut her off. "I may not."

He left the hall quickly, embarrassed by talk of the impending birth. He was embarrassed by her condition, embarrassed knowing what had been done to her, embarrassed that the man who got her that way was still alive. He found it more and more difficult to face Brigitte. She knew how miserably he had failed to avenge her. She had tried to make light of it, but Quintin knew what she must feel. He could not blame her for having lost faith in him.

# Chapter Forty-two

*B*rigitte moved slowly and lazily through the orchard. Every so often she would try to catch the autumn leaves as they fluttered to the ground. And then her hands would go to her waist to feel the flatness there. She had carried her burden a long time, but that time was over. The birthing had not been difficult, or so Eudora had said. Brigitte had thought differently at the time, quite differently.

But she didn't remember too much of the pain, and she was happy being a mother. But when she was alone, as she was just then, misery overtook her. She hated thinking of Rowland, yet she couldn't stop thinking of him. She hated the ache he caused, and the longing, but she thought of him all the time.

Brigitte thought she was imagining things when she saw a rider approaching the gates of Louroux. She moved through the trees to the edge of the orchard, sure the vision would disappear. Something about the horse reminded her of Rowland's Hun. She chided herself for her imaginings.

Picking up her skirts, Brigitte moved toward the manor. Her pace quickened with each step, and when she moved through the gates she was running. She stopped dead in the courtyard, close enough to see the horse clearly as a groom led him to the stable. The rider was not there. Her heart beat frantically. She raced to the hall, stumbling through the doors, and once again stopped dead.

"Rowland!" she gasped.

But no one could have heard her over Quintin's shouting. Rowland and Quintin stood a few feet apart, Quintin in a fury and Rowland ready to draw his sword.

"Stop it!" Brigitte screamed as she ran between them. "Stop it, I say!" She pushed at Rowland and he fell back, staring at her. Then she turned to her brother. "What is the meaning of this?"

"He is not welcome here."

"You would throw him out," she asked hotly, "without knowing why he came?"

"I know why he came!"

"Why?"

"For you."

Rowland had answered. She allowed herself to turn and look at him then, her eyes taking in all of him. She continued to stare, unable to help herself, and he devoured her with those dark blue eyes.

"Leave us, Quintin," Brigitte said softly without looking at her brother.

Quintin grabbed her arm and swung Brigitte around to face him. "I will not leave you alone with him."

"I would like to talk to him, Quintin."

"No."

"I have the right. Now leave us. Please."

Quintin was furious, but he stalked past them. "I will be near if you need me, Brigitte."

"Be damned," Rowland said as soon as they were alone. "Your brother is a belligerent, obstinate—"

"Careful, Rowland." Brigitte cut him off. Her eyes were ice blue.

"He started shouting the moment I walked in. If you had not come when you did, I would have..."

Rowland reddened guiltily, and the hostility in Brigitte's eyes silenced him.

"I know exactly what you would have done, Rowland," she said quietly. "I know you only too well. You would have fought my brother."

"Not that," he quickly assured her. "I only meant to stop his shouting."

"Just tell me why you are here," she said curtly.

Rowland sighed deeply. He was off to a terrible start. But Brigitte was standing before him and, God, how beautiful she was, even more beautiful than he remembered.

"How I have missed you, *cherie*," Rowland said impulsively, surprising her.

He had not meant to begin that way. The words leaped from him of their own accord. She was caught off guard.

"We have been separated many months, Brigitte," he continued softly. "It seemed like many years, for the time was unbearably long without you."

Brigitte's eyes narrowed. "Do you expect me to believe you have missed me so much?"

"I mean all that and more," he replied warmly. "I want you to return to Montville with me. Luthor is dead, and Montville is mine now."

Her eyes widened. "Luthor dead? You did not—"

"No, not I. Thurston came in the spring, and there

was a battle. I avenged Luthor myself. I found that
I...cared for the old man more than I realized."

"I am sorry about Luthor," she said sincerely.
"Were many killed?"

"No, there were more wounded than killed. But
Thurston and Roger both fell to my blade. They will
not bother us again."

"Roger is dead?"

"He stabbed me, and I struck out at him in reflex.
I did not even see him before I fell."

"*You* fell? You were wounded then?" Her eyes
scanned him fearfully.

"In the back," Rowland said slowly.

Her eyes widened. "So, he went for your back again
just as he did in Arles?"

"You know about that?"

She glared at him. "A little matter that you never
mentioned—my brother saved your life! And you
repaid him nicely, did you not?" she added bitterly.

"Brigitte—"

"I know you were unaware that I was his sister,
but you did think he was my lord. You believed he
meant to marry me. And still you took me away! You
betrayed his trust."

"I did so unknowing, Brigitte, when it was assumed I raped you here. The matter was done and
could not be changed. Do you think I was proud of
it? I was furious with myself, furious too that I betrayed him in taking you away. But what was I to
do? Druoda threatened to kill you if I left you here.
In my place, what would you have done?"

"What you could have done, Rowland, was give
me up without a fight when Quintin came for me!"

"It was not as simple as that, *cherie,*" he said gently.

"I could not give you to him, not thinking *he* meant to marry you. I wanted you to be my wife."

Brigitte turned away, the words echoing in her mind. *"I wanted you to be my wife."*

Rowland mistook her mood for anger. "I would never fight him again, Brigitte, now that I know he is your brother. I tried to make peace with Quintin, but he would not listen. I offered marriage, and he refused. I cannot fight him for you, and he will not give you to me. Brigitte, I want you for my lady. I have never wanted anything as much as I want you."

Brigitte felt tears gathering. How many times had she prayed to hear those words? But that was long ago, and she had stopped praying that he would come. Her pride was injured. There was only bitterness now, because he had forsaken her. All the months of her pregnancy, all the months she had needed him, he was not there.

"It is too late, Rowland," she whispered at last.

Rowland's heart stopped. "You have married?"

"No."

"Then it is not too late," he said hopefully.

He reached for her, but she stiffened. Keeping her face averted, she said, "Do not touch me, Rowland. You have no right to touch me. You have no right to come here now and offer marriage. Where were you months ago when...when..." A lump in her throat threatened to choke her. She wanted to cry and fought desperately not to. "I will not marry you, Rowland. You should have come sooner when...when I still felt something for you. I...no longer feel anything."

Rowland grabbed her shoulders angrily and forced her to meet his eyes. "I did come sooner, months ago, but your brother turned me away! I have been wandering ever since. I could not go home. Home means nothing to me without you."

She shook her head firmly. "I do not believe you. Quintin would have told me if you had been here before."

"Damn you, Brigitte!" Rowland shouted. "I love you!"

"If you loved me," she shouted back, "you would have come sooner!"

In desperation, he pulled her to him roughly and bruised her lips with a raging kiss. He had opened his heart to her, and she meant to destroy him. She was tearing him apart.

Brigitte pushed at Rowland frantically, until he was forced to release her. Her eyes damning him, she said, "You should not have done that. I do not love you, Rowland."

Rowland gathered his pride, turned, and walked away from her without a backward glance.

"God, I do not care!" she cried aloud to the empty hall.

"You do not care about what?"

She turned to see Quintin standing in the doorway. She clenched her fists to stop herself from crying.

"I do not care that Rowland has gone," Brigitte repeated stiffly.

"I am glad to hear it," Quintin replied, though there was doubt in his voice.

He didn't know what to say to her, so overcome with remorse was he. He had overheard everything, and he wished he had not. He knew his sister very well. She didn't mean any of what she had said to Rowland. Why had her own brother not understood how much she cared for that man? Why had he let his own anger blind him to Brigitte?

It was not too late to set the matter straight. But how could he tell her the terrible thing he had done? Would the revelation turn her against him? Quintin braced himself.

"Your Rowland has more nerve than any man I know," Quintin began. "Or more love."

"What are you saying?"

"He came here once before, Brigitte. I did not tell you because I thought it would upset you, especially in your condition. He tried to make peace with me, but I refused him. I warned him never to come again, but, as you can see, he did not heed my warning. And now I can only ask you to forgive me for not telling you this. He is a barbaric brute, but if you want him, I will bring him back."

"Oh, God, Quintin!" Brigitte's tears spilled over. "Is it too late?"

He smiled weakly. "I will stop him."

"No!" she cried. "It is I who must stop him."

Brigitte ran from the hall. Quintin followed her to the doors and watched her race across the courtyard to the gates and out of sight. He forced himself to stay where he was. He would not interfere again.

Rowland was riding down the dirt road, but was still close enough that he could hear her frantic cry. But he did not stop. He did not even look back.

She ran after him, crying his name again and again. It was because of her damnable pride that Rowland was leaving. Her pride! To hell with pride. She began to sob, afraid it really was too late, afraid she had hurt him too deeply.

"Rowland, please!"

Sobbing wildly, she tripped on her skirts and fell, skinning her palms. She stumbled to her feet, but the distance between them had widened, and she doubted he could hear her anymore.

"Rowland—come back!"

It was her last pitiful cry, and Rowland ignored it. Brigitte collapsed to her knees then in the middle of the road, her head bowed in defeat, her body shaking with anguished sobs.

She did not see Rowland look back and see her crumpled there in the road. He stopped, hesitated several moments, and then galloped back to Brigitte. She heard the horse approaching and rose to her feet. But Rowland's black rage stopped her from speaking.

"What madness is this?" he demanded furiously. "Have you more words to cut into my heart?"

Brigitte could not blame him. She had been heartless.

"Rowland." She hesitantly reached forward and placed her hand on his leg. Her eyes pleaded with him to believe her. "Rowland, I love you."

His eyes burned into hers more intensely than ever before. "So," he said icily. "What am I to do now? Ask you to be mine once more so you can refuse me again? One thrust of the knife was not enough for you?"

"Rowland, I was hurt because you took so long in coming. I had prayed so hard for you to come, but I had given up hope. I was miserable, and I was bitter because I thought you did not care for me any longer. I tried desperately to forget you, but I could not."

Rowland's expression did not soften. "If you loved me, Brigitte, you would not have refused me."

"It was my hurt pride speaking. I felt that if you loved me, you would have come for me sooner."

"I did."

"I know that now. Quintin just admitted it to me. He did not tell me before because he did not know that I love you. I couldn't tell him because he would not forgive you."

"Are you saying you have forgiven me for what happened with Quintin?"

"I love you, Rowland. I would forgive you anything... anything. Please, don't let your pride come between us, as I did, or I will die!"

Rowland leaped down from the Hun and pulled her into his embrace.

"Little jewel," Rowland said huskily. "No man could love a woman as I love you. You will be mine forever. Nothing in this world can prevent it, now that I know I have your love." He looked deeply into her eyes. "You are sure? You have no doubts?"

"I am sure, very, very sure." She smiled up into his strong, handsome face.

Rowland laughed delightedly. "Now we can go home."

# Chapter Forty-three

$Q$uintin was not surprised to see Brigitte and Rowland walking closely together as they entered the hall, Rowland's arm wrapped possessively around Brigitte's waist. But the look of ecstatic joy about his sister struck Quintin speechless.

They stopped in the center of the hall, Rowland looking warily at Quintin. Quintin jumped to his feet. "For God's sake, Rowland. I am not a complete ogre," he grinned good-naturedly. "And I am not so stubborn that I cannot admit I was wrong. I want Brigitte to be happy, and I can see she will be happy only with you."

"We have your blessing, then?"

"My blessing and my best wishes for a long and happy life together," Quintin said quietly.

"You see why I love Quintin so." Brigitte smiled, going to her brother and hugging him. "Thank you, Quintin."

"Do not thank me, little one. I am only sorry that you have been so long apart from the man you love. I hope you can forgive me for the heartache I have caused you."

"Of course I forgive you. I have him now, and nothing will separate us again."

Quintin smiled down at her fondly. "And did you tell him about...?"

Brigitte turned to Rowland and grabbed his hand. "Come. I have something very precious for you."

She dragged him along after her, up the stairs and down the corridor to a closed door. A shaggy beast lay on the floor beside the door and had to scramble out of her way.

"I hope you haven't dragged me up here just to show me Wolff," Rowland said with mock severity.

She grinned, her blue eyes locking with his. "Not him."

"Then surely it can wait for this," he murmured huskily as he kissed her soundly, molding her small frame to his.

But Brigitte wiggled out of his embrace. "Rowland, please..." She smiled at him, shaking her head, then opened the door very carefully. Brigitte led Rowland inside, cautioning him to be quiet, and pulled him to the center of the room, where there was a bed with raised sides draped in white lacing. Whatever he had expected to see, it certainly wasn't what was inside that bed.

He frowned at Brigitte. "Babies? You brought me up here to look at babies?"

"Are they not beautiful?"

"I suppose so," he grunted.

She leaned over the bed and let a tiny hand grasp her finger. "They look alike, do they not?"

"I suppose."

"Exactly alike?"

He looked from one small face to the other, noting the tufts of blond hair, the dark little eyes, the identical features. Then he laughed, understanding.

"Ha, twins! You wanted to show me twin babies because of Evarard and me."

Brigitte was disappointed. He had not understood.

"These twins are very special." She picked up one of the babies and held it toward Rowland. "This is Judith. Here, hold her."

"No!" He stepped back, much alarmed.

"She will not hurt you, Rowland." Brigitte grinned.

He scowled. "The babe is too small. It is I who might hurt her."

"Nonsense."

But she did not press him. He had obviously never held a baby before, but he would learn.

She placed Judith back in the bed and picked up the other infant. "And this is Arland."

"A boy?" He was incredulous.

She was amused. "A boy."

"But you said they were twins."

"They are."

He looked more closely at the two babies and asked hesitantly, "How did you know which was which?"

She laid Arland down and tickled his belly playfully. "I know, Rowland. You will know, too." She gazed at him expectantly, but he had still not guessed, so she said pointedly, "I think they both look like you."

In that moment, as her hints and her acute involvement with these twins finally made sense to him, Rowland lost a good deal of his color. "Yours— and mine?"

"Our children, my love."

He drew her to him, staring at the babies over her shoulder. "To think you went through that without me. I never even *thought*..." And then he moved her away from him suddenly. "And you would have let me leave here without knowing?"

"I would have," she admitted, her chin tilting in that familiar way.

Rowland shook his head. "You are a stubborn witch," he sighed.

"I am that," Brigitte admitted, her mouth curving.

He pulled her back into his arms. His voice was tender. "But you are *my* stubborn witch. Mine!" He held her very close to him. "And they are mine, a boy and a girl, two jewels from my little jewel. What a wonder you are! And how I love you, lady. Oh, God, how I love you! I will never let you go."

Then he sealed that vow with a kiss, and Brigitte had no chance to tell him how much she loved him. But she would tell him later, and for the rest of their lives.

*Coming soon from Corgi Avon*

**WHILE PASSION SLEEPS** BY SHIRLEE BUSBEE

A novel of searing desire by the bestselling author of *Lady Vixen* and *Gypsey Lady*

Beth Ridgeway was a violet-eyed platinum beauty – the kind of woman who made men burn with desire. Yet her husband didn't want her ...

Rafael Santana was the handsome, arrogant son of a wealthy Texas family. As a child he had been kidnapped and raised by the Comanches. Even now, all his gentleman's breeding couldn't conceal the savage strength beneath his aristocratic bearing.

Beth thought he was cruel and insensitive, a man who used women only for his selfish pleasure and then tossed them away. Rafael thought she was a common wench – flirtatious and unfaithful – who took pride in breaking men's hearts.

Yet something had happened when their eyes first met at a dazzling New Orleans ball. Something their hearts could not deny, something neither the years nor the violent misunderstandings could diminish. Because, for the first time, both Beth and Rafael were awakening to the magnificent passions of love.